A Conspiracy of God-killers

A Conspiracy of God-killers
Tales of the Fallen and the Fragile

Publication of the Modern Library of Indonesia Series, of which this book is one title,
has been made possible by the generous assistance of The Djarum Foundation.
Funding for the translation of this book was provided by
the Indonesian Translation Funding Program
of the Ministry of Education and Culture, the Republic of Indonesia.

Template design by DesignLab; layout and cover by Cyprianus Jaya Napiun
Cover illustration detail from *Interconection* by Entang Wiharso, 2007.
Image courtesy of the Oei Hong Djien Museum of Contemporary Art.

Printed in Indonesia by PT Suburmitra Grafistama

ISBN No. 978-602-9144-43-7

MODERN LIBRARY OF INDONESIA

TRIYANTO TRIWIKROMO

A Conspiracy of God-killers

Tales of the Fallen and the Fragile

translated by
George A Fowler

LONTAR
Jakarta, Indonesia

Contents

Translator's Introduction

One of the pleasures I have derived from my work is a notion (surely illusory) that I somehow have become at least as familiar with the text as the author himself. Indeed, it may even be that the level of scrutiny and cautious experimentation I have applied to alchemize a text from language A into language B reveals insights and linkages that not even the writer was conscious of. After all, Umberto Eco speaks of the *opera aperta*, the "open work" awaiting and encouraging what is in effect its recreation with each fresh reading. And in that light, the translator may justifiably claim to be the ultimate re-creator of a text, if only based on the "each fresh reading". Such speculation aside, what is certain is that, for the reader, no less than for me, these twenty-two short stories of the Semarang, Central Java, writer and poet Triyanto Triwikromo demand, and indeed reward, this sort of repeated "re-creating". And never mind the nagging sense that an ultimate "meaning" may have eluded us yet again.

So it was with delight, righteous indignation, and disgust, and more than occasional mental head-scratching, that I myself read and re-read, worked and re-worked this kaleidoscope of stories. Their plots run a wide gamut of time and place, are studded with symbolism, myth, and allusion, and glow with not only magic, but the fantastic and the absurd as well.

There is a substantial body of textual analysis and literary criticism on Triyanto's techniques, themes, and even his psychological motivations. Unfortunately, being mostly in Indonesian, it is inaccessible to those who do not read Bahasa Indonesia. How, therefore, might a non-Indonesian readership approach this particular work? After translating the book, I found myself grouping these twenty-two stories into three loose categories consisting of the historical, the abstract, and those for which I would use the misleading word "entertainments". Of course, whether or not Triyanto had such a division in mind is another matter. In any case, the moral compass weighs heavily here, especially throughout the historical and the abstract stories.

A favored device of Triyanto's is the prism of history, a magically reconfigured history, firmly grounded in recognizable time, place, and circumstance, but one which veers off in unexpected directions.

Two forceful lines in "A Pair of Death Sniffers" exemplify a very red thread running through the "history" part of this collection:

"Ahmad did not know how such cruelty beyond limit could grow on this earth and could slaughter so indiscriminately."

A paragraph of horror follows and the story ends with simply *"Without a sound..."*

The land, the sky, God Himself, may look upon these atrocities with equanimity, but not Triyanto, whose scorn and anger, while measured, burns at incandescent heat.

We recall Stephen Dedalus in Joyce's *Ulysses* rejecting the idea of history as either an inexorable march to "one great goal, the manifestation of God", or as some impersonal force in the past, easy to scapegoat for all its evil outcomes in the present, when he declares, "History is a nightmare from which I am trying to awake". A lot of people in Indonesia would readily understand this, and more intensely than Stephen Dedalus could ever imagine.

Triyanto, though, shows no hesitation in grappling head-on with the atrocities of history—the violence and cruelty of the powerful against the weak and their treachery against the honorable and upright—as he sees it. For him, history, certainly Indonesian history, far from being a march to apotheosis, is shaped, not "out there" and "then", but right here and now, by quite ordinary thugs doing the bidding of yet bigger thugs or by fanatical religious ignoramuses. Surely these quotidian types inhabit any place and time.

Whether the cynically generated mass hysteria of late 1965 that enabled the great massacres in Java and Bali, the assassination campaign by the security forces of hundreds of underworld figures (damned by their tattoos) between 1983 and 1985, or the terrorism by rape and arson of the ethnic Chinese community in the politically murky events of May 1998, the victims are the vilified, the despised, the fragile, and most pitifully, the innocent "collateral damage" ("Three Painful Stories of Elisabet Rukmini", "Children Sharpening Knives", "Like Drizzle, Pointed Red", and "Kufah's Flying Fish", among others). What earns Triyanto's wrath is the usual raft of clichés and rationalizations trotted out by the perpetrators: "We have to get them before they get us"; "She'd have only become a whore"; "They are the enemies of God/Allah", and so on and on.

And so, these acts of inhumanity against the vulnerable, whether organized by government or by mobs, whether passionately believed in or cynically self-serving, are in effect, if not in conscious motive, conspiracies against Divinity itself. Such conspiracies to commit violence are so depraved, so spirit-bereft, as to seem to be devised and carried out by beings no longer human. In his correspondence with me, the author has used the Javanese term *kropos*, meaning something like "emptied out by rot and corrosion", to describe them. These "conspirators" are "fallen ones", the true "hollow men", far exceeding in hellishness the feckless eponyms of the TS Eliot poem.

While Triyanto's stories are really the symbolic shards of a larger history breaking across the land, "Sultan Ngamid's Wings of Mist" is at once the most "macro", the most historically grounded and most magical history of the collection. It recounts through the comments of the omniscient artist, Raden Saleh, on his famous canvas of the event, the calculated treachery of the Netherlands East Indies government in arresting its mortal enemy, the insurgent Prince Diponegoro, on the Great Day at the end of the fasting month and sending him into lifelong exile from his native Java.

Among the more "abstract" of these stories, oppressors and despots need not have a recognizable face, or any face at all. In "Prophet Bowl Delirium", one of the more enigmatic stories in this collection and a veritable maelstrom of phantasmagorical imagery, the oppressor is a capitalist system that wreaks havoc on vulnerable societies (here, Aboriginal Australians). As banal as that may sound, the protagonist, Vern, recovering (or not) from a brain operation (a lobotomy?) and consumed with schizophrenic paranoia, is convinced he has to rescue his fellow freedom fighters against the system ("terrorists", of course, to the authorities) from their imprisonment in—that icon of consumerism—soft-drink vending machines.

Cynical treachery at the hands of the greedy and powerful is also the fate of the seductress-dancer Nagreg in "Sand Mirror", whereas in the daring Ramayana-eque "Sita's Resistance", Sita is punished (to a degree left to our imagination) by her husband Rama, here an emblem of feckless male insecurity, for having the temerity to simply be Sita.

Such settings and material would make for interesting reading almost no matter who wrote it, but it is Triyanto's moral vision that makes these truly remarkable. Here, as I interpret it, he demonstrates that the cruelties of history's despots never fail to arouse resistance. However weak and futile this resistance may be, no matter how inevitably "crucifixion"—that ubiquitous symbol of martyrdom that runs shockingly throughout most of these stories—awaits its proponents, this resistance to oppression represents a balancing force in a seemingly Godless cosmos ("Three Painful Stories of Elisabet Rukmini"), a redemptive element in the inexplicable nature of humanity, no less salient than its inclination to do violence.

For Triyanto, as for Stephan Dedalus, history shows no evidence of a grand procession to a final goal, only the endlessly repeated cycle of that strange dialectic of cruelties, resistance, and "crucifixion". What is vital and indispensable is the moral stance, most poignantly exemplified by Sultan Ngamid who, in the face of the misgivings of his advisors, says in regard to the untrustworthy Dutch,

"A devil? We're the devils if we cannot forgive people who would kill and trick us."

Triyanto invokes to a degree remarkable for a Muslim the Christian iconography: Mary, Bernadette of Lourdes, and particularly Jesus, along with multiple references to crucifixion and his crucifixion and the several martyrs in these stories who are simple village priests. Triyanto's use of these as points of reference is intriguing, often pushing the envelope of the fantastical, but certainly not intended to make a pitch for Christianity per se. Rather this is to evoke, often ironically, exemplary figures in a moral landscape. Thus in "The Devil of Paris" the drug lord Khun Sa, a mythically bad historical figure, mentions to his lover (whether mockingly or wistfully it is not clear) how "lucky" Bernadette Soubirous, a historical figure of mythical saintliness, had been.

This ecumenical parallelism is most strikingly displayed in "Sultan Ngamid's Wings of Mist". Like Jesus, Sultan Ngamid (Prince Diponegoro) has his Garden of Gethsemane moment when he agonizes over "the fate written by Allah" for him. Like Jesus, he rejects the temptation to appeal to preternatural forces to deliver him from his captors. Most remarkably expressed is Sultan

Ngamid's acceptance of his fate, echoing Jesus's final words on the cross, and later ascension into heaven:

And carefully, too, he cried out, "Allahu! Allahu! Allahu!
All is completed, Lord. I have returned everything to You!"
After that, you know, like Jesus the crucified, he stretched
out his arm, shook his wings, and vanished, body and soul,
and soared right into the mist, disappearing from the sight
of Haji Ngisa, who was no longer astonished.

But even arresting plotlines and an original moral vision, sufistic in its religious dimensions, are not the only attractions of Triyanto's stories. These are rivaled by the sheer fearless exuberance of his writing, dense with vivid and often disturbing, often erotically charged, images: gossiping angels and haranguing devils (lots of devils, of different colors); Jesus's image on a gangster's car in Los Angeles; a Javanese hero prince sprouting and removing his purple wings of power; a freakish village outcast sprouting green wings; herons and mangrove trees protecting the innocent and the upright...

In the end, as I watched the rain occasionally whipping
up the waters into a diamond-like sheen, I heard a pair
of angels chatting away in a madhouse, one year after
Rimbaud had kicked me out of bed. The bed that had
stared at us in amazement, a couple of male dogs, always
panting and gasping as we pawed and kissed and caressed
each other. ("The Ghost in Rimbaud's Head")

Then there are Triyanto's mind-bending literary "tricks": karmic time travel ("Like Drizzle, Pointed Red"), and sudden switches in narrator and point of view ("Sultan Ngamid's Wings of Mist", "The Ghost in Arthur Rimbaud's Head", among others). In what I have arbitrarily labelled the "entertainment" group, the narrator of "Natasha Korolenko's Fiery Circus" is a would-be graphic novelist, while in "Handcuffs of Snow", Triyanto's foray into "LA Noir" literature, the narrator has the starring role in what is surely worthy of a graphic novel itself.

The "entertainment" stories nonetheless tantalizingly defy any easy interpretation. Is "Enter My Ear, Daddy" an elaborate karmic metaphor, one in which a spiritually conflicted professional man of violence, some kind of hit man, but seen here as an ageing but highly valued butcher in a cattle slaughterhouse, weary of his career of bloodletting, uneasy with the moral implications of his work, and unsuccessfully trying to persuade his boss to let him retire, who unintentionally passes on the impulse of violence to his daughter? Or can this story only be understood in reference to the Javanese mystical parable and *wayang kulit* episode "Dewa Ruci" ("The God Ruci") which Triyanto seems to evoke with this title? Is there an intentionally bizarre parallel here with the battle and kin-killing weariness of Arjuna in "Everlasting is Arjuna's Sorrow", trying to persuade his spiritual "boss" Kresna to allow him to retire from the Kuruksetra killing grounds? That is the thing about Javanese culture. It's esoterica all the way down.

"Esoteric" may indeed be the way the general reader describes the many Javanese and Islamic cultural and religious terms, to say nothing of the modern Indonesian historical references used by Triyanto in these stories. A glossary has therefore been compiled therefore to assist with and, it is hoped, enhance the reader's appreciation of Triyanto's artistry.

Do these musings travel far beyond Triyanto's authorial intentions? If so, call it Eco's *opera aperta*, or perhaps even a literary Heisenberg's Uncertainly Principle, at work. Never mind, much can be gained by reading these stories of Triyanto Triwikromo with the intellect. But equally, if not more so, I feel, with the heart.

Selected Sources

Carey, Peter. "Raden Saleh, Dipanegara and the Painting of the Capture of Dipanegara at Magelang (28 March 1830)," *Journal of the Malayan Branch of the Royal Asiatic Society*, Vol. 55, 1, 1982. A superb article that cannot be recommended too highly.

Eco, Umberto. *The Role of the Reader: Exploration in the Semiotics of Texts*, Indiana University Press, 1979.

Kraus, Werner. "Raden Saleh's Interpretation of the Arrest of Diponegoro: an Example of Indonesian 'proto-nationalist' Modernism," *Archipel*, 69, Paris, 2005, pp. 259-294.

Setiadi, Tia. "Fisi, Sejarah, Distopia: Meneroka Gerak Gunung Es Dalam *Celeng Satu Celeng Semua*, Karya Tiyanto Triwikromo" in Triyanto Triwikromo, *Celeng Satu, Celeng Semua* (Jakarta: Gramedia Pustaka Utama, July 15, 2013).

Night Train Sorcery

come back quickly stop our house is surrounded by tibum stop

The telegram came just as I was just settling down to watch *The Day After*, quite a touching film on nuclear war. I was all geared up to see it because, according to its review in *Time*, this film could change the way American society thought about nuclear power and the dangers it presented. Because I was to provide counseling on nuclear dangers the following week, that evening I just couldn't obey Mother's wish for me to go right back home. I preferred to watch the movie.

That morning, another telegram from Mother had come with almost the same demand but in a shriller tone: *come back quickly stop mother almost dead stop our house has been demolished stop.*

I could imagine that when she wrote this telegram Mother's teeth would have been chattering like mad. Her molars would have impacted and her body would have been trembling. At times like this, she'd usually be thinking of my late father and, at the very peak of her vexation, she would say all kinds of abusive things as she left the telegraph agent with a sour look.

"A hero's widow? *Pahhh,* what's so great about being called that if they pay me no mind when I object to all the houses being razed in our neighborhood!" That's how she babbled on one day when the City Planning Board was about to convert our ward into a supermarket.

"Besides," she went on, "is it right to stuff the people around here full of products that they don't know what to do with?"

That sort of grumbling would go on and on until I'd arrive and suggest changing the subject to past times. To the times when Mother felt so very proud to have a soldier like Father for a husband.

But I am not living with Mother now and am finding it very hard to reassure her simply by sending telegrams or writing letters. And because I was afraid of the neighbors thinking of Mother as a crazy woman because of all her scolding and grumbling, I just had to leave for the station that very night (after the second telegram arrived).

I never thought traveling by night train could actually be so free and easy. Even beginning with when I first bought the ticket, there were conveniences that I would never have experienced had I, for example, taken the bus.

And how could it not be? For instance, at the ticket kiosk just now, I didn't have to mention my destination. I hadn't needed to utter a single word, even when all of a sudden the honorable Mr Ticket Agent knew exactly where I wanted to go, what I needed, and so on and so forth.

In an instant, the Ticket Agent and I each understood what we had to do.

"I hope this will be a most memorable journey for you, sir," said he with a smile. "When you ride this train, you are one of the elect. You, sir, will understand some things that would never be understood by someone who has never done this."

I smiled at hearing this invitation so heavily laden with advertising. But when the Ticket Agent smiled back, the hairs on the back of my neck stood up on end. It was a weird kind of smile that suddenly lashed out. Just then my eyesight went all blurry.

"My name is Sisyphus," he continued, "but people often call me Sukarno. I really don't like to give out my name to others. But for some reason I feel like introducing myself to you, sir."

My whole body shook at the sound of his charismatic voice. But not wanting to be swept into the realm of his charm, I dashed out onto the platform. I hoped by doing so, I could be free of him, from his gaze, his smile, from everything that seemed to want to terrorize. There weren't too many people moving about on the platform. It was pretty quiet. And even when I looked more closely, the only things I noticed were a few bats softly wafting back and forth above, several baggage cars that also moved along sluggishly, and the quiet conversations of some people to whom I paid little attention. Elsewhere, in another corner, I saw something that looked like a stage adorned with colorful flags. There were about ten people fixing it up so it would be appealing to the eye.

"They want to celebrate the independence of this nation."

Someone suddenly gripped my shoulder. I didn't need to look back to guess who it was. From his voice I knew it was the Ticket Agent.

"Get on board quickly, sir," he said affably, "I will be accompanying you."

Once again I smiled at him. But weird! My mouth wouldn't open. Even so, I felt that I had smiled at him, so there was no reason to feel I hadn't been respectful.

Actually, I still wanted to stay on the platform watching the people busy setting up the August 17th commemoration stage, but because the spell of the Ticket Officer's words was stronger, in the end I just hurried along to the coach and looked for my seat number.

"Please be seated!"

Oh, God! The Ticket Officer was there beside my seat.

"I hope you are not shocked at the facilities on this special train, sir. Everything has been arranged for you."

Wow, crazy! Since when did I rate such exalted treatment? I was only a reporter who doubled as a university lecturer, no more and no less. Ah, the hell with it all. And the same for the mealy-mouthed Ticket Officer, with his huckstering and services that exceeded even those for royalty. I realized I was nodding off, but I didn't want to tire of my frequent thoughts that so often made me want to write poems or short stories whenever fantastic things were happening, things out of the ordinary. And this particular Ticket Seller was definitely not of the ordinary. But because I did want to rest, yeah, to hell with the "news" I was experiencing now, no matter how interesting it was.

Finally, I fell asleep, even though perhaps my soul wasn't asleep. I say that because when I was asleep I seemed to be on a street that was in an uproarious tumult. I was tormented. I felt my life force being crushed flat by something I had never before known.

I woke up abruptly in the middle of the night.

"It looks like you slept too soundly, sir. Am I right?"

I didn't reply.

"Would you like to take a look around to see what makes this train so unique, sir?" Here came the ads again. "What I mean, sir, is even if you don't want to, I am required to show it to you."

I don't know, for the nth time I just didn't feel like responding to every inducement of the Ticket Officer. Odd, though…. Every time I refused, he had a thousand and one ways to finally beat me down. Like now, yeah, like now, I have to submit in the grip of his charisma.

"This is the generals' coach," said the Ticket Agent as we passed through the first one. "In here gather the generals that once did, that do now, and will in the future struggle for the independence of this nation."

"What do you mean, sir, by saying that they are in the past, present and future?" I made bold to ask. Oh no! I didn't have to ask this. Because, by the time I had formulated that question, I actually already had the answer. It appeared by itself when I happened to see what the sleeping generals looked like.

"There's no need to be surprised," said the Ticket Agent, "Every general that you know is definitely here."

Oh man! That Ticket Agent didn't seem to give me a chance to be surprised. But, still, I had the right to be shocked at seeing on this train several generals who were now dead.

"You don't need to be afraid, either, sir. Everyone on this train has good intentions for our nation. They won't harm you."

"If I am not mistaken…" I plucked up my courage to guess the identity of a general whose face I had often seen on the "national hero" calendars. "The one sitting wearing a head cloth is General Su—"

"Yes," replied the Ticket Agent, pouncing on my words before they were finished. "And you don't need to ask much, sir. Our time is short."

Yet again, I felt I was being muzzled. And once more, I was unable to resist when the Ticket Officer pulled me into the next coach.

"The ones in this coach you are sure to know very well, sir."

I didn't answer him. I preferred to scrutinize one by one the faces of people I easily recognized. There were figures like Rendra the poet, former Jakarta Governor Ali Sadikin, the student activist Hariman Siregar. And on and on.

"History never understood them," said the Ticket Agent sadly. "They were born in a time and place that gave nothing of value to their lives. They were like me."

Strange to say, I felt a sudden compassion well up within me. It passed quickly, though. Adroitly the Ticket Agent, who was in tears, led me to the next coach.

"I can only bring you this far, sir," he said, in a flat, almost listless voice. "In the next coaches, you will find out just why you had to ride this train."

I didn't get a chance to express my thanks when, without knowing why, I abruptly found myself in another coach. Yeah, in another coach where I could see important figures of our nation nodding off and enjoying the rhythmic clashing of wheel on rail or the collision of the endless drizzling rain against the windows.

Nor did I even get to yell when several people crowded around me and kicked me in the stomach with their boots.

"Follow us," shouted one of them.

"You're a reporter, Mister, right?

I nodded.

"Don't write down what you see," said someone. "All this is magic."

I felt there was nothing I could say, so I nodded in assent again. But that gesture turned out to be deadly. Someone hit me hard from behind with a rifle butt.

"Don't believe them, Mister. You've got to write down what indeed has to be written down. But remember, lay it on thick in the newspaper that no one on this train is a rebel. We are trying to liberate this nation for the second time."

To tell you the truth, I wanted to get mad at being treated so highhandedly. But since the one speaking just then turned out to be the Ticket Agent, who had been so friendly a moment before, I was forced to repress all the pain I was feeling.

"So you all aren't a bunch of gangsters?"

Suddenly, for the first time since meeting him, I found the courage to stare right into the eyes of the Ticket Agent.

The Ticket Agent didn't reply, only nodded. After that, I didn't know anything more. My eyelids were just too heavy.

Today is August 17th. Meaning I had to face Mother. Oddly enough, though, this train never wanted to stop. So how was I going to put an end to Mother's grumbling about her house about to be demolished by the Public Order people?

Now it really is August 17th, but when this train passes through the area where my house was, I don't see Mother anymore now. What I do see is only people running entranced to plazas and supermarkets. I only see people who, after leaving the supermarkets, feel clumsy with all the goods they've bought.

I am really sure this is August 17th. But when I try to peer through the train window, I don't see Mother at home.

Where is she?

Has she been eaten up by all the luxury that she had protested against? Was she now buying up everything in all the department stores in my city?

Oh well, I don't care what's going to happen to Mother. It's August 17th, after all. Better that I watch the carnival along the road the train is traveling.

I'm going to watch the carnival. Who knows, maybe I will meet Mother to discuss the home of a hero's widow that had been demolished by the City Planning Board.

I'll watch the carnival. I'll watch Indonesia honor its heroes. I just want to watch the carnival. I want to see Indonesians make fun of my mother.

Children Sharpening Knives

Manyar doesn't understand why the blade doesn't wink as it looks at you. You, who just now sharpened it, think it's sharp for slicing the apple waiting there on the table after dinner. It gleams when it imagines the veins in your neck.
—Sapardi Djoko Damono, from "Blade" in June Rain

The little girl also did not understand why, in Family Welfare Education class at school, she and her friends were taught to hone a knife as sharp as possible if it was only to be used for cutting up carrots or potatoes or tomatoes or anything that should be pared, sliced or skewered. And she knew even less why her father was always waving a knife at her when she caught him biting the necks of various women in the room on the other side of the open door. And what's more, she did not understand at all why the women brought in from the street didn't cry when they were "hurt," and sometimes even giggled or bit back even harder on the neck of the chubby man they called Bardi.

Such scenes started to invade her little eyes one week after her mother died—when she wasn't promoted to fourth grade—right when her big sister Mayang, still a sparkling jewel of a maiden, left for Jakarta.

Whenever she saw Bardi drunk, dragging unknown women into the room, she preferred to slip away from the house. With Nurkhan, her five-year-old brother, on her hip, she would rush off the five hundred meters to the train station and sit in an empty railway coach, lost in fantasies about the big black boxes transporting her to her mother. But she was always disappointed. The coaches never took her anywhere. In her imagination, she was taken by those iron boxes to distant lands where her mother flew alongside little angels with rainbow wings. But this only lasted for a moment. As soon as grown-up men and women wanted her place, she had to be ready to move off again. She was always having to move off, just like she had to when Mayang and her boyfriends—and they were always changing—fooled around in her room filled with dolls.

"It'd be nice to be a grown-up. Always winning," sighed Manyar.

And that night, when the rain splashed onto her house, which was jammed tightly between two others, Manyar had to suffer slap after slap simply because she had just happened to catch sight of her worthy father wrestling with two women she had never seen before, with everyone biting each other there in the room. The door had been left open.

"Rude thing!" snapped the pudgy man as he waved a knife at his own child. "You're spying on your dad again, is that it?"

Manyar didn't say a word. He slapped her cheek.

"Get going! If you spy on me once more, I'll pop out your eyes with this knife."

Manyar obeyed. And even though the rain was forming pools on the muddy road and making potholes throughout the kampong, she walked down the road regardless. She wasn't angry. She felt like every night she had to visit the coaches at the railway station not too far from her home.

"Mother, I'll be visiting you again," she'd say.

Then she started running, getting away from her home with all its noisy moans and giggling. This time Nurkhan was not with her. She knew that Mayang—who was back home with a man with a butterfly tattoo—would be able to look after their little brother. And because she was in such a hurry, she didn't know how many figures had slipped into her house. Her feet made little tracks in the mud as she left behind the moans and the giggling voices, along with the tick-tack of rain hitting the roof tiles.

The moment she arrived at the station, Manyar set out to find an empty coach where she could take shelter from the lashing rain. But as luck would have it, every coach she approached was being used by grown-ups. And because what she saw there looked just like what went on at home, she preferred to get away as quickly as she could.

This time Manyar ran to the platform. She hoped to see other sights. She wanted to see how little kids her age were carried tenderly by their fathers and mothers. Or even if she didn't manage anything like that, she wanted to gaze at the funny pictures on the platform walls.

After getting her fill of the cartoons, she sought out Kabrut, as she usually did. Every night, the young fellow guarded the station toilets, sharpening his knife to pass the time.

"Since you're here this late, you must have been slapped by your dad again. That right?" said Kabrut without even glancing at Manyar.

Manyar nodded.

[line break]

Without a word, the invaders bashed in the doors of the rooms where Mayang and Bardi were messing around with their respective partners.

Tarju, the young man with the butterfly tattoo, and Mayang had no chance break off their kiss when the burly men shot them in the head with silencer pistols. Nor did they even feel the slash of the knives on their necks when, with one jerk, their arteries spurted fresh blood.

"Make sure we get everyone," whispered a tense-faced man.

Before they could respond, the other intruders had already rushed off in search of prey, each ready with pistol in hand.

Meanwhile, the same thing happened in Bardi's room. He was hacked from behind just as he was about to come. The killers moved very quickly so that Bardi couldn't fight back, even though he was considered the neighborhood tough guy.

"You whacked the chicks?" asked one of them.

"Don't leave anyone alive," said the one giving orders.

Without giving them the chance to scream, they slashed the necks of the two naked women. Still not satisfied, the two thickly mustached men thrust their pistols into the mouths of the women and coldly fired.

"They'd only have ended up whores," said one of the shooters.

"So everything's been taken care of now?" said the other one.

Before he could reply, a voice came from the bathroom. The hunters of lives aimed their pistols and without an order being given, the moment the bathroom door was opened, they all blasted away.

Oh no! Almost twelve bullets tore apart the body of little Nurkhan who had just been peeing. Relentlessly pounded by hot lead, he had no chance to scream. He had no chance to groan. And he never did find out who had invited him to play "soldiers."

"My God! It's only a little kid!" screamed one of them.

This shocked the other gunmen as they realized their mistake. "This last one didn't need to get whacked!" exclaimed the skinniest one as he threw his gun down.

"We've got to be more careful," said another.

Now they started blaming each other.

"Who shot first?" someone asked.

No response. They each were sure they had shot last.

"Didn't we only need Tarju?" blurted out the one with a squashed nose. His voice was shaky.

"Yeah, of course we needed Tarju, but we can be sure he infected everyone around him."

"Stay cool! I heard Bardi belonged to one of the banned political organizations. So there was nothing wrong with him getting whacked too."

"But this little kid? This little kid? What did he do wrong?" exclaimed one of them as he threw his pistol and knife down near Nurkhan. "Don't you have children? Weren't you ever kids?"

The room got noisier. They all felt guilty and each felt he had carried out his duty. The uproar calmed down only when one of them who had stayed quiet all along snapped: "A job's a job. It's all over now. The game's done. Go back to your homes!"

Without needing to be ordered twice, the gunmen crept away from the blood-spattered house. One of them almost collided with Manyar, who was coming from the opposite direction in the alley.

[line break]

Manyar and her classmates were sharpening their knives together that morning during Family Welfare Education when a naughty wind raised the skirt of Bu Narni, the pretty teacher. Of course, none of the students saw it happen, for they were all deeply absorbed in scraping their knives back and forth on a sharpening stone. They were carefully sharpening, polishing and honing the blades of their knives so they could be used to shred, cut and pare potatoes, carrots, tomatoes, onions and other things for cooking.

"Oooh! Your knife is so good and sharp, Manyar," said Herman, her bench mate. Manyar said nothing. Her small sparkling eyes were focused on sharpening her knife.

"Where'd you buy it?" persisted Herman.

Manyar remembered where the knife had come from. She had found it next to Nurkhan's body, her beloved little brother. She also remembered a fellow named Kabrut. Every day, all he did was sharpen knives.

"Do you know what knives are for?" Kabrut once asked Manyar.

Manyar shook her head.

"To live," he said. "Yeah, with a sharp knife, I can do my job."

"So what is your job, Mr. Kabrut?"

But Kabrut didn't reply. Instead, he stuck the sharp knife blade up against Manyar's neck.

"This! This is what I do!" he had told her.

Ever since that incident, Manyar imitated Kabrut. She often stayed by herself in the kitchen or the washroom, sharpening her knife. There was a certain deliciousness in the knife blade scraping back and forth along the sharpening stone.

Like now, she would go into a trance the moment her teacher told everyone to sharpen their knives. So of course she paid no attention to Herman, her bench mate. She only had eyes for the gleaming, dazzling knife blade.

"It's really sharp now, Manyar. Why keep on sharpening it?" asked Herman again, trembling a little.

Manyar remained silent. Now she was remembering how Bardi—her dad who liked to get drunk—always threatened to pop out her eyes whenever she accidentally saw him fooling around with those street women.

"I'll pry out your eyes with this knife. I'll pry out your eyes and make you go blind." Bardi said that over and over. Over and over, until finally Manyar had to stop sharpening because Bu Narni told the pupils to stop what they were doing.

"On each of your desks," Bu Narni said, "is a carrot, a tomato, meat and a potato. Now do what you have to do with the knife that you sharpened."

Without asking for instructions to be repeated, the children started cutting, slicing and dicing the carrots, potatoes and meat that had been placed on each of their desks.

And Manyar? Evidently, she wasn't able to obey Bu Narni's instructions. No sooner had Madam Teacher finished telling them to begin the soup-making lesson, but Manyar stood up from her seat.

With the knife in her raised hand, she ran out of the classroom. She kept waving it all day long at Nurkhan's grave.

"Who slashed your neck, Nurkhan!?"

There was no reply.

But the knife blade doesn't gleam at you; you, who just now whetted it, think; it's sharp enough to slice the apple placed on the table after eating dinner; it gleams when it imagines the veins in your neck.

Enter My Ear, Daddy

It's crazy! This old, and I've still got to be a butcher. Still have to herd my victims to the slaughter pit, rope one of its feet, bring it crashing down, and finally whack its neck with a big, sharp cleaver.

To tell the truth, every time I see fresh blood spurting out of the necks of these helpless cows, loathing, queasiness, and disgust always hit me, torment me. But, how could I quit the job that gave me house, wife, and those three cute kids? How could I hang back from blood, when I was a little kid myself and Dad ordered me to cut off the heads of calves infected with the pest?

And, to this day, I can't avoid a slaughterhouse order to butcher ten head of cattle in two days. That's why, by turning a deaf ear to the lowing of those humped beasts, I again and again put my chopper to work at throat-cutting, until I no longer hear the heart-rending cries.

Perhaps I wouldn't be so queasy if I didn't have to cut off the skin that cleaves to the flesh. However, as it would be impossible to sell beef without first removing the skin, I just have to slice off the skin that sticks all too tightly to the blood-red meat.

Actually, if the work of a butcher went no further than this, perhaps I wouldn't mind working another ten or fifteen years. But, once the skinning stage is finished, I still have to cut and chop up various body parts for manageability when transporting them to the market, and there's nothing I want more than to quit this butchering right now.

Once, after many years of revulsion at this sadism, I asked the Boss to let me go without severance pay.

"I'm too old and very tired," I said, putting on a respectful voice.

"Wait a few years more, Abilawa. Without you, this wouldn't be a slaughterhouse any longer. Without you, all the workers and supervisors in this place wouldn't be anything," the Boss said, offering me a cigar.

"But… my energy is breaking down. Sometimes I'm too weak to pull down those imported cows that have twice the strength of our domestic ones. Yeah. And I've been gored time and again."

It was like he hadn't heard my complaints. He just kept trying to persuade me to stick it out there such-and-such a number of years more. "The entire staff still wants you to be the butcher. And what's more, what other job could you do in these uncertain times?"

Unable to turn down the Boss's request that time, I ran towards a barn that was filled with dozens of lowing cattle. I stared into their eyes, one by one, like a soldier staring into the glazed, listless eyes of his prisoners.

I hoped those animals with their folds and dewlaps would be angry and put up a fight. I also hoped they would snort and gore my guts apart without mercy. Too bad, though! Not one of those cows wanted to take up my challenge. Yeah. Not one of them wanted to accept the challenge of a butcher who was fed up with dealing with blood and the pained lowing of his slaughterhouse victims.

"Why can't a butcher die?" I yelled at the top of my lungs.

Our boss and a dozen employees just gaped, bewildered at my foolishness. Ah, maybe they thought I had gone crazy. Maybe they were just letting me vent my indignation and disgust at the routine.

Because the cattle only lowed and kept snorting in what seemed strange and ancient sounds, I took up a horsewhip and waved it about in the air above me. Its cracking and snapping roared, but it didn't panic the animals, some of which were carrying calves. Others merely stared with bulging eyes.

"Why can't a butcher stop being a butcher? Why can't an old man whose sadism is all used up stop being cruel?" I shouted again, brandishing the whip.

It felt like I had been shouting for a long time, repeating my words that may have changed into lowing and snorting. Abruptly, silence crept in and gored my soul into bits and pieces. All the lamps in the slaughterhouse had congealed in darkness. Had night nimbly arrived and kicked out twilight? Maybe. Just maybe.

I started to lose my cool. But why wasn't there a moon passing overhead? Where was the "*cit-cericit*" of the squeaking bats as they flapped their soft wings?

Feeling that if I stayed there I'd go out of my mind, I decided to just go home. Yeah, yeah, and when I got home, I would kiss the brows of my wife and three children. Would express my feelings of unending love, and finally cuddle with my wife the whole night long.

So I ran. Penetrated with all the power that remained in me on a night agitated by drizzle. I coughed and hacked a bit and spewed out all kinds of curses at the gravel that, through no fault of its own, spattered my bone-skinny legs.

When I got home, I saw that my children had not yet gone to bed. Kunti, the little one now only just starting to say *na-na-na*, was sprawled on the bed. Gatot, twelve years old, was still glued to the television that spat out news about the war of stones between security forces and the students. And Arimbi, age six, well, what about my little woman who liked to braid her hair?

"She doesn't want to drink milk anymore. Look, she spilled several glasses of milk I poured for her," said Setyorini, my wife, without looking at me.

"Why don't you want to drink milk, Arimbi?

"Because I hate cows, Daddy."

"Why do you have to hate them?"

"Because I am trying to be like you, Daddy. Don't you hate them a lot too? Don't you kill them every day, Daddy?"

Can you believe it! My own child, and she's wants to wipe out the animals that, for some reason, I wanted to protect after so sadistically slaughtering their grandpas, grandmas, mothers and dads by the thousands.

"The thing is, when I grow up I want to be a butcher, Daddy! I'll kill all the cows, ha... ha... ha..." shrieked Arimbi as she knocked over the tenth glass of milk that had been placed there on the table for her.

Scenes like that assaulted my ever more shortsighted eyes, and not just once or twice. Almost every time I came home from work, with its sadistic routine that I always wanted to get away from, I'd see Arimbi knocking over glass after glass of milk, saying, "I hate cows, Dad! I want to kill all the cows in the world!"

Since I didn't want Arimbi to go psycho and copy me in everything I did, my decision to stop working became all the more inevitable. That's why I once again screwed up my courage to meet the Boss just after I had butchered nine of the ten cows that had to be sent to market that day.

My hands were still spattered with blood when at midday I met the Boss. "Only one left, Boss. I have left it for you on purpose."

"Left it for me?" he said as he blew out a puff of cigar smoke.

"Yes. Some day you too are going to have to feel how killing is not a nice job, or easy or fun."

"Haven't you been having fun all along, O Abilawa the Mighty?"

"Having fun? You're wrong there, Boss. Only crazy men could kill and laugh about it," I said rather philosophically.

"Are you saying that only because you want to quit?"

"Yes. I don't want to be a butcher any more," I said softly, waiting for the Boss's reaction.

Once again, as if not hearing my complaint, the Slaughterhouse Boss still worked on me to stay a few more years. "Only a stupid man would let someone as experienced as you go, Abilawa. Only a stupid manager would lay off a butcher who has made this place the only supplier of fresh meat in this city. Now, go back to work."

"I can't today. Permit me to rest a day or so."

"Fine! Go home. Come back and work this evening."

Without being ordered twice, I ran straight home, which wasn't far from the slaughterhouse. I was still panting in the living room when Arimbi, my child who always wanted to slaughter cattle, startled me with a strange greeting.

"Enter my ear, Dad!" she softly said.[*]

"Yes, enter my ear, Abilawa," came another voice, deep and authoritative. A voice that reminded me of a thunderclap before rain.

"What for?" I asked with a hoarseness I couldn't master.

"No need to ask why. Close your eyes and enter slowly," it ordered.

Not wanting to be terrorized by that voice, I began to think then, could one human enter the ear of another human? *Only to be able to interpret as well as you might whatever is whispered to you,*[**] Must I give in to such persuasion?

"All right now, don't give any more thought to it. Enter my ear," said Arimbi with assurance.

Because I was scared, I closed my eyes and tried to enter Arimbi's ear. My God! A vast chamber stretched out before me as my big body slipped into the ear.

My astonishment had not faded when a loud voice like the mooing of a cow echoed, "Abilawa! Enter my ear!"

---

*) Inspired by the line, "enter my ear", in the poem, "Ear", by Sapardi Djoko Damono.
**) One of the lines from "Ear". Like me, Sapardi may also have been inspired by the episode from the Javanese *wayang* episode, *Dewa Ruci*.

"I've done it," I said in a rasping voice.

"You absolutely have not. Look around you, my vast ear still yawns as widely as can be."

Just plain mad! Before me did indeed appear an ear, which, unless I was mistaken, looked a lot like the ear of a cow. It was ready to gobble up my small, soft head.

Once again, without giving it a second thought, I stepped into the ear whose muscles swelled like a coconut palm.

"What do you see?"

"There's nothing here. No one."

"Don't lie! Open your eyes wide!"

Quickly, I opened my near-sighted eyes wide. Oh my God! Hundreds, no! no! thousands of cows were lowing and mooing together in my ears. Oh, if you could have only heard those disgusting sounds, you would have slaughtered and skinned them all, right down to the last one, I'm sure.

"Do you still want to stop butchering cattle, Daddy?" Arimbi's voice sounded like the clink of a glass being slammed down.

I didn't want to answer that question. Not wanting to traumatize my little daughter, I replied by the anger in my eyes. And yet, the lowing of cattle? The lowing of the cattle truly turned my stomach. Thus, I had no choice. I had to work with the cleaver, the lasso, and the blood that kept gushing out in the slaughter pit.

"Do you still want to stop slaughtering cows, Daddy?" badgered Arimbi. Her voice trapped me, cut away and peeled the skin off my wrinkling body.

"Come on, Daddy! Slaughter the cows and don't ask why!"

Oh Lord God, do you too hear the cold voice of my child? There's no answer. Now I only feel the horns of a thousand cattle butting and ramming me, wounding the part beneath my ear.

The Silent Eyes of
the Takroni Woman

The iron bars bordering the Al-Baqi Cemetery from the outside world are always and ever the same bars. Peering with dazed eyes into the graveyard, the pilgrims will always watch the dozens of soldiers, haughty and wary with their hands on their hips, as if the enemy from Al-Aghwat village would suddenly launch an attack on them.

No! No! Those policemen were only guarding the grave mounds of the companions and wives of the Prophet. Look! They wouldn't dare drive off the hundreds of pigeons that peck at the grains of *habbah* scattered by the pilgrims. They look like benevolent robots who have no job other than to listen to the cooing of the pigeons and the mourning cries of the people devoutly praying.

"Even so, if we've got the nerve to slip inside, they would smack us on our bums and our heads with their clubs," said Zulaikha, a diminutive black woman gripping the bars, to another young maiden.

They were amazed at the sparkle and glitter of the sun as it hit the wings of the pigeons and the packed mounds of grey.

"If we merely gave *habbah* to the pigeons, would we still be chased off?"

"Not just chased off. Thrashed! *Buk! Buk! Buk!* Your head'll be dented and your backside will be bruised like crazy. If you don't believe me, let's go ask my mother."

Like dragonflies, the children stretched out their arms and zoomed to the courtyard of the Al-Baqi Cemetery now filled with pilgrims. From time to time they bumped into people who were deep in prayer. Sometimes they fell and startled the elders of Medina who were guiding foreigners paying their regards and greetings to the occupants of the graves.

And, Medina, that blazingly hot city, still exuded the sun's scintillations as Zubaedah, the daughter of Musa, peddled *habbah* in the courtyard of Al-Baqi. If you get the chance to record the many and varied events with your mind's eye, you will see a pair of pigeons crossing over from the Nabawi Mosque, clucking and cooing in strange voices like the divine recitations in the Masnawi verse form.

As usual, the pigeons did not swerve directly into the cemetery with its beautiful strong walls. By extending their glittering wings, they plunged right down into the two hands of Zubaedah to peck at the grains of *habbah* being specially strewn around the cemetery courtyard by this blind Takroni woman.

"Mother, why can't we feed the pigeons flocking around the graves? How come we can only feed the ones in the courtyard?"

"Because we are women, my child. And, as I've told you over and over again, only the men are allowed into the center where the graves are."

Zulaikha, a young adolescent picked up by Zubaedah from the lanes of the noisy and never-sleeping Medina market, wasn't satisfied with that reply. Her bright eyes suddenly turned to the crowds of pilgrims of all the different races and nations who were now praying and lamenting in all their odd-sounding words before the earthen mounds, unadorned by beautiful tombstones or headstones.

"Come on, Mother, let's go in there. We'll give any unsold *habbah* to the pigeons."

Hearing this unexpected suggestion, Zubaedah stood up straight. A pigeon and her mate that had perhaps been staring amazed at the black woman in the black *abaya*, now were frightened into flight. Their noisily flapping wings startled the pilgrims. Deftly she tried to grab Zulaikha's hand as she was leaving her playmate behind. But Zulaikha had sped forward fast as an arrow and scurried into the hundreds of pilgrims crowding the grave courtyard with its Arabic architecture.

"Don't! Don't go in!" cried Zubaedah as she ran, kicking over the tray of *habbah* and bumping into people hurrying through the cemetery gate.

The pilgrims—most of them walking with heads bowed as they pronounced their recitations—were of course surprised to see a blind woman staggering and crying out in broken Arabic. They didn't know how seriously Zubaedah was struggling to halt the flight of the arrow that, if successful in infiltrating the cemetery, would offend the certainty of millions of people, hundreds of royal families, and all the pilgrims who unquestioningly accept custom and tradition.

"Forgive her, O Allah! Forgive the child who doesn't understand your example, O Apostle!" Zubaedah shrieked again.

Unfortunately, Zulaikha had become the arrow let loose from a blind bow. Therefore, with charming zig-zag movements, she wound and twisted and burrowed through and ran to the edge of the cemetery gate. All the young woman wanted was to give as much *habbah* as she could to the hundreds of pigeons who were flapping their wings above the grave mounds.

I would really like to be like you, my child. I'd like to give as much *habbah* as I could to the hundreds of pigeons who they say protected the Prophet when he was pursued by the unbelievers at Jabal Sur. They say that the pigeons resting in contemplation, together with the spiders which immediately went to work weaving webs, covered the walls of the cave. They acted as shields to protect the allotted lifespan of the Prophet.

Because of that, my child, giving food to them is the same as giving love without end to the Lord Prophet. If you just want to share your love, you don't need to enter the holy grounds of the cemetery. You don't need to weep and wail at the mounds of earth that have been glorified by the people of Medina. Least of all you, a woman, my child. Least of all you, a mere Takroni.

And, as a Takroni, O child of misfortune, as if our water were not *zamzam*. Like Bilal, the beautiful man who would call out the name of Allah in a most melodious voice, you're only the sputum hawked up from a black mouth that is coughing. You are only the echo of the sounds *boekkk* and *plok* from the throat filth splattering on the marble floor, the beautiful paving of the courtyard of the Al-Baqi Cemetery now surrounded by a gold market and dozens of deluxe hotels.

"Oho... there's no need to trouble yourself over what or where you have come from, my child. Like a thing always made filthy by other people, we are the excrement that dirties the beauty of the royal palaces," so said Musa bin Zakaria, my father, when I first asked about the difference between my black skin and the beauty of the skin of the boys and men of Medina who want to play with me in the lanes of the market, but, too bad, are always forbidden to by their parents.

"In fact, you will go blind if you are bold enough to question why mountains are called *jabal* or kings are called *tuan*, why Bilal was born a slave, why you were born as you, and I was born as I, and the *habbah* of Medina is only fit to be pecked at by the pigeons, whose numbers have never decreased or increased since the time of the Prophet and are always sobbing at the graves of his Companions," said Father, who claimed to be the son of an immigrant from Nigeria.

I don't know whether it was because I asked why I had been born a Takroni woman, or because of a disease I inherited, or for some other reason: at the age when I just started to bloom, I went completely blind.

And Father, like other Takroni men, did not bemoan this sorrowful event. "I told you... don't be meddling. Don't question anything. Don't look at things that shouldn't be looked at. Don't..." Maryam—my mother, a woman lovely and pretty as an olive— always argued with Father. "You only know the Black Stone set into the Ka'aba. But you don't know that the Prophet also honored Bilal, our comely ancestor. You only know that the pilgrims put the white *ihram* cloth over their bodies, but you don't know how the Ka'aba is covered by black cloth embroidered with gold thread."

Like the Prophet, Father exalted women. When he and Mother disagreed, he never slapped or got angry with the pretty woman he loved so much. Still, he didn't see my blindness as a curse. Like Mother, he accepted all things that happened in life as a message or even the love of the Prophet and Allah to the *ummat*, the community of believers.

When I was on the eve of adolescence, Mother said, "Of course, you're blind, my child, but you will become the rose of Medina."

Just before Father died, he prayed, "God, Thou Who Seeth All have brought blindness to the eyes of my child and have asked to be given back from her eyes all the beauty of the light of Medina. I will not be angry, O Allah. I will not be angry. But Thou Who Giveth All, grant her the brightest light of a heart in the midst of the darkness that always stalks her."

Since then, no one—including the sellers of prayer beads, veils, and *siwak*, the twigs you clean your teeth with, who cram into the entire cemetery courtyard—ask about my blindness. Only you, oh, who on the nights when silence makes the lanes and byroads shiver, question the source of my blindness.

"Did you ever feel the beauty of the Nabawi Mosque, Mother?" you asked innocently that time.

"Yes, in fact, your mother memorized the shades of gold of the entire door. Your mother could even count the lamps that cast beautiful light in the tower and the carvings of flowers that adorned its domes. Know this, my child, your mother also knows all the colors that adorned the *raudah* of the Prophet. In those days, I often cried and prayed endlessly in that garden of heaven."

"So Mother's seen all of it?"

"Yes, all of it, even all that shouldn't have been seen by humans."

"Why did Mother then go blind?"

"Perhaps because Mother saw something that shouldn't have been seen by a woman."

At those words, you knew, my child, that I really would not go on with my story. I was afraid you would follow in my footsteps. But you just kept rattling on, firing off innocent questions that shoved and stabbed. In the end, you knew why a woman such as I had to be blinded.

Zubaedah never told anyone why she had gone blind. Not her father, not her mother. Least of all Zulaikha. Fascinated by Musa bin Zakaria's stories about the importance of dying in Medina, one night she slipped into the Al-Baqi cemetery.

Tiptoeing softly, she kept remembering the advice of her father: "If you can, die in Medina, my child. The world of our lives as Takroni people is certainly not as glittering and shining as those of the people of Medina. We can never become citizens of the kingdom, not ever. But, if you die here, the Prophet will grant you paradise."

At that time, because of the affliction of a never-ending fever, Zubaedah felt that Death was looking in. "Yes, it would be good to die in Medina, but it would be even better to die in the Al-Baqi Cemetery," thought the girl who was still blossoming.

And so, Zubaedah began to creep towards the cemetery gate. Night blanketed her entire body, and, wrapped as she was in the black *abaya*, no one saw a shadow climb the bars of the cemetery. Oh, no! She had yet to put her foot down inside the place, when suddenly a sturdy hand pulled at her *abaya*. Zubaedah let go of her grip on the fence. And fell backward. The back of her head hit the marble floor. Everything went black. The lights of Medina left her eyes.

She came to from a long unconsciousness at the shrill and strident dawn call to prayer from the Nabawi Mosque. Had a seraph stopped her? Who could know! But what is certain is that, before passing out, she heard the jumbled voices of strong men cursing and swearing something awful.

"What do you expect of a Takroni! What would she steal from the cemetery?" yelled one.

"Right, what was this slave-spawned woman chasing after?" said another, his foot on her chest.

"All right! Enough! Just leave her here!"

Then the voices of the hefty men were gone. Only the sound of their boots slipped back from a distance.

Zulaikha was still dazed at the threshold of the cemetery gate. She didn't rush inside, because she had just remembered Zubaedah's story of the light of lights that always enveloped the Al-Baqi cemetery.

"A dazzling brightness from the wings of seraphs will blind your eyes, child. So heed my advice. Never go into the cemetery, even if you want to die and be buried there."

Zulaikha only knew that to die in Medina she had every day to sell *habbah* in the courtyard of the cemetery, play with the pigeons, and do her daily prayers at the Nabawi Mosque. And from time to time shout out the words *fisabilillah*—"in the cause of Allah"— to the pilgrims in order to be given one or two riyals. But that afternoon the pigeons on the grave mounds looked famished. Fewer and fewer pilgrims fed *habbah* to them. Fewer and fewer women—who normally love and care for animals—approached the cemetery.

And, as Allah willed it, the blind woman Zubaedah staggered and bumped into whatever was in front of her. She supposed that Zulaikha would act as foolishly as she herself had before blindness had pounced on her and imprisoned her. She supposed the small woman was recklessly challenging the dozens of soldiers standing there, hands on hips, in the cemetery.

Therefore, long before she was groping for the cemetery gate, she imagined the police thrashing Zulaikha's cute little body—cursing and swearing with filthy language and seeing Takroni women as unruly slaves.

But, see! Zulaikha was still there standing hesitantly at the cemetery gate. Dozens, no, hundreds! of pigeons that had flocked to the mound of grey soil (*Oh, were they incarnations of seraphs?*) suddenly zoomed over the head of the small woman. They dived toward the Nabawi Mosque, waving their wings, as if inviting Zulaikha to leave the zone of battle.

"Mother! Mother! Look! They won't die of hunger at the cemetery," yelled Zulaikha joyfully.

Like Drizzle, Pointed Red

You would never imagine a November drizzle as sharp as this, Hindun. You would never know how much the sound of the great sunset drum during this recent Ramadan shredded and slashed, and the recitations of *Allahu Akbar* on the eve of the Eid reminded me of your foolishness in reading the victory flags stuck in the skies over Uhud.

Of course, at that time drizzle was not lashing the battlefield, clamorous with the clinking and crashing of swords or spears in combat. Nor, of course, was lightning striking in the uproar of whinnying horses and dust flying about like ashes. But everyone knew, like drizzle, more and more arrows from the heartless bows whizzed through the air, ignoring the cries, ignoring the corpses piling up on the stony hill.

And you, Hindun, why were you still sharpening your sword? Why indeed, at the moments when no swifts and thrushes fly over the graves, do you still remember the fierce battle at Jabal Uhud? Haven't you ceased all your fasting and wild pain?

I had thought you ignored my hoarse cries. Together with the Quraysh tribe—oh, my golden heroes—you hurried to count and to look for the people who had fallen in that great war. Aha! I counted fifty-five soldiers of the Prophet's army who had perished, while only twenty-two had among the Quraysh. Clearly this was an incontestable victory. A most beautiful victory after, long before this, I had heard the voice of Ibnu Qami'ah shouting fit to split the desert, "Muhammad has died! Muhammad is gone!"

Indeed, the war was almost over. But—strangely enough—your face launched no bright fragrance of olive oil at the thunderous news of that death. You seemed not to believe how easy it had been to subdue the Prophet, how Ibnu Qami'ah's sword could strike him in the temple and bring him down headfirst to the ground.

I was indeed stupid. At such a moment, I should have never needed to disturb you, a pretty woman who thirsted after blood. Yet you were more attracted to Wahsyi, the Abyssinian boy, who had succeeded in planting his spear into Hamzah's body. Still, Muhammad dead or not dead did not change your expression into something as sweet as an *ajma* date.

And, I saw you laugh uproariously after learning that Wahsyi had torn open the stomach of Hamzah and pulled out the liver of that Lion of the Desert. Ah yes, your face did shine when you gazed at Wahsyi as he handed the blood-smeared organ to you.

"Look here, Hindun, I have killed the champion who killed your father."

"Yes, you know full well what I shall present to you. Take and possess all that I have plundered and looted. Live happily, after having been throttled by unending pain."

Wahsyi smiled. His chest puffed up.

"Must I hand you this liver?" said the valiant man.

Without answering that stupid question, you just grabbed Hamzah's liver from his relaxed grip. And in a truly unexpected move, you bit off a piece with your sharp front teeth, chewed, and greedily swallowed that tough but pliable meat with the fresh blood still on it. "This was my vow, Wahsyi! I will fast no more. My war is over! See! It's like I'm reborn."

And it would have been a mistake to suppose I could have stopped the thunderous laugh of victory that arose from your blood-smeared lips. After happily tearing Hamzah's body to pieces, you leaped onto a large rock and belted out war songs that stank up the entire desert with its towering hills.

Certainly, Hamzah had perished. But you were mistaken in thinking that Muhammad had been destroyed. And I know about events that you don't. Because, after you ignored all my questions, I sped on wings to another space, to another time. Thus, I knew how, after the Quraysh people were lulled by that momentary victory, the Prophet gradually recovered consciousness. Which meant that you had to keep the fighting spirit of the Quraysh aroused to plant their spears into the chests of the believers, to skewer with their swords the bellies of the army of the soft-hearted, and to hone their wrath once more.

I supposed that with the passage of centuries, after forgetting the stinging November winds, I would not again encounter a bold woman as harsh and foolish as you, Hindun. In fact, in this city— where angels are easily teased and thought of as perfect men, easily flattered and caressed by other men—there you are again.

Maybe you aren't the Hindun of the past. Maybe you are only a dim shadow, quickly fading. But, look, just like Hindun, every day you sharpen your desire for revenge, hone your wrath for something empty, for something useless.

"A waste of time? Nothing's a waste of time. Revenge for the death of my child, you think that's a waste of time?" you ask as you remember the burning city and the wolf-men who incessantly ripped up the evening dresses of every ivory-skinned woman who passed along the streets.

"But the times of sadness are over, Hindun. And besides, why are you always fasting, whereas on the eve of the Eid, you instead…" I said, after I first changed myself into Rosa, your officemate.

"Instead of what? How nice for my child's rapist to be allowed to live. Never mind, don't act like you're an angel. No sermon from you is going stop me from taking my revenge, Rosa. Even if you were an angel, all your stupid advice would mean nothing to me. One thing's for sure, that man has to die."

Uh-oh, I almost admitted who I really am, Hindun. But, I figure you didn't need to know that yet, or why I am so driven to prevent you from doing something foolish. So I am just letting you ramble on, letting you go on sharpening your sword and your hate, while "*Allahu Akbar!*" lashes the night.

"After many exhausting days, Rosa, I finally found out who raped and murdered my daughter. Not someone from far away. Not the wolf-men who burned down almost this entire city."

"Then who?" I asked, pretending not to know, although in truth I knew very well who those rotten wolves were—beautiful men—that she meant.

"You'd really be surprised, Rosa. You'd never suppose…"

"Who?" I again pretended as I watched Hindun's face tense up.

"He is my own son, Rosa. It was… Hamzah!" you shrieked as you hurried away from me, and, taking the sword, dashed off to the cemetery.

Yes, to the cemetery—where your dear daughter had been buried. Of course, I didn't let you race off by yourself. Of course, I didn't let you hide in the bushes waiting for Hamzah to bow his head in resignation at the tomb of his only sister.

Hindun! Hindun! Really, why do you want to repeat that useless slaughter? Why not just let the November drizzle fall like pointed shards without hurting anyone?

No! No! I could not allow this. Hamzah must be saved. I will fly on my beautiful wings and prevent my beloved man from giving up his life in a useless death.

And you, Hindun, you might want to ask: *why must Hamzah be saved?* Surely you'd want to say: *why do I forbid you from cutting off his head?* Hamzah is the lover I adore. Since he was little I did indeed teach him to be a man who neglected the advice of a mother. You of course gave birth to that powerful man. But I only borrowed your belly to breed someone rotten.

So, ever since his youngest years, I infused Hamzah's brain with all kinds of evil desires. At first I told Hamzah how Nur—your most beloved daughter, the one who was murdered—was not his real sister. I told Hamzah that Nur was a whore's daughter whom you found in a garbage bin when she was born. And Hamzah believed this just when he was immersing himself all the more deeply into the beauty of the body and countenance of his sister.

So when this city was engulfed in the blind madness of riots and almost all the women with ivory-colored skin were gang-raped by hired zombies, I whispered wicked words into Hamzah's ears.

"Come on, Hamzah! When, if not now!"—while remembering the soul of the other Hamzah who I was sure was trying to hinder me, if the Desert Lion himself still lived.

At first he was rather doubtful. But because he didn't shut his ears to my evil words, it all happened in the end. He dragged Nur to the end of the lane. Nur resisted. Nur tried to free herself from the embraces and the alcoholic rage in Hamzah's mouth.

At moments like that, Hamzah actually wanted to re-sheath his evil appetites. But I quickly slipped into his soul. I fanned his passions. I fanned his anger. I strengthened his grip on Nur's neck, so that she was nearly strangled.

And after all of that, I flew away, fusing with the smoke enveloping this city. I saw Hamzah standing there dazed, confused. I saw him sorry for his wicked deeds.

"Don't ever feel regret, Hamzah. Don't ever regret anything! Run! Run as far away as you can!" I hissed those words and he obeyed.

Yes, he followed all my commands, at least for a few years. Too bad, though, in the end he wasn't capable of meeting all my demands. And on the eve of this Eid he telephoned you, am I right? Just before this Eid, he spoke of all the bad things you had done, right?

So actually I knew, Hindun. Tonight, when cries of "*Allahu Akbar!*" resound, he will return. He will visit Nur's gravesite before kneeling at your feet, at the feet of a long-neglected mother.

So, if you can just soar along at my speed, you can see how I am blocking Hamzah, making him back off from visiting Nur's grave and meeting you as he intended. And at the station, I will of course change into you. Become the gentle-hearted Hindun. Become the Hindun that doesn't sharpen her sword to kill her own son.

"Don't return, Hamzah. I have just told Rosa about what you did. She has surely told the people in her kampong and they will slaughter you," I said after he got down from the train, after "*Allahu Akbar!*" echoed from the nearest mosque, wounding my ears.

Hamzah only hung his head. He didn't dare look at me.

"Go away again, anywhere, to wherever you will be beyond the reach of the people in this city."

Hamzah kept his head lowered. Nonetheless, he had the guts to hiss the words that I never expected could fly from his ever more tender lips.

"Today is a day filled with forgiveness. Not a single person is going to dirty himself or herself with evil deeds. Allow me to visit the grave of my little sister. Allow me to fall face down in the quiet of that grave."

"Don't, Hamzah!" I shouted, "You can't be as weak as that."

Hamzah sank deeper into contemplation. He began to cry.

"That's enough, Mother! Everyone's forgotten about what happened. Even if in the end someone's going to kill me, I am ready for it, Mother. Maybe my death will…"

"Will what? You can't die! I don't want to lose both my children. I don't want to lose you," I said as I pretended to burst into tears.

My tears seemed to be of no use. Hamzah turned and left me.

Did you too cry at the grave, Hindun? As you whetted your hatred, did you also sense that you would lose your child?

Now understand, Hindun, I am of course Satan. However, even I can feel a deep loss. And Hamzah is the son I adored. I didn't want to lose him. I didn't want you to kill him. I didn't want you to be like the other Hindun, exceeding even me in cruelty.

But my wounds from the piercing sounds of *"Allahu Akbar!"* hurt more and more, and the drizzle is indifferent to all my shouting. Perhaps that drizzle has mixed with Hamzah's blood? Perhaps you have slashed through your son's neck, ripped open his belly, taken out his liver, and bit into that pliant meat as you shrieked your victory? Has Hamzah perhaps fallen and his head has struck Nur's gravestone, sharply pointed and awaiting the death of the man that you had cursed the most? Like Hindun, that formidable woman, would you say, "I've killed my sworn enemy! I have ended my long fast and I will cry no more"?

I can no longer answer that question. The cries of *"Allahu Akbar!"* are shredding my wings. I can't fly. I can't streak over to the grave and kill your majestic anger. But, Hindun, why must it be Hamzah again? Why must it be him again? Why don't you feel the November drizzle, pointed red and hurtful?*⁾

---

*⁾ The phrase *pointed red [meruncing merah]*, I adopted from the lines, *There was a pair of hills pointed red / from the fields that looked straight up* in the poem "Before the Window" (*Di Muka Jendela*) in Goenawan Mohamad's anthology, *Complete Poems 1961-2001*.

Sand Mirror

There are no monster robot transformers on the slopes of Merapi. Just dozens of trucks moving sluggishly, ripping apart the hamlets with an ear-splitting din. Sometimes, when the drizzle stings the air, these iron beasts slither along and writhe like snakes. Sometimes, when they have a full load, they waddle like lizards. But, not infrequently, they forge ahead like dogs when the skies above the mountain redden and the mist of water crystals evaporate.

No one's got the courage to explain why every day more and more trucks claw and comb almost every corner of the village. No one's brave enough to ask why there were more and more landslides, why the hills get more and more pitted or just simply disappear.

And the trucks, the trucks come and go invisibly, like invisible powers. Deep in the night they always carry big bruisers—most of them in uniform—and then disappear after several parts of the hill have been eaten away and the rivers run ever deeper.

There are always disappearances. There are always things that do not come back. Stones, coral, sand, and dozens of women. Not just that! Not just that! There are always disappearances. There are always things that do not return. The stillness after rain, *Ki Dalang* slashing the air with his *wayang* puppets of horn and leather, the chattering of children when the rays of the moon fall on the roof tiles or the silence of the croplands.

All right then, let me introduce myself. They call me a temptress, but actually I am a dancer. Look, even in the bed of the truck that climbs, panting, up the road to the mountain slope, I am still able to enchant the sand miners with my tippy-toed flying turns and my obeisances of pressed palms pointed straight up to heaven.

What's more, when those bare-chested fellows are whispering strange prayer-like sounds, I do my best to steal their attention with the marvels of my fluttering hands and sidelong glances in the manner of a Ken Dedes or a Drupadi.

"It may be about to rain, so why don't you stop dancing, Miss?" someone murmurs.

"I have a bad feeling about this. Stop tempting us!" says an older miner, joining in the whispering as he gazes at my back.

"I have to dance for Kiyai Petruk later tonight. Let me practice for just a bit. I'll stop after I meet with Romo Sentanu and Ayat."

"Later tonight we are only holding our communion meal. Just a gathering at the church to give thanks for the harvest. We aren't going to dance," rasps the older miner.

"But Ayat and Romo Sentanu asked me to dance," I reluctantly reply as I execute *pacak gulu*, my subtle and elegant neck movements.

For a moment all is silent. No one dares stop my dance. Oh yes, mentioning Kiyai Petruk, Romo Sentanu, and Ayat in that village is like invoking the utter invincibility of the gods.

Kiyai Petruk, you know, is a horror that is beautiful. If he is angry, he can spew out from his mysterious mouth *wedhus gembel*—the term for our common goats, of course—but what we really mean here are the burning clouds of gas, ash, and bits of lava. No need to be coy about it, I'd best reveal to you that at first I didn't want to say "Kiyai Petruk" in speaking of Mount Merapi. But since slipping into this village I've been forced to deal with all the taboos and auspicious names for the mountain that stands arms akimbo, so to speak, athwart Java. So even I call the clouds of heat that come boiling and swirling up and spitting out that shard-filled ash, "the Goat." I'm always muttering these odd names when the scintillations of lava dribble down the sides of the mountain.

Now, about Romo Sentanu: oh, he's just the Catholic priest in the village. I'm forced to deal with that decent man because he all too often gets involved in what goes on between the sand mining bosses and the local residents. He even often acts more like an instigator of demonstrations rather than a priest. And one of my jobs in this village, you know, is to tempt and seduce. And, if need be, bring his good name crashing down.

So I'll dance naked in his room. I'll destroy everything he knows about the sidelong glances of women, the coy mewing of women in the early night, and the beautiful nipping of the lioness at the neck of her adored mate.

Sometimes when the voices of the tree crickets and cicadas cut through the village, I have imagined the hefty men in uniform, my friends who don't talk much, spreading Romo's arms against the hill, driving nails though his palms, and thrusting a crowbar into his side. And every time he moans in pain, I take off all my clothes and dance the most erotic dances and ram the tormenting vision into his blinded eyes.

So he was not an opponent that needed much thought. At any time, our strong hands could easily deprive that genial priest of his life.

Ah, for sure you have known Ayat better than I know the stones, coral, moss, and the quiet of this village. You surely must have seen the man in the sarong often performing the wayang kulit episode *Kunjarakarna* in order to unveil the rottenness of the sand-mining businessmen.

Certainly you'll often see this tedious fellow spouting out in Javanese, "The gods aren't fair! The gods aren't fair!" in front of outsiders visiting the village.

Yes, in the eyes of that skinny *dalang*, the gods are definitely unfair. They give their bounty to the strong men who endlessly mine the sand and who never give the slightest notice to the suffering of the impoverished farmers. The gods give only Kiyai Petruk and the

Goat, but forget to stroke the hair of the women who lose their husbands when the lava brings devastation to the village.

And when he performs the shadow play, Ayat can become a god. He can gently get anyone to oppose tyranny. One day, when he said, "Come and dance the whole night through along the road!" all the people of the village danced the *joget* from the edge of the village up to the slopes of Merapi.

It goes without saying: no truck dared to break through the swarm of the dancing villagers. No one was so hardened as to crush the heads of little kids who had come out to watch the lovely movements of the kampong elders, and lay down to sleep by the side of the road.

Ayat also was a good dancer. For the villagers, watching Ayat dance was like the villagers meeting an amiable Petruk. A Petruk who never punished simple folk with lava, burning clouds, and the endless rain of stones. A Petruk who had never spread enmity, strife, or hatred.

But Ayat wasn't Romo Sentanu. In the beauty of his dance were enthroned both angels and devils. I heard from the other dancers that he easily "bent his knee" before women who were the better dancers. Like Samson, he was very easily subdued by Delilah.

Now you're beginning to know why a temptress was needed to get Ayat and Romo Sentanu out of the way. So I'd best introduce myself to you—they call me a temptress, but actually I'm a dancer.

Look, even in the back of the truck that climbs, panting, up the road to the mountain slope, I was still able to enchant the sand miners with my tippy-toed flying turns and my obeisances of pressed palms pointing heavenward.

What's more, while those bare-chested fellows were whispering strange prayer-like sounds, I did my best to steal their attention with the marvels of my fluttering hands and the sidelong glances in the manner of a Ken Dedes or a Drupadi.

"Perhaps it'll soon rain, why don't you stop dancing?"

A little later it did rain. And I stopped dancing just when the truck pulled up in front of the church. Maybe Father Sentanu and Ayat would rush out to greet me. Maybe, as he was bowing, Ayat would say, "O please, Beautiful One, Daughter of my Palace, come dance with me."

Yes, he might say that. "But I've come to seduce you, to bring you down, and to smash you to bits!"

On the slopes of Merapi, the gleam of light in the eyes of Romo Sentanu was more mysterious than the incandescence of lava. So, as he and Nagreg stood face to face, eye to eye, all the wicked schemes of that excellent woman from the city formed a sort of tragic film scene in his calm spirit that always radiated patience.

It wouldn't have been surprising if Romo Sentanu thought that at some point Nagreg would poison Ayat's drink to rob the *dalang* of his voice, so that he would no longer be able to perform the shadow puppet plays and spread criticism of the illegal sand mining businessmen, whose numbers even the sharpest memory couldn't keep track of.

Romo Sentanu also knew that Ayat wouldn't be able to dance again, because while he was dancing with Nagreg in the chaotic *Larung Sengkala* exorcism ritual, in which all bad luck is cast into the river, a dozen toughs in uniform would chop off the feet of the dancer whose every performance reflected the rebellion of the owners of the hill who were being strangled by those greedy city people.

"I only want to dance with Ayat, Romo. I want to quell the anger of Kiyai Petruk with dances of love that no one has ever danced before." Nagreg, who didn't dare look straight at the blazing eyes of Romo Sentanu, suddenly turned sulky.

"Yes, let her dance and be my singer, Romo," Ayat whispered as he dampened his unbearable lust.

There was no reply. And, when from the direction of Merapi, a red light flashed to the white banyan tree at the end of the village, when howling, like that of a wounded elephant, lashed the entire kampong with its cries, Romo Sentanu bit his lips until wet fresh blood trickled down.

"Nagreg will save this kampong, Romo. Let her dance with me," again murmured Ayat as he knelt there, wanting to kiss the feet of the perfect man whom he so greatly revered.

There was no reply. Nagreg gave full rein to a smile within her. And, unexpectedly for Ayat, Romo Sentanu walked away from the church. Ayat worried that if Romo Sentanu could hold out and not return to his own room next to the church, Nagreg might act up by stripping off all her clothes before the serene statue of Holy Mother Mary, or by dancing indecently under the face of Jesus as he grimaced from the wound in his side and the crown of thorns stabbing his head.

Ayat also did not know that in the strange silence and chill of Merapi, Romo Sentanu saw Jesus sobbing under the white banyan tree at the end of the village in a voice as shrill as if it came from dozens of wounded elephants. *)

The procession looked more like a carnival than a ritual of homage to Kiyai Petruk. And, that night, amidst hundreds of torches waved at the heavens, amidst the hot clouds and the lava that kept on dribbling in the stinging November, Romo Sentanu, surrounded by several altar boys, led the ceremony of the *Larung Sengkala* ritual that would be cast adrift at the dam that was steadily losing its water.

Behind Romo Sentanu spread hundreds of villagers imitating the dancing of Ayat and Nagreg, some with elephant head masks, while others streaked their faces to look like tigers.

---

*) The mythology of the elephant and the white banyan has been explored by Elisabeth D Prasetyo in *The White Banyan*.

"Oh Lord, Your commandment will be consummated," whispered Romo Sentanu.

Yes. And I know who the victim will be.

"They will strike my head in the middle of the wild dance, Lord."

Yes. They will stretch out and tie your hands and feet to stout ropes fastened to both sides of the river. Then, as you lay on the water, a hail of bullets will pound into your guts.

"Why must it be me, oh Lord? Why not someone else?"

Oh, not just you, Sentanu. Ayat and Nagreg will be crucified with you.

Truly, there are no monster robots on the slopes of Merapi. Just dozens of trucks moving sluggishly, ripping apart the hamlets with earsplitting din. Sometimes when the drizzle beats the air, those iron beasts crawl along, slithering and writhing like snakes. Sometimes, when they have full loads, they waddle like lizards. But, not infrequently, they forge ahead like dogs when the skies above the mountain redden and the mist of water crystals evaporate.

No one is brave enough to explain why every day more and more trucks comb every corner of the village. No one has it in him or her to question why there are more and more landslides, why the hills are increasingly pitted or just simply gone.

And the trucks keep coming and going like invisible powers.

Deep into the night they always bear big bruisers—most of them in uniform—and then disappear after several parts of the hill were dug out and the rivers ran deeper.

There are always the missing. There are always those that didn't come back. Stones, coral, sand, and dozens of women. And not just that! And not just that! There are always the missing. There are always those who never come back.

And that night they came again. No! No! Maybe it had been several months back, they had sneaked in and lived with the village folk. Like me, (*oh, you know my name is Nagreg, don't you?*), they had drunk in the air, the light, the traditions, the stupidities, the queer dances, the Kiyai Petruk mythologies, the goat—such bullshit, and all the ways Romo Sentanu and Ayat behaved.

So they knew the best way to get rid of Ayat and Romo Sentanu. In the darkness of night, they led those perfect men to the middle of the dam and in the chaotic clamor of the dance of homage to Kiyai Petruk, chopped off their feet, heads, and shot them in their bellies with silencer pistols. Ayat and Romo Sentanu surely never supposed they would be treated that way. For they had never spread suspicion among the villagers. Because they never quarreled with those poor people. But aren't the men who wear uniforms—anywhere in the world—good opportunists, clever at changing themselves into anteaters or pythons? So don't be surprised if they can stab from behind.

All right then, let me introduce myself once again. They call me a seductress, but I am really a dancer. No! No! I am really just a victim. They ordered me to trick Romo Sentanu and Ayat. But after all the preparations for the slaughter at the middle of the dam were complete, I heard from one of the popular strong men, a deserter, that they were going to kill me. There couldn't be any witnesses. There could be nothing to make this event go wrong. Now in all the noise, the torches, the light in the eyes of Romo Sentanu, and the wildness of Ayat explaining the dreams of the burning clouds, the dribbling of the lava from the peak of Merapi, and the shrieks and tears of the dance, I only hope quietly to soon end all this chaos. *Ah, must I face death as I dance the* serimpi?

No reply. Only the shrieks of the gamelan. Only the shrieks in pain.

Womb of Fire

River of Tears

You needn't think of the baby, suspended in the red shoulder sling with little images of phoenixes, as a magical child let fall from the sky. Nor need you ask why a woman lusciously ripe cast a tiny creature adrift onto the river in that rattan basket, after the moon disappeared behind the old temple with its twin dragons.

Perhaps before giving the final suck at her breast, she had asked permission of the *sien bing* [')] —the gods, the pure ones—to dandle the infant in her arms if only briefly. Perhaps she believed the turd-filled river would transform itself into a mother, would protect this little one from the rage and madness, and rock and cuddle it the whole night through, whispering ancient tunes in a nasal humming, in a pained moaning.

"Weren't the worshippers of Hok Tek Tjeng Sien, Kwan Sing Tee Koen, and Kwan See Im Po Sat ["] rushing madly to get outside?"

No. When the bells were ringing and clanging from the church far from the houses of worship full of fruits and incense smoke, it was very possible that the temple had already been abandoned by its monks, its ground keepers, and so on.

So you have to understand, I only heard the crying of the surviving babies, fresh blood still stuck in their hair, the lamps on

---

[')] 神明 "the spirits, the gods".

["] Hok Tek Tjeng Sien (福德正神), Kwan Sing Tee Koen (关聖帝君), and Kwan See Im Po Sat (觀世音菩薩) are "the pure ones" worshipped at the Siu Hok Bio (寿福庙), Jalan Wotgandul Timur, Semarang. In the opinion of Setyono Budy Santosa, Siu Hok Bio is the oldest temple in Semarang.

the pathways along the riverbanks sparkling and gleaming on the water, and a plump hand that was trying to set that baby adrift.

"All night long this city was drenched by rain, right? How could there be a moon disappearing behind the temple?"

Torrents of rain did indeed drench this city. But afterwards, there was only a steady and gentle drizzle that tapped, tapped, and tapped on each roof tile. And, you know, my eyes were still very alertly fixed on infant being washed away, cast adrift among the human filth, plastic buckets, and dead chickens.

A moment later (and to me this was a miracle!) pairs of black creatures (maybe little bats) flew dizzily a meter above the head of that baby. These formed a kind of umbrella shielding the baby from the beating of the drizzle.

"The little tyke wasn't crying?"

Sure, it was crying. Even birds cry when they lose their mothers. No! No! Maybe the baby was chatting away with the bats in a language only they knew. And we only thought it was crying.

So I was really sure that the baby was still alive when it faded from the view of my ever worsening eyesight. Even now its crying is still sounding in my ears. Even now I suppose it had been rocked in the arms of some other woman that longed for a baby sent from heaven.

"Why didn't you try to save it?"

You think I could save it? You think it would want *me* to rock it with all my heart and soul? Its own mother wouldn't, let alone some whore like me who just wants to visit the Twin Dragons Temple.

"If that's true, then the blame's on you!"

Blame? Blame for what? You think just because you didn't see the baby floating among the turds and rotten garbage, you can consider yourself the most blameless of creatures? *Phhh!* You're the guilty one. Why were you just snoring away at home that night? Why didn't you watch the moon disappear behind the temple and stare at the river that passed in front of the house of worship that you're always praising?

And besides, who could know for sure if the little babe was dead. So enough of this, just let me leave! Let me hunt down a good man who will give me a baby. I need a baby that is born from my womb. I don't need an abandoned little thing that has been thrown away by that plump hand.

Dog Woman

"So you want to tell why that that nicely shaped woman threw her baby into the river?"

Yes, of course. Of course, I will tell who the woman is that you may consider the most damned person in all the world. I know best of all why she was drunk the whole night before finally visiting the Twin Dragons Temple, to beg forgiveness of anyone who occupied the house of worship and then throwing that little babe into the river.

And you've got to understand, nobody has the right to blame that miserable woman. She's my daughter. I'm the one who best understands why that baby had to be gotten rid of. I, more than anyone, understand why she didn't want to care for that little creature.

"That means…"

For nine months I kept her shut up in the cellar. All that time, she never spoke a word. And all that time she only paced back and forth in that space. Sometimes she played with bugs, toads, or… snakes.

No! No! I also lit a torch and put a dog into that dark room. So she wasn't lonely. Yes, I know she wasn't lonely. A dog and enough food made her a healthy woman, fully ready to give birth to a healthy baby. And, you know, that dog was really very loyal. Every time my daughter lay down, it would lovingly lick and lick her swollen belly. Its tongue seemed to turn into the hands of a brave and powerful man who never stopped stroking the belly of his lover.

"Why did you keep her shut up in the cellar?"

Because I hated her silence. Because I couldn't stand slapping her face. Because I didn't want stare at her swollen belly. Oh… that belly really set me off. There were times when that belly became a knife that sliced and slashed.

"Don't exaggerate…"

I'm not exaggerating. That ever-swelling belly truly made me lose a lot. My daughter's youth was lost. My confidence in my beautiful body, which had always driven those tough studs crazy, was gone. I lost my trust in everyone in my household. And worst of all, I lost my trust in—

"In the man who secretly got your daughter pregnant?"

That's the problem. You think my daughter got pregnant because she was a victim of those God-cursed brutes. You're sure she was ravished by the mad dogs who burned this city. You're sure those crazy zombies attacked our house, smashed my beautiful china, dragged my daughter to the toilet, and raped her, gang-style.

No! No! It was the girls in the neighboring homes they burned. But not a single one of them dared to touch my girl. You know, when we heard the rioting, she was in the midst of an epileptic fit. That disease, that curse, was the very thing that kept her away from all the fury. That's why, after all the rioting petered out, I no longer saw epilepsy as a curse.

Yes, yes, our house wasn't burned down. But, for the past nine months it has been very hot in there. My daughter's swelling belly would send off sparks at any time. Their heat soared off the wall thermometer. Their flames were hotter than the stove at its highest.

"Enough! Enough! All your nonsense has been noted down. Now, answer my last question: why didn't you try to stop your daughter from throwing that infant into the rushing water?"

Keep her from doing that? Ha ha ha! I was the one who told her to throw that accursed baby in. How could I let the baby from the seed of that drunk live with us? No! No! I didn't want a hellish grandchild from the seed of that dog.

"So you know who got your daughter pregnant?"

(*The woman began to cry. Her lips quivered uncontrollably.*)

"You know? So all right then, answer me! You know who raped your child?"

Him...

"Who?"

(*There was no answer. However, the interrogator knew what kind of a man would be shameless enough to feel up a buxom girl who hadn't the strength to resist the embrace of a pair of hands. The interrogator had heard the tale of a sculptor who every night dreamed of making love to his favorite statue.*)

"Go home now. I'll summon that miserable louse tomorrow."

WILD MOON

Ow! Don't slam your fist down on the table and bark at me like that. You don't have to order me to tell you about the fate of that little baby. I'll tell you all about my dear daughter's and grandchild's catastrophe. And stop baiting me as a messed-up louse. My fate has been nothing but heartache.

My neighbors think I'm a living ghost, married to a demon, and with a devil for a child. It all started from our fear—me, my wife and my daughter with that ripe marriageable body of hers—of the outside world. Of the stinging sunshine, of the wind that mutters and mumbles like the dead, of the ferocious people who almost burned my house down, and those zombies who—

"Get to the point! Tell me why your daughter threw that baby into the river and who knocked her up?"

My daughter? Oh, my poor daughter! My wife had kept that

pretty angel in the cellar with a dog. Couldn't bear seeing her tormented, so I'd always keep her company on the bad days. We often ate together, even when two or three cockroaches were crowding around and our dog kept sticking his tongue onto the plate.

"Did you sleep with your daughter?"

Never! Only the dog and those cockroaches kept by her side until she gave birth to a tiny creature whose birth cord I never got to see.

"Don't lie!'

I never lie. But don't go supposing then that my daughter did anything with that dog. Anyone can think of her as a woman from hell, but she never made love to a dog. Our dog, you know, was the most faithful dog, one that watched over my girl and waited for the birth of a devil baby.

"A devil baby?"

Yes. Of course it's a devil baby when its seed came from the raging men who burned and beat every woman with ivory-yellow skin. How wouldn't it be a devil baby when his father hit me with a club and handled my daughter in front of her old man who had one foot in the grave?

"But your wife said you…"

Oh… don't you believe the wicked words of that devil woman. She's wanted to kick me out of the house for a long time now. For a long time—sorry, since I became impotent—she's wanted to kick me out. She's had me thrown into jail just so she could be free to play around with other men. I'm telling you the truth, I was the first person to disagree with her keeping my daughter in the cellar. I also didn't agree with forcing her to throw that baby into the river.

So, that night, when the moon seemed to be shining wildly behind the temple and my daughter was creeping towards the riverbank, I secretly tailed her. Of course I saw the chubby hands of my daughter throw the basket into the river. I wanted to stop her. But everything happened so quickly, and the current took the basket right to the middle of the water. So don't think I haven't lost something. I was the first one to dive in and grope for the shoulder scarf with the phoenixes that the baby was wrapped in. Look, sir, at that moment I was afraid the little mite would be devoured by the carrion eaters who were always watching for their prey whenever floods hit, when all kinds of things were being washed down on the mighty current.

THE CARRION EATERS

That's right… we do get our food from all the creatures washed down by the river. But we've never eaten little babies, even if they're already dead. That night this river washed down rat, dog, chicken, cat, and maybe even goat carcasses.

While I was with my children and husband, I saw a body the size of a piglet floating by in a sturdy basket amid the garbage, turds, and rotten wood.

"Hurray! We'll be eating goat," I shouted like someone possessed.

"Wild boar! Wild boar! We'll eat wild boar!"

My kids drooled when that carcass sped into sight some ten full arm spans away.

"Wait a second! Don't start dreaming about feasts just yet. Look, that thing in the basket is still moving. We can't eat anything that's still alive," yelled my husband as he stood there on the bridge, hands on his hips.

So we just stayed put. Held back the spit that already was beginning to drip from our mouths. And that meant we had lost a blessing and a gift. The strong tide had sped the basket away and out of our sight.

"Turn around! Look sharp!" shouted my husband, half scolding-like. "That basket ain't got no piglets nor puppies in it. Probably's a baby. Yeah, my eyes ain't totally gone yet. There's a baby in it wrapped in a shoulder scarf with phoenix birds all over it."

I myself was standing stock-still then. But suddenly my three kids—who were just about starving—swam out and fought over who'd get the basket.

And did they get it?

No. The basket—that I figured had a baby in it—sped by so fast, leaving my kids all worn out and wondering what they had to eat that night.

That's all you can relate?

Of course not! At that same time, we saw a big-bosomed woman with a pregnant belly come running up and down the riverside. She cut through the darkness as if she was chasing something being carried away by the water. A bit later, a middle-aged woman appeared too, grumbling. "Damned child, why is she showing off her big belly filled with that devil child?"

And not just that. Not just that. We also saw an old man— maybe he was drunk—babbling something awful. As he ran with a flashlight his shouts cut through the dark. "I don't want to lose you a second time, girl. You can't leave the house. Otherwise those dogs will get you again. Those savages will get you again."

And what I couldn't understand at all, suddenly there appeared all dressed up bright and shiny a woman (a whore, maybe), glaring at me with hatred and spite. I didn't return the vicious lightning from her bulging eyes. I was amazed to hear her hissing like a snake as she kept saying the name of baby in the basket being washed out to the delta.

"My Moses, my Jesus, my Siddhartha, you won't die, my child. You are only sleeping on a river that never sleeps. You are just being carried away. Maybe to the sea. To the sea. To the sea…"

At that moment, you know, my kids were crying. Their hunger was eating them up inside. So enough of that. Don't ask me anything more about a ripe-looking woman casting away a little lump of a baby in the midst of the drizzle that never stopped. Don't ask any more why we weren't able to save the little infant.

Yes, yes, it's not impossible that baby might still sleeping on the sleepless river. Maybe it's just being carried away. To the sea, perhaps. To the sea. To the sea...

The Resistance of Sita

1

Really, Rahwana, in that garden, when the rain beats down on the veranda and in the quiet of the bed, I have seen your ten pairs of lips speaking of the virility of the kings who are always making love. Your visage becomes truly radiant when the blue-eyed maidens invite you for a swim in the stillness of the pool. How strong your hands are when ten women with rainbow faces drag you into the bushes of the garden.

So what more is there to worry you, Rahwana? You've given wings to all the most rainbow-hued of the women for them to accompany you when you fly to the mountains and the valleys, to the sea and to the shores, to the clouds and the stars. To all the most intoxicating women you have given mouths of fire, so that they can create a sublime hell as they embrace you the whole night long.

So you needn't pen me up in this bat-infested garden anymore. You don't have to wrap venomous snakes around the trees anymore, if all you want is a piece of my face from which speech is gone. You don't need to create a ring of fire all over the garden if all you want is the quiet of my burnt eyes.

Yes, yes, even without your watching me with that saw-tooth glare, I am spellbound by your ten-horned faces. Without even whispering words strewn with jasmine, I cannot turn away from your ten pairs of lips that you always smear with that blue lipstick. So put off killing whatever man has already seeded me with a gaze of lust. Put off prying out the eyes of my lover simply because you don't want him to coil around me with looks that radiate sashes of love-drenched silk.

Truly, Rahwana, you don't need to show off by building the most beautiful parkland, a shoreline studded with crabs admiring the muscles of your mighty arms. Even without you reverently seated on the ground like a priest before a carving of a thousand gods, I am amazed by your eyes that are forever spewing fire.

Therefore, you never needed to abduct me. Nor pretended to love me. I hate pretense. I hate your lips which are too cowardly to crush my lips in the racket and bustle of the marketplace.

2

Now, about Rama, my husband, what else could I expect from a fop like him, more in love with his brother Laksmana—a pretty fellow who never stops flapping his wings? You think I love his fragrant studliness? You think I admire his words which ooze slimy worms? No, not at all! Our marriage was only an unavoidable curse. "Marrying me," said Rama, "is to marry the freshness of a watermelon. Marrying me is to wander endlessly in the greenwood. Marrying me is to hide lifelong from the complications of the world."

And as I always need the freshness of watermelon, I wanted to be courted by the man with those snaky dreadlocks. And because I like the greenwood, I sat, legs curled behind me, at his mighty feet, when a greenwood was presented to me. And, to be sure, I followed wherever he went because, naturally, I didn't want to fall into the ravine of a complicated life.

Now I am disappointed. When you (*oh Rahwana, mighty man with silkworm fur*) kidnapped me, he kept silent. I know that he said before the world, "My love, I will pursue whoever abducted you, even to where the winds go!"

However, I also knew this: the day before he sucked on my lips for the last time, he gave a fish fin to Laksmana. And that meant when he abandoned me in the forest, they went swimming down to the bottom of the dark lake and made love without fear of the eyes of a woman blind in her fidelity.

Ooh, he thought Laksmana would give him a lake to be gulped down over and over again. He thought Laksmana, so graceful in his every movement, would invite him to dive to the end of love's endless wandering.

Laksmana, you know, was no more than a snuffling forest pig, confused the moment his owner left him. And Rama didn't know that within the magic curtain—a bed that other men could never sleep in—Laksmana bit my neck again and again. And for me he really was a pig, snuffling and jabbing me all over with his sharp tusks, and drooping when I puffed and wheezed like a bitch dog out of her head.

So the whole world is truly out of luck if everyone keeps on worshipping Rama and sees me as a wife who is as white as a yam bean. Take a look at my eyes that grow ever more wanton. Oh, look at my eyes that yearn for anyone lost in the forest. And now I clearly miss Rahwana emerging from the blue of the pool, coming with his handmaids, and inviting me to give meaning to life.

3

So that's why, Jatayu, you don't have to be so stiff-necked about Rahwana only because you want to guard my purity. You don't deserve to die merely to guard my beauty from the touch of Rahwana's wings.

"But who wouldn't cry if Rahwana happened to kiss your forehead..."

No one will cry over something which someday we'll call a dream, Jatayu. No one will cry over something that someday will be rejected as just a legend. Fly off and find Rama. Tell him that only a dog would be faithful to a heap of flesh without memories.

"I am fated to follow you to guard your purity, oh my revered princess!"

Purity? What do you know about purity? Your pointed beak is purer than my fingers so slender and curved, Jatayu. Your mighty wings, too, are purer than my lips that never stop whispering "Rahwana".

Purity, you know, is only the nonsense of the gods. Purity is only a cracked mirror that always wants to be made whole again. You can't say that you yourself are the purest if you don't kill anyone who claims to have created a garden for sinners. You can't say you are the purest of all if you still see the world only fit to be lived in by pupae, maggots, and low creatures who glorify love over death.

"I will die for you, Lady!"

Don't, Jatayu! Don't! Your death would only become the memories of buffoons. Your death will only be remembered as a useless passion. Yes, yes, I know, Jatayu. Even you want to touch one of my lovely wings in your death throes. So your death would be no more than the last sigh of a bird which had run out of time for chirruping its lusts.

So fly far from this forest, Jatayu. Inform Rama that I refuse to return to the palace. I refuse to be the woman with perfect breasts, if purity is made into a carpet merely to be stepped on. Tell him, I have become a wild and wanton woman, but I am free from all the curses of a life that sees my beautiful demeanor only as a plaything.

Ahh, Jatayu! Ahh! Why aren't you listening to what I am saying? Why are you still fighting with Rahwana on behalf of that fop Rama? Why is it you who will die, Jatayu? Why does it have to be you?

4

I've already said, I didn't trust your ten pairs of lips, Rahwana, but I wanted to have one of them, the ripest one. Your embrace lulled me so, and I always convinced myself that someday sweet children will be born from two pairs of lips that meet with such haste.

No! No! Of course, I was more enraptured by the mantras of love you hummed as we rolled about in the bushes of the garden. Of course, I was more amazed at your fierce bites just before the little bats quickly broke the silence of the trees.

And really it was only your lips that changed the hot, dry evening into a mist-laden sky. Only your lips changed the flight of a pair of birds in their craving for the coolness of a lake at the end of the forest. But, you never gave lips without lipstick, Rahwana. You always smeared your lips with a blue lipstick filled with lies.

"Only you deserve to have my lips, dearest. Only you deserve to nip at them the whole night through," you said over and over.

Weren't these unforgivable lies, Rahwana? Was there ever a night without a maidservant touching your wings and the silkworm fur on your broad chest? Was there ever a maidservant who didn't worship your captivating bat gaze?

"Oh, since knowing you, I haven't touched a bed, my love. Since knowing you, I haven't gasped slimy words all over my maidservants."

Aha! Truly a charming lie, Rahwana. A lie that makes the river dry, the forests sere, and my eyes blurred.

"Blurred?"

Yes.

"Blind?"

Not yet.

"Not yet?"

Yes, not yet. Nothing will end before Rama sets me on fire. Everything will still go on before you're killed and I sob and weep at the edge of the garden. Oh, do you hear my lament, Rahwana? Have you become only a fading shadow that disappears after night grinds down the quiet of the garden? Will you still wrap a hundred snakes around my legs for a love that makes no sense at all?

No, Rahwana! I don't trust your ten lips that do not convince me. When the moment for burning arrives, perhaps only then will I believe that only *your* love was eternal. Only your love—even though it has thrust through the outer skin of the maidservants— can change me into a flower, into a mysterious night, into the sweetest mango. Do you hear my voice, Rahwana?

5

Now even you know who you are, Rama: only the perfect prince who doesn't understand why the caves at the end of the garden are filled with dog-headed monkeys with cruel hearts predicting the day of your death. You are only a dull lover who doesn't understand the meaning of the false loyalty of the garuda-footed dogs that always worship you.

And now I ask you: have you ever considered me a pretty orchid that grows in a swamp infested with crocodiles? To you I'm only a snake, tadpole, rotten frogling, pupa-worshipping insect, or the slime that drips from the sex tools of chickens.

You never adored me like your fish, when I had been the most sparkling beauty of all in the lotus pool. You never fondled me like you did your pretty little dog that panted and moaned, am I right?

"No, my princess, Rama loves you very much," snuffled the comely monkey as he danced.

Yes, he can say that, but I now no longer believe the lips of anyone. Including the lips of Rama. Including the lips of the whole accursed world.

"We no longer have lips, my lady. So there's no need to question the lips of anyone. Just sense it, exalted lady, we can only speak with our hearts."

6

No! No, Rahwana! Now you finally found out, that handsome monkey has finally burnt down the garden, Rama has killed you—although without knowing that it had always been impossible to kill you—and like a plate of ribs I was served up to the mangiest curs.

"Are you still a white deer for me, my love?" whispered Rama then.

I don't have to answer that stupid question, do I? You knew best of all, Rahwana. You were the one who knew best of all if evening would always be called evening whenever a bit of moon gleams in the firmament.

"Say something, my love. Don't just hide behind gleaming lips!" Rama whispered again—exactly like a dog.

And I was still unwilling to fulfill Rama's command. So that rotten prince became furious.

"Aren't you afraid of fire?" Rama said again. "Aren't you afraid of death?"

7

"So did he burn you?"

Yes, he burned me.

"If he burned you, how can you still make love with me?"

Because the fire feared me. Because the Great Fire coiled around me before the stupid matchsticks struck my hair.

"And Rahwana?"

Rahwana reared my children in the lake. The universe had changed them into fish for me.

"And I?"

You only became an ugly monkey, a storyteller waiting for the day you die. You have become only the announcer's helper for my stories previously hidden by the fishermen on that lonely shore. You became only a gatherer of shellfish. You can only stare at mangy dogs running around chasing emptiness.

"So..."

So you needn't immortalize your love for anybody. Now embrace me. Then sleep and dream about a pair of cockles, a pair of dogs, a pair of shorelines, and a pair of deaths that await us in the silence of the sponges. Yes, yes, sleep, dear. You're sleepy, aren't you?

8

I never sleep. I never die.

9

Rama slept. Rahwana slept. Rama died. Rahwana died. And you, woman of fire, your delirium never stops. Ever.

Sultan Ngamid's Wings of Mist

Yes, as you also know, that day, Sunday, the 28th of March, 1830, the fasting month of Ramadhan had ended. So, in my painting, I was certain that only a soft mist and dimmed sunlight enveloped the Residency. No steady drizzle snapped at the old pillars. Nor did lightning bolts lash Mount Merapi, vaguely seen heaped up on this mortal earth. Thus, I wasn't mistaken in embedding a bright color into the whole canvas. There was nothing wrong in my giving the impression of Allah spreading a hue of golden brown on the faces of all who witnessed De Kock rebuking the Prince.

The fragrance of earth was still furling skyward when the uproar occurred. The sounds of squawking poultry still remain fresh in the mind. And people, I especially, believed there would be no fighting during and with the end of Ramadhan. Therefore, even though De Kock stretched out his hand to command the Prince to the carriage that would take him into exile, I still did not want to change that moment of crisis into a Lebaran colored by sadness and melancholy.

Of course, calm and clarity emanated from the newly broken morning; but it was impossible for me to incise the mist and cold of Magelang too deeply onto the canvas. So even though he was surrounded by the tense faces of De Kock's staff and witnessed by the sobbing ordinary folk, I had to paint the Prince upright and defiant. I alone could be sad. Only I—who you suppose had studied the techniques of painting from Horace Varnet and Eugene Delacroix—could slip into the face of a common soldier who reverently bowed before the Prince and the jittery troops worrying about the fate of our Exalted One.[*]

If Raden Saleh had been present at the Residency with Crown Prince Diponegoro, Raden Mas Joned, and Raden Mas Raib, the children of Sultan Ngamid, on that day of wonders, March 28, 1830, perhaps he would not have painted Sultan Ngamid as only a turbaned prince.[**] Yes, if he were standing near Haji Ngisa and Haji Badarudin—the Prince's beloved religious advisors—surely his painting would not have depicted Sultan Ngamid as merely an ordinary person.

Because, as Haji Ngisa saw it—and he was still very cautious and alert when tensions arose and General De Kock expected the Prince to immediately get into the carriage—there sprouted on both of the Sultan's shoulders the dazzling wings of a purple falcon. It was as if those wings would fly Our Exalted One to the pure heavens, to the sky filled with swallows. But unexpectedly, he removed the beautiful feathers that perhaps had been given to him by the Angel Gabriel. He even signaled to Haji Ngisa to remain unmoved by all the wonders that will abound after one devotedly performs the fast. In spirit whispers, the Sultan also asked Haji Ngisa to not be astonished at all the illogical and irrational events that invested the Residency, now surrounded by soldiers.

Haji Ngisa, who understood how mystery could penetrate Allah's chosen ones, just nodded. As he pressed his finger to his lips, he also gave a sign to Sultan Ngamid's intimate retainers,

---

[*] From a painting by Raden Saleh on the cover of Peter Carey's *The Origins of the Java War: The Sepoy Rebellion and Raden Saleh's Painting*, published by LKiS in July 2004. That painting was also used by the choreographer Sardono as the basis of the play *Opera Diponegoro*.

[**] Sultan Ngamid is another name of Prince Diponegoro. The moment he appointed himself Ratu Pangageng Panatagama ing Tanah Jawa (King and Leader of Religion in the Javalands), he gave the name Diponegoro to his son ("the Crown Prince").

Banthengwareng and Jayasutra, to not cry out. Haji Ngisa did not want shouts of amazement to disturb the fate written by Allah. He didn't want De Kock or the stony-faced Kedu resident, Valck, to be alarmed and take flight. "Everything has been set," whispered Haji Ngisa, "and it may well be that Gabriel himself has been commanded to sleep and not get involved in everything that happens in this fine get-together."

Haji Ngisa knew well that if Sultan Ngamid had not shed the wings, or if he spewed out poisonous centipedes at his opponents, Roest, De Stuers, or Perie would consider the Sultan to be performing magic and insulting the officers who had proposed to negotiate an end to the Java War.

"If he wanted to, Sultan Ngamid could disappear. If he wanted to, everything at the Residency could be turned into stone by his curse. Well, sir, would you like to be turned into a dust mite?"

Therefore, Haji Ngisa preferred to gaze at the gleam of the weapons and the uniforms of the soldiers led by Du Peron on the portico, rather than contemplating the visage of Sultan Ngamid, whose blazing brilliance could not bear looking at.

"General, sir, you should not stare at the face of the Sultan. If you must do so, your heart will be burned," whispered the man who always recited Allah's praise so very softly.

Of course, De Kock didn't attend to this subtle signal. Of course, he had not been trained to understand signs that took the form of the mere shake of Haji Ngisa's head. Yes, certainly not all signs are tangible and pregnant with meaning. But, why, after that astonishing look occurred, was De Kock insensitive to it? Why did he not allow Sultan Ngamid return home after this good will visit?

"Why am I not allowed to return home, General? What must I do here? I came entirely in friendship for a brief visit as prescribed by Javanese custom for those who have completed the month-long fast.*) I did not come with kris unsheathed and sword on fire."

"I would like to settle our problems on this very day," said De Kock.

"So you wish to arraign me? You wish to incite a fight? If that is what my General wishes, I don't need justice at your hands, sir. If it is a fight you want, sir, neither do I want to fight with you."

Yes, when he heard this outburst, Haji Ngisa hoped De Kock would quickly back off from his intention to arrest and exile the Prince. However, De Kock had every reason to carry out the order of Governor-General Johannes van den Bosch right then and there. In fact, he was more concerned with the instructions of his governor-general than the outpouring of anger by Sultan Ngamid. Even if it proved impossible to arrest or kill Sultan Ngamid, De Kock had ways to subdue the Prince. *I will demolish your power by any means possible, Prince. If need be, I will slit the throats of your beloved women on the third day of this Lebaran. Then, sir, I will shoot your sons. And, do not forget that we will also throw Haji Ngisa and all the attendants into the old well.*

Sultan Ngamid could read De Kock's thoughts. Therefore, as he raised his head, he spewed his final wrath at the general, whom he now considered the lowest form of criminal.

"Now, General, know this. I, whom you have always called Prince Diponegoro, am not afraid of death. I am prepared to be killed at any time. Death is just a fine mist, anyway. Death is only a curtain that will allow me to unite with my wife at Imogiri. So go ahead and kill me. I am sure this will be the very summit of triumph I have gained from my month of fasting."

It grew harder for Haji Ngisa to keep listening to this outburst by Sultan Ngamid from which emanated all manner of fragrances.

---

*) Words spoken by Sultan Ngamid in the *Babad Diponegoro* (The Autobiographical Chronicle of Diponegoro).

Therefore, he tiptoed next to Ali Basah Gandakusuma and whispered several unexpected questions.

"Friend, did our Sultan not understand that something like this would happen?"

Gandakusuma nodded. At that very moment, he saw Sultan Ngamid begin to gather up the purple falcon wings that he had removed. He carefully put on the wings. And carefully, too, he cried out, "*Allahu! Allahu! Allahu!* All is completed, Lord. I have returned everything to You!"

After that, you know, like Jesus the crucified, he stretched out his arm, shook his wings, and vanished, body and soul, and soared right into the mist, disappearing from the sight of Haji Ngisa, who was no longer astonished.

Why were you no longer amazed, oh clear-sighted Kiyai?

Because, in truth, not all things have to amaze. Be amazed at why Sultan Ngamid dared to die in the very space and time that provided him the opportunity to live. Be amazed at why he did not display those wings of purple to De Kock and the soldiers, who were also blinded. Know you well, Tuan, that if De Kock and the soldiers knew, the entire Residency would have gone up in flames. De Kock would have been just a piece of charcoal and the soldiers would have been lifeless ash.

Were you not worried, sir?

I could no longer be worried after De Kock was bereft of sensitivity.

So you knew that everything would end so tragically?

Tragically? Why "tragically"? The miracle of Gabriel's wings on the Prince's body, you consider that tragic?

Oh, so Sultan Ngamid really did have wings?

Whether or not he had wings is none of your business, sir.

Then whose business is it?

Mine, Haji Ngisa's, business.

Did Allah send millions of angels to escort Sultan Ngamid to heaven?

Why do you ask that?

Why can I not ask that?

I suppose I wasn't the only one to see the millions of angels escorting Sultan Ngamid to heaven.

Does anyone else know about that magic event?

Ask Gandakusuma. Ask the man who prayed together with the Sultan in every dawn prayer.

May I ask De Kock?

Why not? Would he view the Sultan as the lawless Tempter? Did he seize Sultan Ngamid because he imagined himself to be the messiah who could end the war?

Haji Ngisa did not want to answer that question. Lightly touching Ali Basah Gandakusuma's hand in departure, he withdrew from the Residency that seemed all the more like a ravenous apparition.

"Tell no one what you have seen, sir. I believe you will not spread anything that would mislead the community of the faithful. Wonderment, you yourself know, sir, often can distance us from the Sower of Wonders!"

Yes, it was Ali Basah Gandakusuma who, ever since that dawn prayer of March 28, 1830, really did catch sight of wings growing from out of the shoulders of Sultan Ngamid. "The wings of death", thought he, "wings that will end the war".

Nonetheless, Gandakusuma lacked the courage to question matters of war and death. It would not have been good on this newly blossomed Lebaran to question the stench of death, the fragrance of grave flowers, and Matesih village on the eve of Sultan Ngamid's negotiations at the Residency.

"I think all the soldiers must accompany you, my Sultan."

"Allah makes no such requirements, Gandakusuma."

"Your pardon, Sultan, but I worry that General De Kock will—"

"Yes, yes, you can worry. But, I am more worried that our soldiers will alarm them."

"So we shall only be making a goodwill visit to celebrate Lebaran with General De Kock, Sultan?"

"Yes. Don't put on your signs of rank or office. Just wear casual clothing, as if we were going on a pleasure outing or just taking a walk."

At that point, when this exchange was becoming less and less comprehensible, Gandakusuma saw the purple falcon wings on Sultan Ngamid's shoulders starting to unfold and engulf the pillars, posts, and everything that could be felt and touched by hands. Therefore, once again, Gandakusuma objected.

"We will indeed be making a friendly visit, Sultan, but De Kock has become a devil. And as a devil he will kill whoever does not submit to him."

"A devil? We're the devils if we cannot forgive people who would kill and trick us."

This time, Gandakusuma couldn't bring himself to look directly at the Sultan's face. He knew that in a little while, after eight o'clock that morning, the Sultan would depart for the Residency and De Kock would be mobilizing hundreds of devils to arrest the Exalted One, who now cared less and less about the cries and shouts of victory on the battlefield. He was very certain that the Sultan's wings would fall to the ground the moment De Kock snapped at the Prince, commanding him to step toward the coach of his exile.

"Everything has been arranged by that damned general, but why does my Sultan believe that that everything that happens has been set by God and can no longer be avoided?" whispered Gandakusuma in a whirlwind of wild thoughts.

"It's all right, Gandakusuma," said the Sultan, as if he understood everything that was being thought by his leading general. "When we are at war, think of war. But when it is Lebaran, think of Lebaran. Come on, then, let's relax and enjoy ourselves with General De Kock and his officers. Later on, I'll give you a new horse. Later on, I will give you a prayer mat and a new turban. Later…"

Gandakusuma knew that later on, he would only get wings that had fallen off, eyes that had lost their power, and a spirit no longer enchanted by the mists of Merapi. *Oh, why does defeat smell so fragrant? Why does it appear when the apex of victory comes naked in the form of an angel?*

Now you know, don't you, why I didn't want to paint Sultan Ngamid with the purple falcon's wings. Portrayed with or without the wings, Sultan Ngamid is Sultan Ngamid. He will shed whatever does not belong to him. Including wings and earthly majesty. Including wings and everything beloved.

Yes, my name is Saleh, and you have seen Sultan Ngamid in my painting""") in the evening when your prayers are mostly absent. I am happy because I don't consider him an angel or a god with purple eyes.

****) Historical Tableau, the Capture of the Javanese Prince Diponegoro.

The Ghost in Arthur Rimbaud's Head

THE STICKUP OF THE PRETTY FELLOW WITH THE HANDS OF SNAKES

"In 1876, or forty-six years after the Java War ended, only an angel or a devil could have sped through the air from an army barracks in Salatiga to messy Semarang. Therefore, I don't believe Van Dam's notes. I'm not going to be hoodwinked by nonsense about Rimbaud being able to walk forty-eight kilometers. So, Raden, let's create a story for *Archipel* or *Le Tour du Monde* about that spoiled fellow who joined a Dutch infantry battalion. Who knows, maybe the world will use our notes when it dissects the life story of this poet, this genius!"

Madness! I'm no historian. Just a simple-minded chap who's fond of sketching whatever appears amazing to his eyes. That's right, I've drawn a tiger that has suddenly leaped onto the back of a wild buffalo and plunged its sharp claws into its pliant flesh. I have also depicted a Prince of Java standing steadfast when dozens of soldiers all aimed their rifles straight at his golden eyes. And from my doodlings on this canvas, anyone would know I could hardly be called the savior of life stories. But why is that pretty fellow, whose fingers stick out at me like snakes, forcing me to write a story about a man I didn't know very much of at all?

"Come on, Raden, you can surely do it. I only want you to write the story of that loony soldier from a rather problematic angle," said the man with the plump lips who claimed, as he clasped and wrung his hands, to be an old enemy of Van Dam's.

A problematic angle? Oh, I'm just a simple, straightforward draftsman. I don't want to get mixed up in anything you'd find outside the rational or logical. When I depict Javanese people bravely and heroically subduing tigers, wild buffalo, stags, or lions, I haven't the slightest desire to tell the Dutch soldiers how one day they're going to be chopped up into little bits by people who've been oppressed and ignored.

Also, when I paint a cliffhanger of a fight between a wild buffalo and two lions, I'm not showing the eternal fray of good against evil. I am not confronting something problematic when I scratch lines and lay colors on a piece of canvas. So how can I recount an event from a problematic angle? How could I ever string together strange words or phrases if I tremble whenever I confront something strange—including this man with the wild lips?

"Oh, I don't care if you know history or not, Raden, sir. But clearly you are Javanese, and Rimbaud once stayed in Salatiga. I will pay handsomely for what you'd write, and more than you'd get for ten paintings."

Hmm... this crazy fellow really knows nothing about all the stuff I was doing in Paris after January 23, 1845. And he doesn't know how I got drunk on the flowers in the garden full of snakes and all kinds of fruits. If he only knew how much I hated everything that smacked of Paris in my paintings, I am sure he wouldn't be wheedling me to write a story about a romantic soldier or a poet who thought he just had to get a feel for the thunder of battlefield cannons.

Yes, yes, in July of 1875, I did actually go back to Paris, to look for my pictures in the collections of France's grandees. Because the war had destroyed these pictures, I came back to Java. After that, I preferred life in a town where every day all you had to do was hum a tune and the skies would drizzle. I wasn't in the least bit interested in living in Semarang or Salatiga. Therefore, it's a mistake for the man who's spent his whole life trying to defeat Van Dam, to ask me in this stuffy café to create a new history of Rimbaud using precisely those bits and pieces of information discovered by that same Dutch military historian who published an account of Rimbaud's travels in *De Fakkel*.

But, all right then, someone who draws, you know, may be able to write the history of somebody from the colors, lines, planes, space, time, and storms that suddenly make a mess of the veranda or the studio mottled with paint and memories. It's not impossible that someone who only knows salt-laden fog would write of Rimbaud wrapped in drizzle and hundreds of pelicans flying hither and yon.

Rain of Fire

A draftsman did write the life story of Rimbaud in wildly surrealistic prose. Raden, painter of Java, supposed that Rimbaud's frail soul would have been easily taken over by ghosts and those subtle beings called *mambang*. That's because he knew he had been a slaver, a gun runner and mercenary. He assumed that for the poet who had surrendered to the forces of darkness, it would be more suitable if his story were written in a style that combined sufistic fantasy with a brief whiff of Tuntang Forest village magic.

I suspect that, just before writing one of most wildly absurd of Rimbaud stories, Raden read Rimbaud's poems, which dwelled on every Parisian intellectual's bookshelves. He may have even cried out, *"My hunger, Anne, Anne, flee on your donkey"*, over and over.

The spontaneity and the uninhibitedness of Rimbaud's verse deeply influenced all the writing I discovered in the garbage bin not far from the *De Fakkel* office. So, when Raden wrote: *Rimbaud by now had been given wings by Lucifer when he left Tuntang*, all I can say is, this stupid draftsman really did deserve to be called the unluckiest guy of all. Nor can I say anything about when Raden confidently wrote: *Rimbaud flew in a flock of twelve angels. And with those angels, he formed part of a bizarre configuration so that if you saw it from a distance, it looked like a sunflower that was forever radiating tears.*

And in order to bring out a mystic effect, he also dragged the name Nyai Danyang Tuntang—Lady Guardian Spirit of Tuntang Forest—into Rimbaud's adventures. *Actually, when he ran from the barracks, Rimbaud was drunk. And in the depths of that drunkenness he felt he met with a woman with the face of a bird. It was she who asked the fallen angels to fly Rimbaud as quickly as possible from Tuntang to Semarang.*

Wild stuff, this! Not even Van Dam, I think, would consider Raden's writing nonsense. Rimbaud did arrive in Java as a Dutch soldier in 1876. He had commenced his reckless journey and mentally unbalanced adventures in 1874, after he wrote the poem "A Season in Hell" that drove a lot of people wild about him. On May 18, 1876, Rimbaud went to Haderwijk and enlisted as a Dutch soldier in what was also known as Europe's foreign legion.

As you know, he received at the time an allowance of 300 guilders. Naturally, a treasure of that size could change into a drunken ship taking Rimbaud to heaven, *dang dang ding ding*, to the song of the highest tower, to the feasts of hunger, the poor man's musings, or the endless winter.

Finally, as he sailed to Java, he no longer imagined himself a soldier or brave volunteer, but in fact a disturbed devil unfit to live in even the filthiest barracks. And even when the vessel Minister Fransen Van de Putte arrived in hot and dusty Semarang, according to Raden's version, he said, "Wait for me, sick city. I will be visiting you very soon again, once these silly soldiers release me in Salatiga."

Oho, I knew he wouldn't feel at home in Salatiga. This town was too cool and orderly for the wild spirits that danced and screeched in Arthur Rimbaud's head. So, before arriving in that flamboyant city, after getting on the train from Semarang to Kedungjati and walking in the direction of Tuntang as he watched the clear river flow by, once again in Raden's version, he muttered, "Someday a devil will fly me to the big port from Tuntang River's rustling waters."

Yes, you then knew, from Van Dam's notes, that on August 30, 1876, he was reported missing from roll call. History cannot record Rimbaud's path after that. And it was Raden who slyly and wittily provided us with the flight of the spirit-haunted Rimbaud. According to Raden: *Rimbaud in truth was no poet or soldier. He was a ghost who tried everywhere to incarnate as a soldier or whatever could disturb the lives of people, and who deserved to live in hell. The Tuntang Forest was the place most frequented by Rimbaud during his two-week stay in Salatiga. In that forest filled with pine trees, snakes, and bats, he often performed ceremonies wherein he flapped his wings with the fallen angels. Flames licked the sky in that region when Rimbaud exploded his incantations with twelve winged spirits. As you know, ever since then, I have called that blazing red forest hell.*

You know, they say that hell will someday be reborn as the painting of a blazing forest fire and its panicked animals.

"I actually would like to present that painting to Rimbaud. It's a pity I can't afford to pay the price it's going for," said a friend reputed to have known Raden very well when that damned draftsman lived in Paris.

Ah, I, the cashiered editor of *De Fakkel*, know a bit about Rimbaud. I think it impossible that this mad poet accepted a gift that utterly mocked his life in the grey forest he would never see in Europe, filled with its glass windows and ominous castles where vampires nested.

Confessions of the Flying Snake

They call me "Snake" only because my fingers are skilled at slithering everywhere over drunkards sprawled in front of the little apartments on Avenue des Veuves, near the Champs-Élysées. And because I so easily streak from one apartment to the other in matters of love or merely its act, they also have named me "Flying Snake".

I didn't mind being teased like that. Names, nicknames, titles, or gentle greetings aren't too important. What's most important for me, you know, is getting the moolah, and the more of it the better, writing biographies of great Frenchmen who liked deviant sex, and demolishing my old enemy, Van Dam.

"You'll never beat Van Dam," said a friend whom I often invited for a debate about Rimbaud. "Pretty fellows like us can never write proper history. You can write accurately about the history of suffering of your lips or your hair, but you'll go right off track the moment you record the little hobbies of your customers. Including your eternal ones, Rimbaud and Van Dam."

"But I have collaborated with Raden. And I think he wrote the best Rimbaud story there is, and in such an appealing way. I am sure *De Fakkel* will kick Van Dam out after we finish the section about Rimbaud in the Tuntang Forest..."

Whispers of a Pair of Angels

In the end, as I watched the rain occasionally whipping up the waters into a diamond-like sheen, I heard a pair of angels chatting away in a madhouse, one year after Rimbaud had kicked me out of bed. The bed that had stared at us in amazement, a couple of male dogs, always panting and gasping as we pawed and kissed and caressed each other.

"Actually, when Rimbaud was lost in the Tuntang Forest, I had prepared a burial service for him," sobbed the angel with green wings. "But you made a mess of it and flew the lost man to Paris. Now... we can't control him at all. Lucifer has given him a pair of iron wings that can be used to pierce the dark heavens."

"Don't feel bad! Perhaps soon someone will shoot him smack in the forehead. Maybe death will end his craziness," said the angel who was half horse, flapping its red wings.

"Ah don't talk nonsense.... This year death couldn't take a thousand lives of this infernal chap! He's still going to make love to all those women and all those dozens of men!"

"So... I should have killed him in Tuntang..."

Ah, neither of those bat-brained angels understood Rimbaud at all. Even though it was their duty to escort and guard him in all seasons, it turned out they never really lived with that satanic poet. If they were truly guardian angels, they should have known who I was. They should have not only flown hither and yon, perching on the roof of this madhouse, but also from time to time should have slipped into my room.

They once even snuck into the toilet when I was taking a shit. But at such moments, they only gaped when they saw me muttering Rimbaud's poetry. They didn't react one bit when I said, almost whispering, "Come, yes come, when you love. Come, yes come when you love!" *)

Yes, yes, I remember... it was only after I left the toilet that they discussed my silly behavior.

"This guy never knew who Rimbaud was."

"Perhaps... if he had known Rimbaud fully, entirely... might he not kill himself?"

"Kill himself?"

"Yeah... this guy loves Rimbaud too much. He doesn't know that Rimbaud was never able to love anyone, no matter who."

---

*) "Song of the Highest Tower" by Arthur Rimbaud

Heh, heh heh... those two angels thought they were so smart. They really never saw Rimbaud and me as a pair of male twins who were always changing roles at any time and in any place. Nor did they know how I had stalked Rimbaud when he was burned out from studying Charles Baudelaire's poetry or making love with Paul Verlaine.

Didn't they also know I was at Rimbaud's side when he bought and sold slaves in the African bush and when he got lost in the Tuntang Forest? I don't need an answer. All answers in the end are just ridiculous verses from the dreams of biographers allied with Satan. Ultimately, all answers only want to tell about how there was the ghost of a loony soldier screaming in Arthur Rimbaud's head.

So don't believe anyone.

Including a pair of angels who in the gleam of the forest eventually appear like that ghost...

Handcuffs of Snow

In Compton, there are no crows whose wings always give off the rancid smell of garbage, cheap wine, and corpses hidden in the ghetto slums or in the big houses that just squat there in the dark. Also, no snow or strong winds freezing the electricity poles or making the black people shiver as they do their messy dancing or loud rap on just about any sidewalk that night. But in a city that seems untouched by the hand of Christ, I always listen to those birds of death cawing without let up all day long. There's always the sound of a salvo of bullets which people just take to be the sudden braking of inner city drag racers. There's always the whispered deals in cocaine, morphine, or hash, but all the hissing and whispering only sound like the whistled codes of kids calling their little gangs to scope out a pair of lovers in the darkness of the park.

Naturally, in May, with its useless rumbles between *pachucos* and blacks, I shouldn't have been shivering from the cold, but I always felt as though I was enveloped in snow as I patrolled slum areas that would never see the likes of Paris Hilton's car or hear the footsteps of Pamela Anderson. And a spring that did not release millions of caterpillars still got me itching whenever I slinked through dark alleys full of graffiti. I get into an acute psychosomatic condition and end up half-paralyzed before I ever shoot my pistol at anyone bent on disturbing the peace and tranquility of Los Angeles County.

And the damned thing is, as deputy sheriff, or before that, when I was still a policeman, I could never avoid the booby traps of disaster in this city of no angels. Just supposing Grace—a pretty kitty in a

blue dress who often claws my back when making love with me—
hadn't lived in a crummy apartment in Compton Center, I'd never
have stepped foot in the hell that reminded me of the slums on the
edges of Jakarta, the home of thousands of zombies with the faces
of pigs or boars. And just supposing J Morgan, king of the coal-
black gang, who always called me a lousy police dog, didn't hide
out in the confusing labyrinth that spread out everywhere here,
I wouldn't be wandering around at night in the middle of all the
shooting, the snorting and snuffling of drunks, and the bitching
and wisecracks of people who've given up seeing the dawn of hope
in the moonlight over the cathedral steeple.

"Hey, come on, Grace, move into my apartment. Get out of
this stinking hell," I said three years ago when I was sure I was
going to propose to this African-Mexican woman.

"Oh, Tito, baby, of course this is one ugly lookin' city to you.
But out there on the streets with all that rappin' and the hip-
hoppin', I be sprayin' foul graffiti and shoutin' out everything my
poor and hopeless people want," Grace said, sounding a lot like the
politicians.

Not wanting to get into an argument over the complaints of
this nude dance instructor I met on Sunset Boulevard, I went back
in my mind to my childhood in Alas, Java. Up to when I was the
same age as my little comic book hero Sinchan, I lived in a small
town full of rivers that linked the cities of Semarang and Solo. In
the middle of rubber tree forests that you'd never see on any map of
Indonesia, I even became a little street punk who liked to strangle
cats in front of my friends.

"If your granny hadn't rescued you and brought you to Los
Angeles, I'd bet you'd never have left the city you were born in.
Probably you'd never have been a cop. You might even have become
the baddest gang-banger back there."

Even though everything that Grace was babbling was half hogwash from all the martinis she had been gulping down non-stop, once again I didn't try to argue with her. At moments like that, Grace seemed to be transformed into a mirror that could reflect everything I had done in the river that flowed behind the house. I remember the paper boats that I set adrift. The same too with the rafts made of banana tree logs that shot off crazily. Nor do I forget the snakes that appeared from all the holes alongside the river every Saturday evening and sped to the waterfall.

But there weren't any rivers with snakes in them in Los Angeles. Nor were there rubber tree forests in the midst of the big buildings. Even from Grandma's apartment, I almost couldn't see the moon. Still, Grandma tried to give me everything I wanted through the TV. On the TV, I could see snow that was beginning to melt on the hills or the moon looking like a tiny winnowing basket for rice at the far end of the sky. Also on television I could watch the police or the LA County sheriffs being beaten up by the bad guys in Compton, but always come out on top after reinforcements from headquarters showed up and smacked down the bandits who sometimes were armed only with rusty knives or baseball bats.

Aha! Television was what became a true mother, always whispering in my ear before bedtime. "Okay, Tito, go ahead and be a policeman. Wallop all the thieves. Bop their dumb heads with a baseball bat. Shoot 'em in the back if they take off when you're going after them."

But Grace never lets me daydream about the faraway town of my birth, where my father and mother were slaughtered by the army in that painful year of 1965 just because they were considered to be in cahoots with the communist bureaucrats. Always at the very moment I just want to enjoy quiet—which, sad to say, I can only make exist in my head—she's always hugging me from behind, giving me intoxicating little ear-nips, and whispering words of love as if they were mantras, like Christ's prayer before the soldier thrust the lance into his soft and yielding side, before the clouds were enveloped in black clouds.

"Come on, baby, you ain't got to force me to leave this town I've always thought was hell. I'm just your gone-bad angel or your blue cat from the Compton ghetto. Or that moon you moanin' for in the cracks in the dark rundown warehouses left by them rich folks, taken off to wherever in their limos on the LA freeway, all so nice and frozen.... Oh, why you so quiet, baby? Didn't you sneak into my room just so's we could make love and look out the window to spy on the people plottin' and schemin' in them skinny alleys? Wouldn't you always be telling me, just now you frenched my ear, snow would fall in Compton the day you popped the question to me? Why do you trick me like that, Tito? Why don't you just bring the climate and the hills around Tahoe down to my lousy ghetto so we can really feel how beautiful snow is?"

I regret now never answering Grace's barrage of questions properly or a little seriously. I'm always responding to sentences I think are silly with long kisses and whispers full of BS about a couple of angels who will live forever, and no need for cathedrals or prophets or God.

As you know now, that was Grace's last snort of love to me before she was torn to pieces in the wild volley by a mysterious shooter who thought my fragile dancer was a police snitch. The way it looks, the gang-bangers who were always claiming to be the saviors and Robin Hoods of the poor couldn't accept that anyone in Compton might love a cop. They saw cops—especially colored ones—as devils who had to be eliminated in the nastiest possible way. According to them, everybody who wasn't white should be brothers and shouldn't have to threaten each other. And since I was a traitor as far as they were concerned, they got to me by first murdering my lover. What was even more fucked up was that Grace never got to make a "dying declaration" when I and my partner, Gabriel Lee, barged into the bullet-ridden shambles that had been her room. With blood gushing out of her everywhere, she could still hug me and move her fingers across my back. But the moment I asked who did such a vicious, awful thing, her mouth seemed to lock up tight.

"Come on, just tell me, who shot you, baby doll?" I shouted, almost in tears.

"Oh, my God, please—don't go yet, Grace! Tell us who hurt you!" yelled Lee—a guy I always considered my guardian angel— like a man possessed.

But there was no reply. Fifteen valuable seconds gone, just like that. Yeah, a dying declaration, a fifteen-second-long statement Grace could have made just before going, which we could have used to do a grab or a warrant-less search, was really only stuck in her throat. Just think, if only she had said it had been Morgan who did her in, at that very moment I would have torn apart every inch of the Compton labyrinth and grabbed the stinking punk and blown his brains out again and again. No! Better to send the rat to San Quentin to feel what it is like to go stiff in a tiny cell. If I had to, I'd ask permission to give him the injection or bring back the gas chambers to that lowlife bandit. Oh, the threat of death row, the rows on rows of deathly cold cells, even these didn't feel cruel enough to repay Morgan for what he had done, the slimy bastard who always dodged the cop's bullets and never got caught.

Suddenly Lee cried out, "Look, Tito! The word 'Jesus' is written in Grace's blood on your back. Couldn't we use this as her dying declaration?"

Hmm... Jesus's blood is certainly useful for sinners. But "Jesus" written on my back may only have been a futile expression by Grace to face death that had her in its grip. Only graffiti without meaning on clothing that I sure wouldn't be wearing again when I set out after Morgan or the backsliders out on the streets. Still, you know, that Jesus on my back—finally I saw it more as a cross I had to bear as I schlepped the Compton sidewalks, never clean, although Spring perched on the branches of grape and mulberry trees.

And three years after that shooting, of course I still can't forget the beautiful nights in Compton. Okay, I've watched the comedy *A Night in Compton* over and over, but right afterwards I recall Grace's uneasy laugh when I splashed her in the shower. That's when I remember how she did the new dance moves she created right before she died like a cat cut to shreds.

When I mourn her, I sometimes figure that I have been looking for love in the wrong places. If only I could write a poem, maybe I'd call it, "Looking for Love in the Wrong Place". But I'm a cop and poetry's not my thing. So the way I remember Grace is just to play "No Woman No Cry" real loud, and promising, promising not to die before killing the mysterious gunman now hiding out in the labyrinths of Compton that I have traced inch by inch.

Strange to say, after passing the long exhausting nights and every second up to my eyeballs escorting bad guys on their way to the death row at San Quentin, I am more sure than ever that, still, it'll snow in Compton some day. In spite of that, everything was like normal. The rap just kept flowing. The filthy whispers kept steaming up the air. Any patrol car that passed through slowly was still bound to get sprayed by crazy volleys of bullets.

Turns out I've been wrong. From my car radio I heard a report of a highway chase of the Morgan gang by the police. It would be easy for Lee and me, now just wrapping up a mutilation and murder case not far from Grace's apartment, to catch the old enemy of the LAPD and LA County Sheriff's Office. And, there it is, the line of roaring cars headed for the streets of my turf. It'd be a snap to shoot out the tires of Morgan's junker. And after that, there's no way that crazy devil and all his devil underlings, all blood spattered, wouldn't be crawling around just begging for mercy in their crazy talk.

Cra-zy! My fantasy didn't pan out that way. The crazy junker—which amazing! had been painted with a totally clear picture of the man from Nazareth and the name "Jesus"—actually outran the pursuit and sideswiped our car after evading both Lee's and my volleys.

Staring at that graffiti, my memory is jolted back to what Grace wrote in her own blood on my clothes. It made me leap from the car as if possessed by devils and run after the color-chocked sedan. Yeah, believe me, in a moment more I'll be cuffing Jesus whose shots had spattered Grace's body three years back. In just a moment more I'll be putting him behind bars or crucifying him in San Quentin or, if I have to, shooting his face full of holes. Then, I hope that an all-blue snow would fall in Compton. All blue, yeah, all blue. *Are you still saying that snow won't ever fall in Compton ever, my pretty little kitty?*

Of course, Grace can't answer me. In the whizzing of the bullets, after colliding into the statue of the angel where the road turned, past the white noise and static of Morgan's microphone barking like a police dog, just like Prince Wolf who couldn't be killed by ten or one hundred bullets. *Really, won't it ever snow in Compton, lover babe?"*

Still no reply. Now I feel the labyrinthine streets swallowing up our car and Morgan's car that goes on howling and roaring, enough to split the night.

Mother's Quiet Light

A Rhino Without Makeup

No matter what, don't let Mother get lonely, Ros. Loneliness, perhaps you haven't learned yet, is like a crematorium. Hot, dark, mortared grey walls, and very stifling. In the nursing home, when I attended Caroline's funeral, Mother flew into a rage simply because I didn't rush her friend (the one always telling stories about the beautiful seagulls' wings at Santa Monica or Redondo beaches) to the best hospital in Los Angeles.

"Now that Caroline's gone, I'm sure I'll be like an old, feeble pigeon who's lost the desire even to move its wings. I'm sure it will be like staying in a room filled with the light of nine suns," said Mother, who I knew frequently spoke in the metaphors of the Book of Revelations when describing the awful conditions that she would experience.

I didn't respond to Mother's fevered imagination. A sixty-year-old woman as elegant and vibrant as Mother shouldn't be talking about nursing homes that resembled hell or a night clamorous with nine dragons spitting fire all around a room filled with dolls.

I supposed Mother's and Caroline's dependence on each other—including in their care of the orchids and roses in the garden—has made it seem those two women had nothing else to keep them going. They were never able to trust other people, not even Nora, the director of this old folks home.

"If Caroline dies, it won't be long before I die too, that's for sure," Mother said one day. "So, while she's still alive, you should treat her with the love you and Rosa have for me."

As far as I was concerned, all Mother's nagging was merely a strategy to keep her friendship with Caroline going. Loving Caroline, you ought to know, meant I had to join in financing her life there in Glendale. Caroline, that eighty-year-old witch, had no children whose wealth could be plundered to pay for an old age without hope, without grandchildren, with just a little garden with a bunch of trees and flower beds.

"Were Jesus still living, if he hadn't been all entwined by nine dragons from the south when he was on the cross of wood, I'm sure the King of Golgotha would help Caroline. So if you want to follow the example of the Son of Nazareth, then go ahead and invite Rosa or anyone at all to keep us going. Just tell me, in the freezing wintertime, would you have the heart to make us sleep in the doorway of Jack in the Box or Burger King?"

Oh, damn it all! Why did Mother always involve Caroline in everything? To tell the truth, from the very beginning I didn't want anything to do with that messed-up woman with the face of a cow, who was always dressed garishly. The first time I met her, I felt I was face to face with a monster that would charm Mother with her evil sorcery. With her Jewish blood, she was good at reciting strange incantations, and had, I was sure, turned Mother into her little lap dog. Perhaps into something even worse: a mynah bird parroting only what that infernal woman expected of her.

Of course, I've never known firsthand what happens in nursing homes, Ros. But from all the whispers of the elderly people I always meet in the rehab room, especially Angela and Gertrude, I've gotten to know whatever Mother does and how she behaves.

Angela, a sixty-five-year-old woman with the face of a lotus, once said in a guarded tone and a beat guaranteed to persuade anyone she was speaking with: "I often keep an eye on them. Caroline loves to suck on your mother's lip in the bathroom. Oooh! They're an awful pair, the two of them. If the attendants aren't there, they'll sleep together under one blanket. Hmm, if that happens, it often makes me think there's a pair of dragons wrestling together in the dense grey heavens. Snorting and hissing, they make those of us who've lost the passion for living hope we're not dead tomorrow morning. Oh, Rafli, you handsome guy, are you still going to let them make love all day and all night?"

Mother makes love with a Jewish woman? Do I have to believe such cheap gossip? How could Mother, who still understands the proper behavior in love of the people of Alas—our city whose rivers are almost lost from everyone's memory—be in love with this slippery, dangerous eel of a woman? Perhaps Angela is spreading rumors like that because she can't get Caroline's attention. Because Gertrude once said to me that Angela was the one who longed to be fondled and caressed the whole night by that weird woman who, I must say in all honesty, is still entrancing—though sometimes I think of her as a rhino without makeup.

"There was no one in the nursing home who wasn't attracted to Caroline, Rafli. Even John, Nora's husband, often tried to hit on that beautiful woman when she was with your mother, strolling around the garden. And Angela, snide lesbian that she is, wanted to take that woman she was so infatuated with into her arms. So don't be surprised if she hated Tari, your mom, as much as she did," whispered Gertrude, a woman who, at her most luscious, had been a dancer in all the various Las Vegas hotels, and who seemed about to lick my ear.

Nuts! Common sense won't let me digest everything said by strange old people who, if they were in the examination room, looked like morons who could only stroke their dolls and shake their heads or nod listlessly. Nor can I clearly process all the grumbling of halfwits without faces who gap at the television shows of stupid LA cops up against the whores in Casa del Mar.

Buijsen's Testimony

But, understand, Ros, I also got a different version of how they were behaving from Martin Buijsen. Buijsen, a fit seventy-four-year-old who claimed to have been a soldier in the Second Dutch Military Aggression and to have lived in Yogyakarta, by contrast knew them as a pair of angels who saved his life when he had almost gone crazy and had no future.

"If it weren't for them, maybe I'd just be wasting my time in the Las Vegas casinos. Yeah, with gambling, you know, you get a better chance to express your sorrow and happiness compared to talking with ignorant sheriffs in bars. In front of the slot machines and the gaming tables with all their eagle decorations, I could actually laugh or cry my heart out. Was that why I didn't want to shut myself up living with the crazies in the nursing home? But after getting to know your mother and Caroline, I grew used to listening to their weird stories about dragons, rivers inhabited by tigers with the heads of elephants, or anything at all that could make me forget about the blood gushing from the bodies of young Javanese whose heads I had cut off just about anywhere I went," whispered Buijsen as he pulled my arm and tried to move away from Angela and Lortha.

"I've heard that no one here wants to talk to you, Buijsen! Even Caroline and my mother."

"Yeah, they didn't want anything to do with me because they were scared I'd kill someone with my old gun," said Buijsen, bursting out in laughter. "And that's because I really have rambled on and on about the slaughters I committed in Maguwo. In fact, you know, most of those atrocities were merely things I made up. What really happened, before emigrating to America, I had been with a bunch of nasty and cowardly Dutch soldiers hiding out in a lonely cave with shade trees all around it at the foot of Mount Merapi when the Sultan led his general attack."

"And what about Tari and Caroline?"

"They're the ones who want to hear my stories, even though they knew I was pulling their legs."

"Did you like to spy on them? Did they to make love with each other?" I asked anxiously.

I hoped by digging up everything about my mother and Caroline from Buijsen, I'd find out something new about them. Who knows, maybe they really were inseparable lovers.

"That's crazy! How could a couple of angels make love in public? Don't ask such idiotic questions. Only depraved women from Las Vegas like Angela and Lortha or Gertrude can kiss each other anywhere they please. You know, Rafli, I actually often saw your mother and Caroline as if in prayer for a long time in the garden with all its orchids and grasshoppers…"

"What were they doing?"

"They said that was where Holy Mary always appeared in the evening, carrying on her hip a child shining with light and escorted by seven angels and nine dragons. They also said the birds and the moon always would accompany that Chaste Woman on her way."

"Do you believe that, sir?"

"And why shouldn't I?"

Ah, Ros, when Buijsen tried to persuade me about the appearance of Holy Mary, in all honesty, it made me think of Bernadette Soubirous at Lourdes. Caroline and Mother clearly were not beautiful women blessed by Mary to bring light to the world. Mother remained an Alas woman whom you and I resettled in Los Angeles and who always believed that Jaka Tarub of legend could imprison an angel with his tricky powers. Even though she was quite capable in Dutch and English, she remained a pious communist who was absolutely sure that Nyai Loro Kidul— Queen of the South Sea—sat enthroned on the south coast of Java and with all her powers could invite the kings to make love with her in her diamond palace at the bottom of the ocean. And, I am firmly convinced, even though Mother was a devout churchgoer—perhaps to bury the dark past times at Crocodile Hole and her hiding—she was in no way interested in the odd legends about Mary or the little miracles of Bernadette Soubirous.

I guess the stories about the appearance of Holy Mary are just Caroline's schemes to stay at the center of attention. I have to admit that, when relating Bernadette's mindless worship of Mary, or when telling about the caves without bats, where the Mother of Jesus gives spiritual sustenance to the poor at Lourdes so they can free themselves of suffering, Caroline does more resemble a troubadour than an old granny with no understanding of the lineage of the prophets or apostles.

"And so, believe me, Rafli! They were a pair of angels sent from heaven to save us old people neglected by our own children—by, let's say, stories about the wonders of roses and orchids, fragrant devils, and the colors of strange evenings that you'll see from time to time at Redondo Beach or Santa Monica. Have you ever seen the seagulls on those beaches, Rafli?" asked Buijsen softly as he kept dragging me to the yard behind the home.

I shook my head. I very much wanted to tell the old man how much I disliked beaches, salt air, weird crabs, clammy evenings, white sands, little waves, or birds that perched on black rocks. Even though I had to go to Santa Monica occasionally with Mother and Caroline, that was out of a need to pretend I was being filial.

"Caroline and Tari were very happy looking at the sky far out over the ocean. They say after people get past the age of seventy-one, they can see their face in the cloudbanks."

"Yes, they also said that to me. Have you also been able to see your funny face?"

Buijsen shook his head.

"Hah! If that's the case, you, sir, have not truly discovered the essence of life," I joked.

"The essence of life?"

"Yeah, the essence of life, Buijsen, comes about after you can conceal your bad self in crannies as deep as those under an outhouse. The essence of life comes about if you can scrutinize your strange mask behind the cloudbank," I said, jerking Buijsen around with some philosophies of life I just cooked up for the occasion.

Buijsen and I then had a laugh. I couldn't make out for sure just what he was laughing at. Perhaps he knew I was just a silly clown who was confused in confronting the odd behavior of old people who lived in the nursing home with his mother. Maybe he knew that my conversations with people in this refuge for the aged were only nonsense blabber that shouldn't exist in a city as practical and pragmatic as LA.

Oh Ros, to tell you the truth, to this day I can't believe one hundred percent of anything Buijsen said about Caroline and Mother. As we accompanied Caroline to the burial ground, he didn't look to me like someone who knew Rhino Woman very well. There was nothing in his face reflecting a man's loss of his beloved companion as he brought up the rear of dozens of people seeing Caroline to her grave.

I was also shocked when he kept grumbling, "Why cry over someone who should have croaked when Hitler baked the Jew cockroaches?"

So how can I believe in people who don't value friendship at all?

ORCHID ROMANCE

Of course I never gave up trying to understand Mother, Ros. And I knew a bit of the mystery of her friendship with Caroline a day after Caroline's interment. I try to be like Angela, Lortha, and Gertrude in keeping a close watch on what Mother does.

The little bells in the nursing home kept moving in the Glendale wind that night. The 55°F chill slowly seeped through her outer skin, but, just as she always did, Mother walked gracefully towards the garden, to where she and Caroline prayed to the statue of Mary and communed with the orchids and roses, and maybe one or two grasshoppers as well.

"Oh, lovely Lady of the Orchids, they still don't know how Caroline and I were preparing your marriage to the Prince of the Roses. And now that Caroline has left us, do you still want to make love with your very best sweetheart?" Mother said, gently stroking one of the orchids.

Naturally, this was startling; but I tried to keep myself from making the slightest sound. If I could just stop my heartbeats, I would also stop the sound that only God could put to rest.

"Hmm, they also don't know that all along Caroline and I were only pretending to worship Holy Mary. What they don't know is how we were always talking about ways to escape from this place that sees us—wretched old folks—as broken-down junk to be given sleeping meds all day and all night long. It's okay, my Lady, I am always praying to the Lord God not to take the lives of those who have only now seen the color of the morning. Caroline also told God to take just the lives of those who have stared into the night. So, without being poisoned by all kinds of drugs, we've been longing to die."

Nora gives just sleeping pills to these old people? What kind of wickedness is this? My teeth are chattering, but I still don't want to disturb Mother's conversation with the orchids.

"Yes, yes, I agree with you, Lady, our children will always see us as fragile vessels, vessels that, if only they could, would be soon removed from their cunning eyes. But I don't want to be that fragile vessel. Let me tell you, Lady, tomorrow, I am going to escape from this damned old folks home together with my friends. We're going to Redondo, Santa Monica, and Marina del Ray. We're going to be human, free to do anything at all on the beach.... We'll look at the moon for as long as we want and refuse Nora's demand that we go to sleep before 7:00 pm. We're going to..."

EVENING TRICK

So, Ros, I now doubt my initial findings about the people who live in this nursing home. At first I thought Caroline was only a woman who hid her Jewishness by giving herself over to worshipping Holy Mary in front of everyone. In actual fact, she was a martyr who raised a rebellion against Nora's cruelty. At first I thought that Mother was a woman who could conceal her communism in the country that most hated the ghosts wafting out of the smelly mouth of Karl Marx. But it turns out, she's only a woman of Alas who sees flowers, leaves, and insects as having mouths to tell about everything in this world. I also thought of Buijsen as only a coward who wanted to keep a gun under his pillow, but now I see he is a vicious fellow who has no appreciation of friendship.

Thus, Ros, for you to truly understand Mother, now comes the moment I invite you to the beach. I will invite you to listen to Mother talk with the moon. I will invite you to listen to Mother humming strange mantras as she imagines herself a seagull flying to the edge of evening, to the quiet of the moon over the horizon.

Do you think Mother will become a moon bird, Ros? You don't have to answer that question. I more hope that Mother will go by herself to this beach and find a pair of children who love her as they gaze awestruck at a maharani, the gleam of whose hands can change the ripples and waves into a silent light that calms the heart.

The Devil of Paris

Yes, if on a wild and hot night, your lover suddenly sticks a
pistol in your belly, you'd better listen to this very fucked-up
story of mine

Everything changed so quickly with Khun Sa's death. I, the golden doll of the Golden Triangle's Opium King, hidden away and whom someday you'll know as Zita, could never have attended the cremation ceremony together with the Shan guerrillas. I could never have smelled the fragrant ashes of my lover or merely imagined dying bravely in a raging fire of love. Nor could I have staggered along behind the coffin and tried to blow my brains out with a pistol before his other lovers simply wept and wailed to display their faithfulness. Since that painful year of 1996, the Lord of Death of course had ordered me to go to France and disappear. He was very sure the Mong Tai Army, his trusted soldiers, would not be able to protect me from the cruelties of the junta bosses, and so he asked me to slip away to a country not in the grip of the gunmen and prisons of Burma.

"Don't you long to meet with Mary at Lourdes? Wouldn't you like to be as lucky Bernadette Soubirous was?"

Deciding against the land those pilgrims find so beautiful, and suffering a tremendous disappointment at leaving, I flew to Lyon. In that cathedral-filled city, he bought me an ancient house and I quickly transformed what looked like the Bat Lord's castle into a modest hotel. If some day you go astray on Rue Saint-Michel, believe me, you will find me and Anjeli, my younger sister, running a hotel for low-budget tourists.

"In the land of Napoleon, you don't need to deal heroin any more, Zita. Believe me, until I die, the hotel will stay standing."

Even without him saying that, I had indeed made up my mind to break free from anything reminding me of whatever I had done together with the 25,000 soldiers along the jungle borders of Thailand, Laos, and Burma. I didn't want to be chased anymore by those damned cockroaches who wouldn't ask to be paid too much money to cut off my head. If I had to defend the Shan people, I didn't want to send the devil's powder to every corner of the earth anymore. Yes, yes, I still had other means of wiping out those cruel soldiers. A sidelong glance, a curve of the finger, and passion that just keeps exploding when I dance—I figured these were weapons enough.

Only, I was surprised that he didn't return me to Dhaka. To the city where he first picked me up when I was playing with Anjeli in the Buriganga River after the monsoon flooding had receded. I still remember in 1971—when my city became the capital of Bangladesh—Khun Sa asked Ghuslan, my father, to manage the heroin trade along the Thai-Burma border. Not wanting to be separated from his family, Father asked Mother and us two daughters to join him.

"Our future isn't in this country," said Father to Katra, my mother.

I was just seven years old at that time and hadn't the slightest idea of what he meant. What I know is that, a year before that happened, Father and Mother never again suggested Anjeli and I go to church, didn't want to talk about the wings of angels, nor wear a cross around their necks any more.

"Sooner or later, we are going to be driven away," Father said, "and so we'd better accept Khun Sa's offer. Believe me, this is only temporary, Katra. After we have enough saved up, we will emigrate to France. Don't you want to live your life bathed in Mary's love at Lourdes?"

I've half-forgotten, but as far as I know, Mother didn't reply. Only, on that very night, we were met by a jeep and left Dhaka. Left the strains of our Gombhira-Bhatiyali-Bhawaiya folk songs, and the Ganges-Brahmaputra Delta so fertile. Only recently have I come to know, we also had to erase memories of the tropical winds with their winter coolness from October to March and their summer heat from March to June. And, of course, I could never forget the monsoon season that's so hot and humid and the city of Chittagong with its beach, the longest in the world. If, at that moment, I could have had my choice, I wouldn't have gone far from the Dakeshwari Temple, the Bara Katra Palace, the Hossaini Dalan, and the Lal Bagh Fort that made me proud to be a daughter of Bangladesh.

Apparently, Father never expected that after that night we would only live in the jungle with the army of the Shan nation. But don't imagine that, surrounded by the forest, we didn't know the world. Khun Sa wouldn't let beautiful girls like us not know how to count the number of stars in the heavens. By hiring private teachers from England and ex-French Foreign Legionnaires, he made sure we became familiar with the maps, the speech, and even the weapons of various nations. And surprisingly, the wives of that taciturn prince taught us to dance, learn the language of the body, the awful groans of lovemaking, and understanding the beauty of opposing the cruelties of the junta.

So there is no need to be surprised that at twenty years old, I could kill anything that dashed by with my trusty pistol. Also, you needn't be surprised that when I was twenty-five, Khun Sa asked me to be his secret lover.

"No one will ever know that you have become the sole heir of my power. Someday the junta can finish me off, but you'll never be touched. Some day, I might pretend to surrender, but you will save the Shan people from persecution," whispered Khun Sa as he raked and clawed my back.

Ah, to be a hidden lover is very saddening. No matter how you try, you'll find it hard to express your love. It will be hard for you to only look on amazed at the power of the man of your dreams there in front of the other soldiers. Only stealing a glance when the man—old enough to be your father—addresses his army and other eyes are glaring at you. So I exist only in the sad secret of my lover. Only when he invites me—secretly—to distant countries can I lay my body against his chest. Only when he leaves his scores of lovers behind in Burma can I strengthen myself as spouse.

"In the end, I'll get old, Zita. In the end, only you will be able to continue the struggle of the Shan people," he said, right before he asked me to emigrate to France. "And I am not asking you to return to Dhaka, because you could never lead a movement in a country that only gives you beauty…"

Beauty? I have forgotten beauty ever since all I've known is battling with the police, who pursue us from forest to forest. I have forgotten beauty ever since the junta forced us to surrender at once and to move to Rangoon, bereft of our pride as fighters. I have not known beauty since my love for the Lord of Death could be concealed only in jungle foliage. Beauty, you know, only appears when the moon, like a slice of citron, radiates its light at the very top of the steeple of the Cathédrale Saint-Jean-Baptiste. And, sad to say, for a person imprisoned in her routine work as a hotel manager, it is really not at all easy, and requires a long struggle to reach the religious site not far from Forvière. At the very least, I have to hobble along to the Saxe Gambetta Station, and keep changing the Métro packed with immigrants, in order to finally

creep and crawl to the slope that was almost straight up and down
by funicular, by a train that looked like a snake slithering through
the lanes of the silent buildings that I always imagined to be filled
with bats.

You might suppose that after the Khun Sa's life story came to
its end, the fates of the old hotel and a pair of lonely women also
came to an end. Not at all, for it's precisely at this moment that life
has really begun. Now that I am not tied to anyone, I am actually
game enough to deal in the devil's powder again. You can't get an
uprising going against the junta's brutality simply by relying on
the prayers of monks and the rusty coins from the savings boxes
of the Shan fighters. I'm also beginning to get sick of Aung San
Su Kyi's softness in not immediately beating the junta to death
with bayonets or just claws. So when I look in the mirror, I often
imagine myself a soldier again, and camouflage my face with green
watercolor. I'm also beginning to fantasize and imagine all the old
houses in Lyon to be the giant trees along the Thai-Burma border.
All black, magical, and full of snakes that can prey on their trapped
enemies, now without the means to rediscover the sunlight.

Of course, I still love Khun Sa, even if my Algerian-Spanish
heroin courier with the naughty eyes, Aljir Duarte, is now bold
enough to give my bum a squeeze and ask me to shower with him
under the often-jammed nozzle, or to come up behind me with a
hug when I am making up in the gloomy mirror in my own room
by the warehouse.

And loving the late Khun Sa, you know, means having to always
see yourself as a deadly knife or pistol to his enemies. So I have
never told anyone about Khun Sa's birds and his hundreds of geese
with their crazy racket every time they hear the hoofbeats of our
horses clomping on the dusty soil, or when they see us clinching
and kissing in the shade of trees dripping with creepers and vines.

And I am always cautious as well towards Duarte and haven't said why I've never wanted to live in Paris or just pray in Cathédrale Notre Dame and enjoy the warmth of the winter sun from the River Seine.

"Paris is hell. Sweet devils will kill you if you dream of staying in that bad, bad city. You must realize, Zita, from the very moment a person I completely trusted knew I loved you, from that very moment he has intended to kill you. They think you will weaken the struggle. Therefore, once they know that you will emigrate to France, that's when they will send your murderer there. So believe me, Zita, don't go to Paris. And when I am dead, also never fall in love with any man from that city of devils."

At the time, I gave out a great laugh when Khun Sa whispered those evil words into my ear. And now I also burst out laughing when Duarte displays a pretty little room in the neighborhood of a former convent on Rue Notre Dame, which in the photo looks like an alleyway filled with reptiles, toads, beggars, and beat-up bicycles.

"Come on, Zita, I will turn everything that looks like hell into something that looks like heaven. Every day I will invite you to make love in the white boat before the storm comes," panted Duarte as he dragged me to the dusty warehouse.

Hmm, at first I was in fact quite tempted to leave Lyon. I also began to think of ending all my dealings with the Shan people. But, when Duarte's breath quickens in lust, I always imagine my perfect man turning into a red-winged devil with a stinking, drooling dog's snout. I can never embrace or even just kiss the brow of the beautiful man who has begun his metamorphosis into that spiky-furred creature.

When that happens, Khun Sa appears in the mirror and whispers weird words like mantras from Land of the Dead and orders me to get rid of Duarte.

"You're sure it'll be him who murders me?" I say softly, hoping that Khun Sa will shake his head, no.

Khun Sa never moves an inch. He doesn't shake his head, or nod it, either.

"You're sure, he's the last enemy I have to kill?" I say, feeling for the pistol that I always keep at my waist.

And because I quickly point the pistol at Duarte's forehead, I see the man who wants to fondle and caress me with his boiling lust, now quivering with fear.

Quivering with fear? Not a bit of it! It's my nearsightedness. In one swift and surprising move, he snatches away the pistol I'm on the verge of firing. Now it is Duarte who sticks the end of the pistol barrel into my stomach.

"Oh yes, I have been stalking you for a long, long time, Zita. I have been going to kill you for a long time. But Khun Sa's dead. And with the other generals scurrying off to neighboring countries, what more is there for us to defend?"

I don't answer Duarte's question. I shut my eyes, and on that black screen, I see Khun Sa, together with hundreds of mounted soldiers shooting their rifles into Duarte's heart, which is unprotected by anything at all.

And because that event happens over and over—even when Duarte proposed marriage to me in all sincerity—now I am all the more sure, in Paris I will never leave a pair of sandals, a gown, and a wedding ring.

In Paris, you know, there are only devils that hurry to knock on the door and stick pistols in your tender and unprotected gut.

Is God dead, too?

Prophet Bowl Delirium

LIKE GUERNICA, LIKE SCHIZOPHRENIA

You think I'm crazy? You think that after they operated on my brain, everything in my head is just a strange world of people murdered for nothing in Spain when the Nazi planes bombed the Basques during that bitter April of 1937 in Picasso's *Guernica*? You think I'm schizoid? You think that after the doctor rummaged through my brain, all my energy was centered only on counting the corpses sprawled on the Kuta streets, their guts pouring out, when those proclaiming to be the fanatic worshippers of Allah killed themselves with simple jerry-rigged bombs? So was that also when I appeared in your eyes dandling an Aborigine baby, all blood-smeared, and then you thought that strange creature from heaven was only an ordinary plastic doll?

And don't think I am suffering from delirium either.

Wu u u u u fffff Z z g g g g g g Wu u u u fffff Z g g g g g 1 4 1 4 Ciqummmzqq987rcirqumzzzzzzzKlingKlangzzzqircum1426 zqqstdpKling12KlangxxxxxrwKlang. aotqwuuuufKlang. xyrqxruk Klingklang14ktpnkk. rzowqtk90000. Kling Klang!

You know, when just for fun I took the train from Newtown to Circular Quay, Redfern, Town Hall, Museum, Saint James, even to Bondi Junction and Sydney International Airport, I actually always wanted to sling across my chest the red babies thrown away just like that in the park by the crazy, wild pig-faced women and take them to the verandas of barren women at just any old house.

There are always devils with green faces asking me to do those stupid things. Everything I do—like sometimes dragging the corpses of babies on the road and not caring about the sound of their heads scraping along on the sidewalk—is driven by the whispering, like the hissing of snakes, that runs wild within me.

"If you perform all my commands, you will get the Prophet's Cup."

"The Prophet's Cup?"

"You'll only know the secret of the Prophet's Cup if you do everything I order you to without questioning whether it's good or bad. If you don't do what—"

If I don't, that rude devil will bash me on the head with a hammer. When its anger peaks and is uncontrollable, it always saws away with thousands of tiny little teeth deep in the labyrinth of my brain with all its nerve nodes.

"This time bring the babies we've kept in the showroom at the National Gallery to the Botanical Gardens. Hide them under a tree full of bats. Some Abo women dancing for independence day will take and care for them. Don't let the police know..."

Couldn't ask why the babies had to be hidden in the National Gallery and no way to refuse that command. So I dashed to chilly rooms whose walls are filled with the Sidney Nolan's paintings of Ned Kelly's fight against the greedy British colonial police always oppressing the poor. Not knowing which room the mites were crammed into, I had to sneak in and out of all of them. That's why I found out how Nolan shifted the actual police hunt for the indomitable fighter of Irish stock, clad and masked in iron, from the grey cities to the dense forests of wild Victoria, onto the canvas rich with leaf green, earth brown, and iron black. I found out how one time Kelly—why was he painted starkers?—rode totally knackered into the forest on a horse equally so.

Unable to bear the sense of suffering in the paintings coated in earth brown that radiated sadness which Christ himself probably found hard to bear, I just had to get out of the place which I could justifiably call Kelly Hell. However, I hadn't yet found the exit when the Green Devil's nasal scolding knocked sharply in my ear. "You don't want to end up like him, right? Or, starkers like that? Maybe you even wish we'd be crucified right there on the Sydney Opera House steps?"

I didn't answer the question. Rather than being tormented even more painfully—sometimes the Green Devil put ten red fire ants into my eyes—I then went looking for those little tots. As it turned out, right at the hoofs of Kelly's red horse, I discovered three babies still coated with blood.

And after that, I don't need to say how I hid them, right? However, you've got to understand, sir, in the morning before day had fully broken, when those Aborigine blokes danced in the park with tourists from all the corners of the earth looking on, five pairs of cop eyes were peering from behind that tree of caterpillars. They could have just shot me. And if they killed me, that would have been the end of my career as a wedding dress designer. Ended too would be my hobby of collecting classic paintings from all over.

So before they send a bullet flying square into my brains, before they explode my heart with fury, I ought to hurry over to the vending machines. You know, my mates are held by the police in that cold prison of soft drinks. I'll release them first thing.... I hope we'll all struggle together against the greedy cops who want to change this continent into just cheap burgers.

Like Jail, Like a Gaping Chasm

There's no other way, I've got to hurry to the train. I have to find the coach that would be the hardest for the bloody murderers to reach and immediately get the vending machines that suck in most of the fighters in this country.

And of course, as anyone can guess, I will go to the drinks machines all over the airport, because that's where it's impossible for the police to arrest the fighters wanting to emigrate to countries or continents beyond their reach, other than by using the magic of the vending machines.

No idea who designed that absurd prison. What's always obvious—in my increasingly short-sighted view—every time my mates they suspect of being rebels hurry to the aircraft, the imprisoning machines suck them into a sort of maze of dark hoses and freeze them.

So to free them, I have to insert as many of my favorite coins as I can right away, so that many can quickly pop out of the machine and help me collect the babies abandoned in the lanes—especially those that pile up in the centers of prostitution like the King's Cross red-light district—and give those future prophets to mothers chosen by nature to raise them.

You don't have to believe how the fighters—suspected of being rebels and recidivists—come rolling out of the vending machines and startle the mobs of tourists, astonished at the sight of them dashing through, something they had never witnessed before. But, together with the choreographer Shaun Parker at various bus stops, stations, and airports, I really did over and over again witness events that sometimes made me conclude that God had old and painful stories in this city.

Of course there're no rain lights at that stop. Still, almost everyone who is piled up in that place surrounded by mirrors seems to be playing with mercury lights reflected by the heavy rain. Two twin women whom I saw then, for example, tried time and again to express to each other just what the color of the pain suffered by Christ was when he was crucified. Before the mirror, they stretched

out their hands and grimaced and then cried together. After that
they whispered to each other, cried, and finally shrieked out, "So
when will you crucify us, you child of Satan?"

There was also a bloke with the look of a snide Italian playing a
violin and from time to time imitating every movement made by
all the people at that bus stop who had gone astray. I suppose every
move that nutter made was simply driven by sheer boredom. At
first he imitated the butterfly dance of a young fellow with Chinese
eyes who always shouldered a skateboard. After that, he acted like
a tree duck flying madly about. And finally, he moved toward the
vending machine, put in several coins, and shouted with joy the
moment he saw several humans—yeah, real humans!—tumbling
out of the soft drink and snack machine in fragrant and colorful
clothes and with bodies that were fit and refreshed.

Wu u u u u u z z z z z z z z z g l b r g l b r 1 4
q m w z z z z z g l b r q m 1 4 z z z z z z z o p p g l b r g l b r q m z z z z z w
kmqmwzzzzzzzglbrglbr14qm14qmqgbrgbr

These things always go on for only a moment. And always after
that, several cops would arrive and seize Mister Italian face, and
then crucify or hang the crazy bloke from an electricity pole and
ask the evil machine to suck in everything that was milling about
or loitering at the bus stop. Oh no! For it wasn't only people who
got sucked into the dark and yawning maw, but the stop itself
disappeared in a second and turned into a lilliputian object in the
vending machine.

Wu u u u u u u u u z z z z z z z z w r r r r r r r r r r r r r r r r r r r r r r r r r
wuzzzzzzzzzzzz wrglbrglbrrirzirqwirzirqwr

From that moment on, my view was that God, or anyone who
wanted to become a messiah for a sick world, had been sucked
in by that foolish imprisonment machine. Since then, I've also
believed that the rain light or anything that sheltered your life
was imprisoned by the police and not given the chance to be free,

unless there were sincere people who inserted their favorite coins into that creepy, strange prison.

And because I, so often possessed by astonishing dreams at the touch of the flowing, unfurling notes of the music of JS Bach, would—unintentionally of course—be at those vile bus stops, so that I was moved to constantly free whoever the cops imprisoned simply for ending up at a bus stop, a station, or an airport being cleansed of roving terrorists.

At first I wasn't brave enough to be involved in such improbable things. However, ever since they operated on my brain—ever since I met with the devil with the green face who asked me to become a messiah of some kind to save Australia from the police who were now controlled by an international network that wanted to wipe out the Abos, even as babies—I learned how to fight fear.

Like right now, I have to fight my fear as I run from coach to coach avoiding police pursuit, avoiding the punishment of being crucified in the middle of the city, avoiding the possibility that God will have one more story of the painful past because He couldn't save one of His beloved sons whom He had sent forth from the pursuit of the devils of Sydney that infest the lives of those accursed cops.

I hope that at moments like this, it is the mercury light that blurs in the rain beating on the windows of the train. I hope that if the police can catch me, they will crucify me in beautiful surroundings, not like when Jesus grimaced in the darkness of the hill of Golgotha.

Now I ask you: Are the cops still after me? Will they send a bullet into my guts?

Like a Green Devil, Like a Green Cross

It won't take long to get answers to these foolish questions. Turns out the Green Devil has been tailing me all along. I shouldn't have hid from you that he's a pretty pommy with violet mascara who reminds me of Paul Capsis in Melbourne's Malthouse Theatre production of *Boulevard Delirium*. He doesn't have wings, but he always seems to be able to chase me wherever I am rushing off to. He never stayed with me in the same house in Newtown, but it feels like he's lodged in my brain. Like now, when he is in the last coach. He waves his hand and asks me to sit beside him.

"Finally, I have to tell you, the cops have intentionally trapped you in this carriage, Vern. If you want to save yourself, there's no other way, you're going to have to jump off. Hide in a garbage dump. Wait for another train and head straight for the airport!"

"What'll happen if I'm caught? You're not going to defend me?"

"If you're arrested now, you won't find out the secret of the Prophet's Bowl. And what's worse, you'll be dragged off to the crucifixion room at the back of the machinists' shop."

"The crucifixion room?"

"Yeah, in that room with the green curtains, a green cross is stuck in the floor specially prepared to crucify you. From the prophesy I've read in the Book of the Green Cross, the victim will be crucified without blindfold and then the cops will shoot the guts out of someone that they consider a backslider. And before dying, they'll put red ants into the eyes of the crucified one."

"So..."

"Now jump..."

Like a Red Gown, Like a Red Sky

You definitely don't know what's in the world of garbage. At first I found a rotten apple. Shiny streaks of red lipstick were still on it, and the hissing of weird words. Words that reminded me of Eve's lament when she was betrayed by a snake in the Garden of Eden. There were also pieces torn from a magazine showing Christ crucified and the sentence, "Every God Has a Painful Past. Does He Have an Un-healable Wound As Well?"

I never expected there'd be a Zippo lighter with a picture of a kind of rain that glowed red. On the lighter was the sign of the cross and some blurred writing saying "I hate J." Don't know who threw that beautiful thing away here. Clearly, if I wanted to spend the time lighting it, Sydney could get burned. But you know that the Green Devil commanded me to be a savior, so it was totally impossible for me to do something that would bring suffering to so many people.

The garbage I hated was junk-food chicken and rancid french fries in the narrow bin that luckily that could be used for throwing out any kind of waste and was bigger than this grown man. In the world of chicken pieces, now all maggoty, it was like I was in a slaughterhouse with no air—disgusting, and totally creepy.

Very fortunately in that garbage pail there was the fragrant scent of a red dress. In a sexual sense, I actually do not like women of any kind. But the scent of that dress reminded me of my mother. Mother, who Dad always struck. Mother, who had the courage to run away, wearing only the red dress. Mother, murdered in the cabin of a cruise ship at anchor while wearing her favorite outfit. *In this world is there anything more beautiful than the red of blood?*

Can you see the red sky in a garbage world? Maybe you can. But because everything happens in the mornings stained with all the blue-tinged rays of light, the evening colors definitely cannot be seen with the naked eye. Still, really, you can see the refractions of the evening light any time at all. Everything that you see is only illusion and so you can arrange those illusions into anything you want. And I'm like that. Peering out of the garbage bin whose cover I open slightly, I stare at the sky filled with bats in whatever color I want, the color of Mother's captivating dress.

"The train has arrived... don't be too spellbound by the illusory evening colors. No matter how beautiful the evening is, it's not yours if you don't get the secret of the Prophet's Bowl." The nasal voice of the Green Devil suddenly reverberated loudly off the wall of the garbage bin.

"I've got to jump onto a train again?"

"Yes, you've got to get to the airport right away."

LIKE A WHIRLPOOL, LIKE A DOLL

I arrive at the airport. Unexpectedly, so many shadows flash by in the same direction, toward a vending machine standing there in the transit lounge of people hurrying out of the country. A few of the figures dashing by I've seen on television. Most are activists who defend the rights of Aboriginal citizens. Others are opponents of Australia's involvement in terrorism issues in neighboring countries. Only, what I don't understand, the faces of the people who flash by are like the purple masks of zombies that had run out of makeup. They look like Frankenstein ghosts who lived in the dark, dusty castles of Europe.

Wuuuuuuuuuuzzzzzzzzzwrrrrrrrrrrrrrrrrrrrrrrrrwu zzzzzzzzzzzzwrglbrglbrrirzirqwirzirqwr

Crazy! This is just soooo crazy! No one—not even the Green Devil—shows the initiative to rescue fighters who haven't got the strength to refuse being sucked into that evil machine. So there's only one thing to do: I've got to whip out my favorite coins and put the most valuable things in my life into the vending machine.

"You're going to understand the Secret of the Prophet's Cup very soon now, Vern," says the voice of the Green Devil emanating from the hidden microphones stuck on the walls of several perfume shops.

I ignore the nasal voice.

"Only by saving them and mobilizing a resistance to wipe out the police will you win the heaven you've been hunting for all your life."

Still ignoring that stupid voice, I rush as fast as I can over to the vending machine. Really, my main purpose now is to save the fighters trapped inside the machine, and I couldn't care less about all that stuff about the secret of the Prophet's Bowl. Even if that secret could make me an intimate of Christ, this still would not be the jumping off point for my rescue efforts. Even if such a secret could make me the main messiah to save this sick world, that still wouldn't be give me the power to save lives.

"Now hammer that machine! Smash it! Smash it!" shrieks the Green Devil in a deranged nasal voice.

I'm not going to bash that damned machine. As usual, I'm going to put in my favorite coins so that those trapped in that musty and cold prison can come barreling out, breathe the fresh air, and commence a new battle.

"Smash it!"

Oh madness! Forget about smashing it—I can't even manage to insert the coins. Then suddenly, that wicked machine tries with all its might to suck me into it. Of course, I stand my ground and fight back.

Wuuuuuuzzzzzzzzzzzglbrglbr14qmwzzzzzglbrqm14 zzzzzzzzoppglbrglbrqmzzzzzwkmqmwzzzzzzzglbrglbr 14qm14qmqgbrgbr.

Of course, I try to back out until I feel some of my skin peeling off.

And yes, God, it turns out that I am so weak and fragile. It turns out that the machine can suck me in with all sorts of things: chairs, posters, perfume bottles, airline travel brochures, a statue of Mary rocking a baby and the crucified Christ, along with this grand airport. Everything has become lilliputian there in the labyrinthine hoses inside the vending machine. It's like we've become dolls in a mysterious vortex that we've never known in the riot of Sydney's street lights. We're like a pile of worthless things about to be sent to the final garbage dump at Coogee Beach.

Wuuuuuuuuuuzzzzzzzzzwrrrrrrrrrrrrrrrrrrrrrrrrrwu zzzzzzzzzzzzwrglbrglbrrirzirqwirzirqwr

Now I'm telling you: rescue us! Drop your dear coins into the vending machines that just stand there at the airport, very soon to be blown up by these terrorists. We will tumble out of this cold jail. *Kling klang!* We will form a resistance that will just keep on snowballing. *Kling klang! Kling Klang! Kling Klang! Kling Klang!*

We will..............

Wuuuuuuuuuuzzzzzzzzzwrrrrrrrrrrrrrrrrrrrrrrrrrwu zzzzzzzzzzzzwrglbrglbrrirzirqwirzirqwr

Kling Klang!

Natasha Korolenko's Fiery Circus

1

I don't know why Natasha Korolenko always calls Virginia Grey's house on Bondi Beach's Jenison Street an animal prison. As far as I know, there isn't a single animal in the building with the wild architecture all wrapped up in candy colors. But at the end of nightlong vodka parties with me, that Moscow woman who always wants to be called Pelagia Nilovna will shiver and say that every time you go into the rooms or toilets in Virginia's house, you'll hear tigers roaring, snakes hissing, or the racket of thousands of disgusting black rats.

"The first time I slipped into Virginia's room, I was blanketed by thousands of bats. And when I made love with that Englishwoman, my neck was covered with little bites, and bleeding, as if the Bat King's fangs had poked into it." Natasha gave a snort as she scuffled along on the sand of Bondi Beach.

I didn't challenge the story of that butch sixty-year-old whose own life story as a Russian immigrant to Australia was something I'd love to make into a graphic novel. Whenever the miracle of my brain stops working, it's really better to see Natasha Korolenko as a Scheherazade who never stopped thinking up her entrancing Thousand and One Nights stories. Were I to stop Korolenko's prattling, it would be like cutting off her head, the contents of which I'm grubbing around in with such effort.

"I suppose the tattoo on Virginia's back can really turn into a dragon. Have you ever heard a dragon snort?"

I shook my head.

"If you want to know every musical score snorted by the honorable Mr Dragon, at some point you'll have to sleep in that madwoman's house."

"Just dragon snorts? Didn't you say just now there'd be tigers roaring and a thousand rats clamoring?"

"If you want to hear all the beasts in the jungle making a commotion, you'll have to make love with Virginia."

"Make love?"

"Yes, Ivanovna, that's the only way can you can get a close look at all the creepy tattoos that cover that woman's entire body, the woman who was my lover for the past twenty years. Besides the dragon on her back, you'll be charmed by the pair of rats tattooed on her calves, the scorpion and dragonfly on her neck, and wolves on the palms of her hands. That's the only way you'll understand why I call Virginia's house an animal prison."

"Make love?" I asked again. "You think I'd be able to do that?"

"If you can't do it, just pretend, Ivanovna. Pretend like Madonna imagines making love with all the pretty women."

Of course, I took Natasha Korolenko's suggestions as the babbling of a strong and inebriated woman. Nonetheless, to be perfectly frank, I imagined that in my graphic novel I would draw Virginia Grey as a deranged woman who wanted to get every one of the jungle denizens onto her body. Except for her face, I wouldn't leave a single spot of her body free from the tattoos of the wild and horrible animals I had seen in the zoo.

2

To tell you the truth, I'm not at all interested in seeing whether the spirits of all the animals are stuck to the walls of Virginia Grey's home. If finally one dusty April day, I managed to slip into the house on every wall of which were pictures of Christ in various poses and suffering, including being crucified, with his drooping head full of caterpillars à la Salvador Dali, that was because I wanted to get a more complete picture of Natasha Korolenko's character from the love of her life. Also, if I finally got a look at all of Virginia's tattoos from the round mirror in the room which I just happened to glance at from the other side of the door, I also didn't want to see whether all the beasts on that beautiful sixty-one-year-old really were weird creatures that could turn into demons, terrifying anyone who wanted to solve the devilish secrets in that house.

Everything I did there, while naturally continuing to enjoy the magic of vodka, you know, was merely to sharpen the dramatic aspect of the lives of two women blessed by nature to love each other from the depths of their hearts.

"Do you really and truly love Natasha Korolenko, Virginia?" I began my interview, aware of a Picasso engraving of a pair of Christs embracing each other on the ceiling of the sitting room.

"Yes, I love her, Ivanovna. Living with Natasha Korolenko keeps me from thinking of suicide or even of making love with the strongest man possible."

"Do you really know who Natasha Korolenko is?"

Not getting Virginia's reply to this, I glanced stealthily at a statue at the edge of the balcony of Christ's bloody face wrapped up in leaves and all kinds of seaweed.

"Is…?"

"Yes. I know who she is, just as Natasha knows who I am," Virginia whispered.

"And you both still love each other?"

"Yes, we still love each other."

I wasn't surprised to hear Virginia Grey's answer, which was spoken in an irritating near-inaudible whisper. Long before I had insinuated myself into the home of the artist skilled at presenting all the versions of Christ's crucifixion, starting with the sketches of Vincent van Gogh right up to Jean Michael Basquiat, Natasha had leaked something to me about Virginia's love life.

"What if suddenly Natasha left you?"

"She can never leave me."

"Or the other way around, don't you want to leave her?"

"Do you mean, I have an urge to leave Natasha?"

I couldn't answer Virginia's unexpected question. And so as not to appear stupid, I cast my eyes on a painting of Christ being scourged by soldiers in masks. To look expert, I went up close to the canvas with the all-green background stuck on the all-black wall.

"Would you like to see the demon that always stalks Christ in that painting?" asked Virginia abruptly in a nasal voice that reminded me of the giggling Bat King in French-style vampire movies.

"The demon that always stalks Christ?"

"No need to be surprised, Ivanovna, anyone at all can be stalked by demons."

"Yes, but not Christ," I protested.

"Would you object if I gave its title as *The Demon that Hunted God*?"

I nodded, even though I knew that in the Bible, Christ had of course stood firm against the devil. And of course, too, I didn't believe in God; but I wasn't prepared to listen to an Englishwoman, who claimed to be intimate with Christ, belittling the Nazarene by thinking a demon hovered in the picture and sometimes is stuck to the wall in a crucified pose.

"Hmm, all right then, you can call him the Green Demon. Natasha Korolenko and I together painted that ugly devil in my favorite colors, yellowish green or greenish yellow. I hope some day you'll meet him before I invite you and Natasha over for vodka or champagne on my balcony or veranda. Do you have any other questions, Ivanovna?"

I shook my head. To tell you the truth, I was trembling and amazed to see the painting of Christ being scourged by masked soldiers who, according to Virginia, were shadowed in the background by a demon, completely green in color.

I promised myself that the next time I went to Virginia's home I would bring a sword and slash to bits that painting that so disgraced Christ, the son of Mary, whom I worshipped half to death.

3

I put on hold for the time being my desire to dig up everything connected with Natasha Korolenko and Virginia Grey. I even neglected the leak about Virginia's involvement in the poisoning of Alexander Litvinenko, a former Russian secret agent who had settled in the UK. Even if Natasha Korolenko claimed to have helped Virginia hide the car and murder the nurse who took care of Litvinenko, I wouldn't be concerned with such silly ravings.

Actually, from various friends in Moscow, I knew that the poison used to murder Litvinenko was a radioactive substance that could be found only at super cutting-edge nuclear laboratories. I also understand that President Vladimir Putin was behind that murder. But I'm only a painter who wants to illustrate a graphic novel that shows the dark sides of human existence. I am not in the least interested in bringing to light political conspiracies that expedite the murder of opponents as if they were lousy pigs to be put down.

So, if finally I was forced to realize that Natasha and Virginia were actually double agents working side-by-side to kill Putin's political enemies, I wouldn't consider such information as anything unusual. I'd think I'd be touching something really special only if that pair of lovers suddenly sharpened each other's fangs and in the end both were killed by funny wounds in their necks.

"Were you in the end able to see all the demons enthroned in Virginia Grey's home, Ivanovna?" asked Natasha when we met at the Torongga Zoo.

"Yes, I saw them all, Natasha."

"And also all the wild animals on Virginia's body?"

"Yes, all the wild animals on Virginia's body."

"Hmm, at first I thought you really wouldn't be able to make love with her, Ivanovna. But actually…"

"But actually… of course I never made love with her, Natasha. I just…"

"Just what?"

"Just got drunk and talked about any silly old thing, any useless old thing…"

"Did she tell you about a pair of angels who couldn't get back into heaven because their wings were sunk in the mud? What I mean is, did she ramble on about a couple of women with cat faces who lost their desire to obey God and preferred to live in a snake-infested jungle?"

"Maybe."

"Why maybe?"

"I don't really remember what Virginia Grey talked about. I only remember she complained about Russia being in almost total collapse, so it didn't need a paid spy in Australia…"

"Did she also tell about the possibility of Putin sending an invisible army to Sydney?"

I shook my head.

"Did she talk a lot about my first meeting with her at Mardi Gras in New Orleans?"

"As far as I recall, she talked about the Bat King who always made love with ten village women in ten boxes. The Bat King, you know, always invited those plump and buxom women to dance and prance about in the tomato field before killing them on the vilest possible night, his victims with their bad-luck eyes."

"Didn't she talk about Hitler who burned thousands of humans he considered useless only because he never could watch a pair of men kissing passionately in the corner of a park? Didn't she talk about the cruel Gestapo who cut well filled-out women to pieces only out of jealousy from watching a pair of girls squeezing each other's hands in the darkness of the apple orchard?"

I shook my head. I think Virginia preferred to chatter on about the rain of ash the moment Christ slumped over in the painting *Silent Transformation* that she scratched and scrawled in the style of Andy Warhol. I think Virginia almost never talked about anything that was hazy or mist-enshrouded or anything that resembled darkness.

"If that's the case, Ivanovna, you really don't know anything at all about Virginia Grey. You only have a superficial grasp of all the things you consider the truth. So once more, make love with Virginia, and you'll know everything. You must experience it. Don't just take notes. Don't just scratch your pencil stub on a piece of paper."

This time I couldn't refuse Natasha Korolenko. At least in my brain, there arose the desire to imagine squeezing the mysterious Virginia's hand as she sketched the soldier thrusting a poisoned lance into the side of Christ in the manner of Chagall, sketches permeated by René Girard's theories of human sacrifice.

"You won't be jealous, Natasha?"

The woman with the Brazilian bead necklace shook her head.

4

It wasn't easy to seduce Virginia Grey. It wasn't easy to bring out the spirits of the animals stuck to the body of the woman whom I've always imagined as that marvelous person who gave birth to Maxim Gorky, the Russian writer, intimate with the determination and fortitude of those warrior women. As a pretty creature of forty, who had never been thrashed by nicotine and had never been touched by animals with vertebrae, moon-beauty worshippers, I thought I could be a woman, ripe and endlessly devoured by Virginia Grey.

As it turned out, though, the mind of this astonishing devil almost never shifted in the slightest from its enchantment with Natasha Korolenko.

When she began to open up and wasn't going to keep any secrets at all from a person always there before her, scribbling and noting down all the words that flew by, Virginia in fact never said who she was. Instead, she invited me to understand Natasha's character.

"Don't you become Natasha's slave, Ivanovna. That Korolenko is a magician who can easily get someone to do what she wants. You were asked to become my lover only to discover the secret of the spirits in this house, am I right?"

I was startled, but I hid the sudden surprise that hit me out of nowhere.

"Without even using you, Korolenko will be able to free all the beasts that, according to her, I have imprisoned in this house. She can just easily burn this place down, skin me, and remove all my tattoos in an instant. But she's never done it. She really and truly knows how I—I am revealing this for the very first time—am the main enemy that has to be killed because of my unshakeable loyalty to Vladimir Putin, a beautiful man who sent me to act as a British immigrant in this land of kangaroos. But she doesn't want to kill me. Love, you know, has changed the insatiable lioness into a tame swan."

Speechless, I tried to figure out where this conversation, dominated by Virginia Grey, was headed.

"On the other hand, I am totally unprepared to kill Natasha Korolenko, even though on several occasions she sent me animals for the slaughter like you, merely to trap me, to trap her perfect woman, whom she loves so much. She is, you know, an enemy who is forced to go down on her knees in surrender before going to war because she can't shoot a pistol into the belly of the person she adores.

"And so, she and I aren't good Russian agents. She and I are lousy foot-soldiers who may someday be caught red-handed by the leaders and not be able to resist their brutal guns and knives. So, in truth, we are frail human beings, Ivanovna, but we put on a brave front. We tattoo our bodies only so that other people tremble in fear and can't hurt us by even so much as by a tiny scratch from the end of a dull knife."

I still could say nothing. I only thought that, of course, no one could ever hurt Natasha Korolenko and Virginia Grey before they lost consciousness. Really, even in a vodka frenzy, they never lost the means to bark at or strike anyone they considered an enemy. As you know, even toward me they never truly drew back the curtain of darkness that covered the secret of their lives. I am certain that, if at this moment, they leaked the slightest bit of their life stories, the consequences would surely have been thought out beforehand. Perhaps they were entrapping me. Perhaps they saw me as a counteragent, so that all the leaked secrets about their lives as spies were nothing more and nothing less than a tactic for outwitting their foes.

"So take note, Ivanovna: get out of our lives and stop pretending to be someone who designs graphic novels."

I wanted to laugh at Virginia Grey's nonsense. But this time I strongly wanted to savor that foolishness and nonsense. I wanted to taste what it felt like to be a frail woman thought to be a Russian secret agent.

"And what if I don't want to get out of your lives?"

"Natasha and I will kill you" she said with a menacing snort.

Hmm. I sensed the snorting and snuffling of a dragon creeping through the house. I sensed the souls of dozens of wild beasts struggling to surround me. Feeling threatened, I raced out of the house which for me—what can I say?—seemed more like a zoo for demons.

5

After five months had passed, you'd be very mistaken if you thought I wouldn't go back to Virginia Grey's house.

"Ivanovna, dear, you will get your beautiful ending for the graphic novel very soon now. You're at Bondi, right? Go quickly to Virginia's place. We'll have a surprise for you," Natasha Korolenko chattered away at the other end of the phone.

"Surprise?" I shouted at the top of my lungs to overcome the rustling of the wind on the shore, so my feeble voice could be heard on Natasha Korolenko's telephone.

"Yes, you know what happens when a house becomes a crematorium, don't you?"

I didn't answer that question. I actually imagined a room filled with flames lashing fragile bodies. I also imagined the bodies in that house slowly melting and giving off little explosions, the oozing of foul liquids and the sound of cracking bones.

"What're you two going to do, Natasha?" I asked after I was able to get a grip on myself.

"We are going to set ourselves on fire, Ivanovna."

I didn't need to ask why they were so desperate as to do that. I was sure it was all connected with the pressure of fundamentalists who didn't want Australia filled up with beautiful women who made love all the time in the quiet of the parks and the noise of the streets. I strongly believe that the parade of crucified women who were marched and motivated by Virginia Grey and Natasha Korolenko on Oxford Street and Hyde Park during Mardi Gras had offended a lot of people.

"If we're physically gone, if they can't find our bodies..."

Natasha didn't have to go on. I already knew where that lament was headed. So I slammed down the receiver and without requesting permission from either of them, I told the Sydney Fire Department to rush over to Bondi Junction, to Denison Street.

I didn't want Natasha and Virginia to die for nothing.

6

Too late. Virginia Grey's home was burned down.

7

Accident? Arson? Who knows? I don't want to tell how the fire department tamed the flames that seemed to have every intention of licking the sky. I only want to tell you that in the midst of the fire and smoke, I thought I saw mice without wings, bats, a pair of twin dragons, all kinds of snakes, as well as dozens of crucified men—all of whom I had stared at in Virginia Grey's paintings and as statues—floating in the air with a pair of hands that stretched out streaking through the clouds.

Accident? Arson? Who knows? Rather than imagining Virginia Grey's and Natasha Korolenko's incinerated bodies in the ruins of the house with all its demons, I preferred to imagine Natasha Korolenko intentionally burning Virginia's house, dragging her beloved to the Sydney airport, and getting on the fastest flight to Russia. Natasha, you know, could create a hologram of the dozens of crucified men who soared in their own ascension to heaven amid the fiery circus that turned the house on Denison Street into ashes, into something that someday you can remember only in my graphic novel.

Accident? Arson? There's no sign that truly gives me a chance to answer this question: *Why did the fire so easily char a pair of lovers into nothing but brittle wood, into nothing but a beauty that was rotten and horrifying?*

Everlasting is Arjuna's Sorrow

1

I have put down my bow and arrows on your field, this Kuruksetra, Kresna. I have unscrewed my courage for hacking off the heads of Bisma and Durna, our true enemies.

I will let the sons of Destarastra kill me. I will let their chariots grind to dust my limbs that grow ever more fragile and painful.

Truly, I am unwilling to war on my relatives. I tremble and lack the courage to stare into the raging eyes of those horses, elephants, and bloodthirsty soldiers.

2

You may think me the weakest of *ksatria*. You may think me a repulsive animal that deserves to be slaughtered just because I won't avenge the attacks of Bisma and Durna, my esteemed ones, whom you never considered beloved of the gods.

Thus allow me to become a beggar rather than plunder the lives of glorious spirits. Let me be a coward rather than live in a storm of blood, in a tempest of disgrace.

So, enough! Why do we live if we have killed the ones we love, the ones who love us? Oh, is it a secret that I have not yet read from the signs of the dust flying above the Kuruksetra that you want me to be the *ksatria* who butchers the Kurawa? If I can kill Bisma, will that make me happy? If I can cut down Durna, will I gain heaven?

Truly, Kresna, I will not do battle for you. There are enough battles within me that I bury daily in the quiet aftermath of the

Kuruksetra, in the calm of the victory of the *ksatria* of Destarastra, in the victory of your enemies.

So do not force me to fight. Let my anger be buried. Let my conceit perish. Let me topple face down when you hear the cooing of doves.

3

You say I will attain perfection if I am not afraid to fight with anyone. Is there anything more false than those words you whisper so arrogantly? You say that you will always bless every combat of mine. Is there anything more mendacious than the sutras that you breathe into ears that I have made deaf since our chariot penetrated the swirling dust?

Are your wars also for your own perfection, Kresna? Are these fallen soldiers also unblemished victims for you? If I don't fight for you, will you see me as a shameless thief?

Believe me, the world will not be destroyed if I will not do battle for a triviality suitable only for the parties in your gardens and parklands. Believe me that, without your forcing me to fight, the drizzle will turn into green birds that will flap their magic wings into your heaven.

Those green birds, oh my Esteemed One, are my final prayers before the Kurawa chariots smash my head to pieces.

Do you hear the bitterness of my voice?

4

Have you discovered the secret of my death?

"I understand the secret of your birth and your death, too. I know you will not die in this battle, O Subduer of the Kurawa."

Have you ever sensed the beauty of death, O Kresna?

"No one gave birth to me, but I have felt birth again and again. No one brought death to me, but I can feel death before the time comes for you to feel it."

Oh, how will I attain that beautiful knowledge?

"You must first attain my eternal home. But not now, Arjuna. Not now. Fight first until your arrows sever Karna's neck. Fight first until Durna and Bisma are destroyed."

5

I'm still filled with doubts about doing battle. I still don't want to be pummeled by the blood-drenched storms of your wars. I want to leave the field of combat and knock again on the nine doors of my home. I want to return to my own peace and quiet, O Kresna.

"Your home is on the Kuruksetra, my child. You can only open those nine doors after you have killed the Kurawa. So never return before the miraculous caves and forests invite you to lead a hermit's life in praise of the beauty of my universe."

6

Once before, in a garden filled with butterflies, you had spoken of there being no difference between noise and silence. You've said that gold and gravel are only names whose sublimity you needn't squabble over. But, truly, I would be forever sad if you keep forcing me into battle, if you keep forcing me to let fly my Pasopati arrow at those lovely horses and elephants of the Kurawa. I will be sad if the singing of the birds still differs from the humming of the rainbow. I will be sad if the buzzing of death differs from the joyous melody of your green growing grass.

So how could I possibly go forward into war and not prefer to return home? How could I possibly prefer to let fly my arrows instead of enjoying myself in the shining sunlight on a clear pool?

All right then, I will just meditate for you. I will empty myself of all my desires until I see the crashing of the seas are no different from the creaking of the sky, until my desolation is no different from your happiness.

Do you hear me shudder when I pray for you, Kresna? Do you hear the sizzling of my tears?

7

"I regret that, after all, you really don't understand who I am, O Arjuna." You whispered those bitter words to me.

That was my regret, too. I regretted that I didn't understand you as I understood cracks in the earth, the muddiness of water, the sharpness of fire, the poison of wind, the creepers of thought, the sting of intelligence, the falseness of a frail body and my crushed spirit.

"Oh Arjuna, I am the taste of water, the light of the sun, and the moon. I am the voice in space and the passageways to your innermost spirit. I am the fragrance of earth, the place where all that lives plants love with resignation and surrender. I am the heat of fire, the taste that drives your beautiful desire to prostrate yourself and worship my majesty. Truly, I am the silent cave where the *ksatria* meditate in search of my heaven— but why do you still not know me?"

Why must I know you, Kresna?

"So that you understand how shallow your life is, Arjuna."

8

Must I also know the color of doom? Must I also rush into battle to better know the meaning of the shadow of my body that creeps on tiptoe through the burial ground full of carcasses?

You aren't answering my question. You even ask me to look upon the enemy's chariots that are now hurrying to pierce the heart of the Kuruksetra that grows ever more silent.

9

"If one night in the stillness of the lake you find out the secret of your death, harken to the shrieks of the leaves that suddenly drop from those wondrous trees, Arjuna. Attend to the soughing of the wind suddenly caressing the lotuses that will not shout for joy from attaining the very peak of the stillness in their meditation."

Why can I not remain mute?

"Because you are my voice. Because you are my sacred chant."

10

If I am sacred, do I still need to worship you, O Invulnerable Commander? If I am sacred, do I still need to quaff the grapes of eternity from the golden cup you offered before you began the sacred war to crush the Kurawa?

"You are not Mount Meru, Arjuna. You are not my lightening bolts. Fight for the sake of my serpents. Fight for the death of your enemies. Fight for the sake of your sanctity."

11

Now I want to blind my eyes. I don't wish to see you incarnated as a river the very moment I want you to become carrion. I want to deafen my ears. I don't wish to hear you hissing the wrath of the Serpent Ananta when I want to hear you roar the sadness of the God Yama.

"Have you also cut off your tongue, Arjuna? Can you no longer whisper miraculous visions to all the flowers?"

12

I am understanding your teachings less and less, Kresna. At first I knew you as a door, but actually you are only a window. At first I knew you as my certainty and perfection, but actually you are just hesitation and doubt and the cracks and pulvering of my wretched life.

I understand your love less and less, Kresna. At first I saw you as my beloved who kept kissing me in the stillness of the cave of meditation, but it's clear you are the tempter that drags me to make love in the uproar of the forest, filled with droning bees and poisonous snakes.

How much longer must I hold back my fear of soon leaving your heaven?

13

"Before, your hands were very stupid, Arjuna, and now your feet are stupid too. Before, your ears were very stupid, and now your mouth is stupid too. Before, your face was very stupid, and now your chest is stupid too. Why don't you learn from the smoke that thins in the stillness of the air? Why don't you learn from death creeping about in the stillness of the mist? Don't these disappear before the storms rage, before the rain rebukes and lashes you?"

Do I suffer because I have not instilled within myself the secret of doom that wants to free itself from the door of the Hell of Lord Yama, who shouts and calls for the *ksatria* who tremble on the battlefield?

14

"You are the most repugnant of the Pandawa, Arjuna. You, the son of Pandu Dewa Nata, who refuse to see the grandeur of our battle."

15

I want to be annihilated immediately in this the most stupid and useless of battles, Kresna. Why do you still look to me to be your champion? Fame such as that is just plain false. Why do you still hope I will become your moon and stars?

16

I am ashamed. So I am, after all, only dust. I am afraid. So, after all, I am only grass.

17

Truly you are the Sacred Text, Arjuna. Truly, you are perfection without peer.

18

No, Kresna, I am your sacred victim.

19

Therefore, I will go and do battle for you. I will loose Pasopati even though fresh blood gushes from my anguished guts.

Kufah's Flying Fish

You don't know where the bodies of Kufah, Kiyai Siti, Zaenab, and the flying fishes have disappeared to, do you?

Kufah didn't believe that in the end the city people really would break up the tomb of Sheikh Muso standing at the end of the promontory that was surrounded by mangroves and the harsh croaking of herons in their thousands. They were going to build a resort in the kampong that was filled with those flying fish. Kufah was concerned, not because Sheikh Muso's gravestone frequently emitted a dazzling green light, but if at some point in time that headland also disappeared, she would not be able to spend long hours gazing at the moon while splashing her feet in the clear sea water, which at high tide often brought all kinds of unexpected things swirling in with it.

Sometimes, you know, when she was playing with the other young girls, Kufah would see little boats drawing close and discharging several men—she and her playmates supposed them to be angels with red wings—who then swarmed around the tomb of Sheikh Muso. They made their voices sound like the squeaking of bats, like the prayers raised by Kiyai Siti—Kufah's father—whenever the raging seawaters lapped at their veranda, the mangroves were submerged, and the darkness crept and crawled to the ancient mosque whose foundation was buried in the salt water.

And also one night with Zaenab—the watchwoman of the graveyard, in her thirties, whose whole body was covered by scales, every bit of which she wanted to peel off—she felt she had met with a pair of angels with dimly glowing lanterns who had lost their way in the cemetery.

"Why're they here?" asked Kufah.

"Because they're making a pilgrimage to Sheikh Muso's tomb, Kufah. You know that visiting Our Reverence's tomb is the same as making a pilgrimage to the garden in the Glorious Country."

Kufah did not understand Zaenab's hissings. Even so, she still watched everything that was happening at the grave with unblinking eyes. She was astonished when there appeared the tattoos of wings in dazzling rainbow hues on the shoulders of the radiant-faced men and women who were always holding hands. Even more startling, they bowed their heads towards Zaenab, the very woman who had been driven from the kampong purely on account of her scaly body, her habit of talking to herself, and her split tongue.

Several times, Kufah also saw a boat mooring and tall men wearing turbans hurrying to the mosque. At moments like this, Kiyai Siti—together with five grown men who lived on the land that had sunk as a result of the erosion mentioned earlier—would listen to whatever was said by the creatures with the shining red eyes who were always pointing and jabbing their fingers at the sky.

Kufah loved to spy on and listen in on what she could catch from the sermons of the bearded visitor who was better known as Abu Jenar, Heaven's Commander. Only, because in Kufah's mind Abu Jenar looked like a cruel voracious giant, ready to gobble up anything and everything, she always left the house when Kiyai Siti and the snot-dripping demon spoke about the great struggle and the mangrove forest that would be cut down. She also did not like Abu Jenar because the Heaven's Commander always stared at her with naughty eyes whenever their glances met. She hated him all the more upon hearing the rumors that Abu Jenar would make her his fourth wife.

But for some reason, tonight Kufah wanted to listen to whatever Abu Jenar was saying. It wasn't easy to eavesdrop from such a distance. Almost no words of importance words slipped into her ears, and to Kufah it was like listening to the droning and buzzing of bees, that then turned into the croaking and squawking of herons, the roar of the waves, and occasionally the thunder whenever Abu Jenar waved his hand. Kufah tiptoed closer.

Now the voices that at first had sounded strange to the ear began to be audible. Only heard, though… Kufah, about eleven years old, couldn't yet understand what they signified.

"There's no other way… we'll just blow up Sheikh Muso's tomb ourselves rather than letting them wreck it…," said Abu Jenar with fire in his voice.

Kiyai Siti's face revealed his tension. Even so, Kufah didn't know why her father wasn't brave enough to reject the proposal to raze her great-grandfather's tomb.

"If need be, we'll burn down the mosque and the kampong. If they try to stop us, we'll have to be ready to die!"

As on earlier days, no one dared to oppose Abu Jenar. So, in the deepest recesses of her mind, Kufah, whose mind couldn't grasp logic, this meant that Abu Jenar's order would be obeyed. Sheikh Muso's tomb would be destroyed. Fire would devour the kampong and its inhabitants burned up needlessly.

"And I think that tonight will be the best time to blow up the tomb. So be ready to carry out this great struggle!" said Abu Jenar, making Kufah's flesh crawl.

As she imagined fire devouring the tomb, Kufah remembered the fish splashing around it. She didn't want to see its fish boiled by the heat.

So she tiptoed away in search of a savior for the fish. She was looking for Zaenab. Zaenab surely would never allow Sheikh

Muso's tomb be burned, blown to pieces, or smashed by anyone. And if the tomb was saved, her dear fish would be saved too.

The tide came in just at that moment. The veranda was underwater. The only thing Kufah could do was to use the little sampan to reach the tomb, which had never been submerged by the roiling waters. And it was true that Zaenab was in the calm of the tomb. She was in meditation there, extolling Allah as she fingered her prayer beads. Kufah seemed to see one of the fallen angels now weeping and sobbing. She saw on the shoulders of the woman expelled from the kampong, wings of dazzling green opening and closing in the rhythm of her laudations and in time with the breath of Kiyai Siti after praying.

Hmm, here is the protector of the tomb. Here is the one who'll protect my fish. Here is the one who'll protect the place where I play with my friends. So thought Kufah.

A little later, Kufah moved off to the side and hastily made for the roofed tomb and immediately began to meditate before Sheikh Muso's tomb. She wanted to ask Allah first of all that Heaven's Commander and the kampong people not blow this miraculous place to pieces. She wanted to tell Zaenab to quickly leave the tomb and flee to the next kampong.

"What're you doing here this late at night, Kufah?" hissed Zaenab, waggling her forked tongue.

"Heaven's Commander is going to blow up the tomb... I want to save my fish. I want it to keep flying around the tomb. Really I want that fish to recite the Quran to Sheikh Muso, but Sheikh Muso's going to be burned up," panted Kufah breathlessly. "Leave this place..."

To her surprise, Zaenab's expression never changed at all. She kept on meditating and felt nothing was going to happen.

"No one has the courage to blow up the tomb of the line of the rajas, Kufah. As you know, even though outsiders see Sheikh Muso as a communist who disguised himself as a famous *kiyai,* he was still just the son of Raja Pemangku Bumi III, whose wife was descended from Raden Patah." And Zaenab began to relate the story, unconcerned whether Kufah knew what she was talking about or not.

Indeed, Kufah didn't know who Raja Pemangku Bumi III and Raden Patah were. She only knew that if the tomb were to be blown up or burned, the amazing stories about Sheikh Muso, the builder of this kampong in one night, would disappear with it. And more importantly, she didn't want her pet fish to be boiled and Zaenab to be charred to death.

"We only need rain. We have to pray to Allah to give us the magic of rain!" Zaenab hissed again.

"Rain? For what?" asked Kufah, not understanding what Zaenab meant.

"Isn't rain the only thing that can put out fire?" Zaenab explained. "But there can never be rain when there's a full moon, Kufah."

"I can summon rain!" shouted Kufah stretching her arms apart, like a person crucified.

Then she raced to the center of the headland. She prostrated like Kiyai Siti did when he prayed for rain. But not every wonder came in response to Kufah's wishes. Rain did not fall at once. Rain did not come promptly.

Unbeknownst to Kufah, Kiyai Siti asked Abu Jenar why Heaven's Commander insisted on demolishing the tomb of Sheikh Muso himself. It seemed that Kiyai Siti was beginning to sniff out the stench of treachery. He feared that Abu Jenar himself was the city people's errand boy for the immediate destruction of the kampong.

"If it's them who will blow it up, we'll be the losers," said Abu Jenar. "But enough of that… I've placed the bomb at the tomb. All we need to do is detonate it from here and our great struggle will be accomplished."

"Don't! Don't blow up that holy tomb" said Kiyai Siti. "Allow me to save some important books there. You've got to know that we keep the entire history of the kampong and the family tree of Sheikh Muso at that memorial site. If you blow it up now, we won't have a single memory." Kiyai Siti was trying to play for time.

Did he really want to save books? Who knows? But clearly his eyes were peering into every corner. He was searching for his wife. There she was. He searched everywhere for Kufah. She wasn't there.

"Kufah must be at the tomb," thought Kiyai Siti.

So, without paying the slightest attention to anyone, Kiyai Siti left the mosque. He dove into the sea. He swam out to the headland, to the tomb of Sheikh Muso. He didn't want to see Kufah's body all burned up or torn to pieces by the blast of Abu Jenar's bomb.

But he was too late. Although Abu Jenar and the other residents never expected it, Kufah discovered the bomb that had been hidden behind the headstone in a place unknown to Zaenab.

"Who does this toy belong to?" asked Kufah as she bounced the bomb up and down in her hand.

"Toy? That's not a toy, Kufah. That—" Zaenab was suspicious of the thing that she, too, had never seen in her whole life.

"It's… what?"

No reply. Then a blast. Then cheering and shouting. Then Kufah's body lit up, spitting fire like the flapping of an angel's wings and licking anything that was still or that flashed by at the tomb.

Now you know where the bodies of Kufah, Kiyai Siti, and Zaenab, and the flying fish have disappeared to, don't you?

The Eleventh Wali

The envoys of the headman of Lading Kuning wanted to kill Sheikh Muso and throw his corpse into the sea. But Sheikh Bintoro wanted to show to the kampong folk how this purveyor of false teachings was nothing but a rotting dog's carcass.

He was no religious preacher. Nor had he ever invited the people of the kampong—which with the arrival of each evening became the paradise of herons—to pray in the mosque. Suddenly, these people were calling him Sheikh Muso. He couldn't walk on water, but it was whispered everywhere in that fishing village that he could cleave the waters of the sea with his staff. He could walk on the bottom of the sea and see pools of giant fish behind the walls of the sea he had split in two.

Not only was this man thought to be capable of miracles that the Prophet Moses could perform, one of the kampong folk had related in detail how Sheikh Muso had once been swallowed by some sort of dragon, or dugong, or a giant shark, and didn't die, although he was in the belly of that animal for a day and a night. That's why the kampong was certain that Sheikh Muso was really the Prophet Jonah who had been sent to save them from destruction and their disobedience of God's word.

And not just that. During the time he was inside the shark or at the bottom of the sea that was pressed back by the cloven walls, Sheikh Muso, as heard in the deliberations of little kids, could chat with all the fish and other sea creatures. Of course, like the Prophet Solomon, he could speak with every manner of flying bird, fowl, creeping animal, buffalo, cows, goats, and all wandering beasts.

"Did Sheikh Muso tell the fish about our lives?"

"No. It was the flying fish who told my grandpa about their suffering. They said humans were getting greedier all the time. Before, they never wanted to eat flying fish, but now the flying fish are being roasted all night long," said Azwar, the young grandson of Sheikh Muso, to his playmates.

"What did Grandpa Muso do, that time he was in the belly of the shark?"

"Grandpa asked the gills and all the things that could vibrate to chant the praise of Allah," replied Azwar again to the other little boys, who all wished they could have a grandfather as mystically powerful as Grandpa Muso. "My dad says Grandpa can also fly and disappear!"

"Did Sheikh Muso fly on the steed Bouraq that carried Prophet Muhammad to heaven?"

"No. Grandpa flew on his sarong."

"Did he disappear like a ghost?"

"No. Grandpa disappeared like Prince Diponegoro."

Because he could fly and disappear, the word always went around that Sheikh Muso could perform his daily prayers at the Grand Mosque in Mecca or simply go into seclusion in the Prophet's Mosque in Medina. And because he was alleged by the villagers to have created a kampong community and built a mosque in only seven days, he was revered as the Eleventh *Wali*, or "Governor". In Java, as you know, the history of the Wali ends with the glory of the Ninth Wali. But only on the headland, crawling with these lizards whose tails had broken off, years and years later, it would be told to children as bedtime stories that there lived a Tenth Wali, invulnerable to all the weapons and the martial arts champions.

The name of this holy guardian was Basir Burhan. He had a twin brother named Said Barikun, better known as Sheikh Muso, or the Eleventh Wali.

Basir Burhan, or Sheikh Bintoro (as he was also called), lived in the neighborhood that was previously known as the Raden Fatah Palace. He came only every Friday congregation to give the sermon. He never allowed Sheikh Muso to utter even one sentence to the kampong folk. "The moment he delivers one sentence in the mosque, this promontory headland will be drowned," said Sheikh Bintoro, who considered every word that emerged from the courteous lips of Sheikh Muso as heresy.

Sheikh Muso indeed had never become a teacher. However, every action of this Eleventh Wali was considered an example to be imitated. Because he never killed herons, the kampong folk saw these birds as sacred creatures that ought not to be hurt. Because he spent all his time planting mangrove trees, they considered it forbidden by a higher law to damage or kill those trees that were a barrier to the waves.

But not every act of Sheikh Muso was easy to imitate. Even though they tried again and again, no villager was able to become any kind of healing *dukun*. Any flower, when mixed with a cup of water by Sheikh Muso, could be used to heal various kinds of sickness. Only one or two knew the secret of Sheikh Muso's healings. And even then, their healing powers weren't as strong as those of Sheikh Muso.

Nor did Sheikh Muso have a congregation. Nonetheless, every night many kampong dwellers gathered at his tranquil home. Even though Sheikh Muso did not teach anything, the villagers felt that every night they were learning from that wonderful man.

If some child asked where its parents had gone, "Your daddy has gone to the well of knowledge and your mommy is learning to understand life at the home of Sheikh Muso," would have been the response.

Sheikh Bintoro felt things were awry in Sheikh Muso's teaching. The sharia was being violated. So, one blustery Friday, he visited his twin brother. Naturally, that night, as on previous nights, the kampong folk were swarming around Sheikh Muso as they discussed the nature of herons and mangroves.

"Help us understand about herons, please, Sheikh Muso," said a woman who had a face as pure as a rabbit's.

"I know nothing about herons."

"Come on, sir. You have taught us to not kill herons. Surely, sir, angels have whispered to you that those birds are to be left perching in the forest, am I right?"

Sheikh Muso neither shook nor nodded his head.

"Have these herons never died, so that all this time, they cannot be counted on the hands of all the people of this kampong? Or do some of them die on Tuesday and are raised back to life by Allah on Saturday?"

Sheikh Muso still did not shake his head, or nod it, either.

"Why do you say nothing, Sheikh Muso? Do Allah and the angels sometimes appear in the form of herons, so that you forbid us from killing them, sir?"

Sheikh Muso only smiled.

"Will you tell us, sir, that the only angels are those herons? Would you say there is no Allah but Sheikh Muso—but you yourself, sir?"

Sheikh Muso still just smiled. He didn't shake his head no. He didn't nod his head yes.

"All right then, what do those mangrove trees mean for us?" asked a young man with a face as sly as a rat's.

"I don't know anything about mangrove trees."

"If you don't know about mangroves, why, sir, do you spend all your time planting them on this headland? Are all those the trees you brought from heaven?"

Sheikh Muso tightened his lips in silence. He shivered because a tempest raged and beat against his frail body.

"Who knows, maybe on each leaf are scratched Allah's beautiful verses? Maybe those trees are forever chanting praise to Allah?"

Sheikh Muso stayed tight-lipped. He was shivering more now and felt that it was ever more impossible to reply to the questions of the kampong people, who had an unquenchable thirst for the secret of life.

"Are those mangrove trees more important than all the other trees, so that at *subuh*, *zuhur*, *asar*, *maghrib*, and *isya*, all the five times in the day when we pray, you still devoutly plant them, sir?"

Sheikh Muso did not respond to that question and in fact got ready to leave the house. He wanted to be by himself at the end of the promontory over the sea.

"Don't go just yet!" shouted Sheikh Bintoro, who had all along been hiding behind a tree.

Sheikh Muso ignored this booming voice. He kept on hurrying to the headland.

"Stop your false teachings!" Sheikh Bintoro yelled more loudly.

In Sheikh Bintoro's mind, Sheikh Muso had preached heresy because he hadn't answered the questions of the kampong folk in accordance with sharia. Not answering their questions meant he had agreed with everything they had said. And that was dangerous for the enforcement of religion. And that was dangerous to himself, because he seemed to be fighting his own shadow. Seeing everything that Sheikh Muso did was like seeing his own reflection muddying the pond water that just before had been as clear and sparkling as glass.

"If you don't cease your heretical teachings, Allah will kill you! Believe me!"

Sheikh Muso just continued to ignore him. He rushed off, leaving Sheikh Bintoro behind, leaving behind the suspicions and doubts that tightened all around his chest.

"I know nothing about heretical teachings. So why would Allah kill me?" whispered Sheikh Muso, staring out to sea, staring at the lightning bolts that scored the gloomy and ever-lowering sky.

Sheikh Muso was sad because he felt that no one understood him. Not the people of the kampong. Not Sheikh Bintoro. All the figures he dearly loved.

Did Allah actually kill Sheikh Muso? Allah never becomes involved in small issues. Allah was involved with the miracle of Prophet Noah, who in a fragile boat saved his people from a great flood; but Allah had absolutely no desire to interfere between Sheikh Muso and Sheikh Bintoro over the issues of herons and mangrove trees. Allah had to do with the miracle of the spider that protected Prophet Muhammad in the cave, but He didn't want to judge who was a heretic and who wasn't, in their worship of Him. Was Sheikh Bintoro, who felt obedient to the law, the more correct? Was it the more heretical Sheikh Muso, who never uttered a sentence? Allah didn't want to answer such petty questions.

So did in fact Allah kill Sheikh Muso? Allah was in no way at all involved in the murder of Sheikh Muso. Compared to Allah, it was the headman of Lading Kuning who wanted to take the sheikh's life more quickly. He considered Sheikh Muso the most dangerous enemy because, in addition to now having many followers, this fellow who could do no wrong, together with his gullible disciples, were also accused of being burglars, who on every *Kliwon* Friday would steal from the houses of the hamlet head, the district head, and the head of the kampong.

Not wanting to be seen as incompetent in guarding the safety of the village and wiping out these ruffians, the headman of Lading

Kuning then contracted eleven killers-for-hire to subdue Sheikh Muso. In fact, the headman of Lading Kuning wanted to thrash Sheikh Muso himself. But because he didn't want to look like a cruel official, he borrowed "the hands of others" to get rid of the sheik from the headland, a place that looked increasingly to be the most prosperous neighborhood of the kampong. He told the eleven assassins to murder Sheikh Muso.

Why did there have to be eleven of them? Because the headman of Lading Kuning was sure that Sheikh Muso would be able to transform himself into eleven martial arts adepts whom eleven ordinary humans could never defeat. He needed people who possessed cruelty and extreme killer instincts in order to slaughter Sheikh Muso.

"Of course, he never stole for himself. Of course, he always shared the harvest of his thefts with the poor folk, but still and all, he was a nasty crook, even if you all will call him 'The Good Thief'," said the headman of Lading Kuning, moments before giving the eleven assassins his order to kill Sheikh Muso.

The eleven killers didn't much care about the reasons given by the headman of Lading Kuning.

"Actually Sheikh Muso submits to Sheikh Bintoro. But Sheikh Bintoro asked my help in removing Sheikh Muso," said the headman of Lading Kuning again.

The eleven hired killers didn't listen to his explanation. After receiving their payment, they hurried out of the village. They hurried to the tip of the promontory.

However, at the tip of that headland you would not find a fierce battle between Sheikh Muso and eleven hired assassins. Long before arriving there, as they passed the mangrove forest, the killers were blocked by roots that spread out and twisted around their bodies.

Those roots, as if ordered by a miracle, twisted and turned and coiled like serpents and finally entwined and slammed the thugs down until the bodies of these failed killers were sunk into the mud. And because the eleven of them could not move, from a distance they looked like statues from ancient times standing stiffly in the dark of the night.

But those mangrove roots had not been ordered to kill. Those loving growths were only to terrify. When finally their entanglements loosened and the mud had not buried them alive, the killers took off in a hurry.

"It was impossible for us to kill him," one of the assassins reported to the headman of Lading Kuning.

"We couldn't even get to see his face!"

"His body was enveloped in light!"

The headman of Lading Kuning did not argue with the assassins.

"Don't be afraid. You will win. I am going to ask Sheikh Bintoro to help you."

The assassins trembled. They felt they would be facing a frightful death. They imagined the mangrove roots strangling them or the pointed ends of the branches poking into their eyes.

"Sheikh Muso will be defeated by himself," said the headman of Lading Kuning. "And because Sheikh Muso and Sheikh Bintoro are twin brothers, only Sheikh Bintoro will bring down that almighty man."

The killers didn't understand what the headman of Lading Kuning was saying. They just kept on trembling and shivering. They felt the angel of death with boats from heaven drawing ever nigh, ever nigh.

Sheikh Muso was still in meditation at the end of the land when Sheikh Bintoro and the eleven assassins came to the place the local folk considered awe-inspiring. The roots still spread out like serpents, so that anyone who was there was faced with a feeling of horror that would never go away.

And Allah presumably did not want to be involved with all the actions to be performed by Sheikh Muso and Sheik Bintoro. Nor did Allah order the mangrove roots to be killers, so that the headland was calm, the headland was tranquil. At that point, perhaps the Angel Gabriel whispered to Sheikh Muso, "Do what Sheikh Bintoro asks, even if he wants to thrust a kris into your belly."

Just then, Gabriel may also have whispered to Sheikh Bintoro, "You need not kill your twin brother. Your task is only to ask him to *muksa*, to be transported in extinguishment."

Then the twins came face-to-face. In the sight of the eleven assassins, they spoke not a word to each other. Each one only tried to stare down the other. Yes, of course they did not speak, but they held a secret conversation in their hearts.

"Once more I say to you, I do not teach the slightest thing to your congregation!"

"But you have become an idol."

"I only do whatever Allah requires me to do."

"Yes, but your actions have become commandments. Everything that you do, even what is in error, has come to be considered the Written Word."

"I have said to them that I am nobody."

"But they're blind. They think you are a *wali*. They have forgotten the teachings of the Prophet."

"If that is so, then I shall leave this headland."

"Go inland."

"Yes, I will go. Now leave me alone."

Sheikh Bintoro then backed away several steps. He joined the eleven hired killers.

"You all don't need to kill Sheikh Muso. He has died. Of course he is standing upright in meditation at the end of the promontory, but in truth he has died. That is only Sheikh Muso's body. His soul has gone on."

The eleven assassins trembled at hearing these words from Sheikh Bintoro. They felt they had witnessed a terrible battle without having to stare at the splattering of blood as it gushed from the belly of Sheikh Muso.

Had Sheikh Muso died?

"We succeeded in killing him. We tossed his corpse into the sea," one of the assassins reported to the headman of Lading Kuning.

"It turned out that Sheikh Bintoro had no mystical powers after all. He ran like hell when he came face-to-face with Sheikh Muso!"

"We know Sheikh Muso's weaknesses. I stuck his gut and fresh blood just gushed out. It poured out so strong that the sea turned red when we threw his corpse in it.

"There's nothing more for us to be afraid of now. There is no Good Thief. There are no roots with tapering ends to poke your eyes out. It's all over."

The headman of Lading Kuning smiled to hear those reports. He imagined the rulers, the ministers, and all the creatures would praise the beautiful success in eliminating Sheikh Muso from the promontory of land that had increasingly appeared to be land that everyone must venerate.

Had Sheikh Muso died?

Not a single person reported the news of Sheikh Muso's death to the kampong folk at the edge of the headland. That night, Sheikh Bintoro—after remembering the death of Sheikh Siti Jenar—carried in his arms a body fragrant with sanctity and clothed in his burial shroud. He then invited several residents to offer an occult prayer.

"Who's that?" asked one villager.

"Sheikh Muso, is it?" said another.

Sheikh Bintoro did not answer. He signaled for someone to untie the neck cord of the corpse shroud. And when this was undone, all the kampong folk present shivered with fear. They saw the face of a dog that had rotted away, grimacing behind the blood-spattered cloth.

"Is that you, Sheikh Muso?" shrieked someone hysterically at the stinking dog.

No reply. And Sheikh Bintoro distanced himself exceedingly quickly from the astonished villagers. Silence filled the mosque. Death filled the mosque.

"Did your grandpa return as a rotting dog?"

Azwar, the beloved grandson of Sheikh Muso, didn't answer. But he knew precisely that Sheikh Muso had evaporated, body and soul, into the sea. He had walked on the seabed and saw fish chanting praise to Allah on the walls where the sea had been cleft by the staff of the sheikh.

He was also certain that a moment later, Sheikh Muso would be in the belly of a giant shark and talking of the majesty of Allah with the small creatures which one night had also become the prey of that sea monster.

"Come on, answer, Azwar! Sheikh Muso turned out to be just a rotten dog, right?"

Siti's Fire Birds

The fire birds hurled themselves forward and pierced the hearts of the butchers. The murderers caught fire. Their bodies burned brightly. Siti asked, "Why have the herons all become so fierce?"

There's no beauty as elegant as the dance of herons in the act of making love. And Siti stared amazed at the hundreds of pairs of herons in their encounters of passion. The birds croaked and squawked all at once in the most painfully ear-splitting cries, but at the same time they moved like palace dancers. They waved their wings in movements that were by turns indolent, urgent, rhythmic, and random. They also leapt, ran, leapt again, and ran again. And what amazed this young boy of ten years even more, the herons stood straight up staring at each other with their beaks piercing the sky. He didn't know why the male bird only let out one cry while the female did so again and again.

This was a sight that Siti saw repeatedly and it always left him speechless with amazement. However, on that day in October of 1965, when the sea breezes were laden with the smells of salt and fish, these birds hardly moved at all. The evening prayer had come and gone from the kampong at the end of the headland, but the tropical wildlife here still made no sound at all. Siti supposed hundreds of giant snakes were swallowing them. And the mind of the young lad saw repulsive creeping beasts first pouncing on their wings and then striking and crunching their heads.

Siti, though intending to hurry home from the mosque, out of curiosity abruptly turned and headed back for the open field surrounded by mangrove trees, not far from the tomb that had become a sacred object of veneration. And from that field, he would be able to accurately see everything that happened to those herons crowding about on the muddy dirt between the mangrove trees. Of course, if it were true that huge snakes devoured his beloved birds whenever they felt like it, Siti would chase those hideous creatures away with a torch that never burned out.

"You may not hurt my friends," said Siti waving his torch at the serpents he imagined were so ferocious.

But it wasn't as he had suspected. There weren't any giant snakes roaming about. There wasn't even one heron's bloody carcass. Rather, hundreds of those birds were standing listlessly, wings folded, though they were still wildly croaking and rasping in a deafening clamor.

"Why aren't you dancing?"

There was no reply. Siti had no idea that nature truly has a way of keeping all the bad things secret from children. That night the herons and the mangroves seemed to be a strong fortress impenetrable to Siti's weak eyes. Because of their gathering so closely together and hiding everything that happened behind the stands of mangrove trees and the "heron fortress", Siti saw only a thick wall that separated the open field from the land's end. As it was now low tide, that place had turned into a kind of public parade ground, filled with sand, snail shells, and all kinds of shellfish.

"Come on, why aren't you all dancing?" Siti shouted again.

No answer. Only the wind with its sea stink kept buffeting Siti's body, too frail to confront the raging of night.

What was hidden by the herons and the mangrove trees? If only Siti's ears had not been deafened by the clamor of the herons, he would have heard long and final heartrending screams from eleven grown-up women and men whose necks were being severed by killers from the next kampong. Those butchers shouted Allah's name over and over, before coldheartedly brandishing their choppers, before happily thrusting their bayonets into bellies.

"We have to kill them because, before, they were going to kill us," said one soldier.

"We have to slaughter people who deny this religion, because, before, they killed the generals," said a young man wearing a long Arab robe, one that was completely white.

What was hidden by the herons and the mangrove trees? If only Siti's eyes had not been blinded by the hundreds of herons that formed the barrier wall, he would have seen that there were in fact dozens of grown-up women and men, along with children from the next kampong, parading eleven wretched rope-bound creatures to the end of the promontory. These creatures, considered the most accursed of humans and in league with Satan, were forced to dig their own graves in the open field of sand. After all was finished, the people who saw themselves as the most holy thrust bayonets and swung their choppers to their hearts' content into frail necks or backs.

"Don't think of us cruel.... If they were not dead now, in the future they would slaughter every one of our descendants," hissed a woman in a voice almost inaudible to the other people.

She was talking to herself.

"This is a national duty. You needn't think this is an unforgivable cruelty," hissed a soldier in a voice almost inaudible to the other soldiers.

He was speaking to himself.

What hadn't Siti seen and heard? The tears of the herons and the shrieks of the mangroves. They were terrified to witness all that was happening then, because Allah did not conceal from them the cheers and dancing for joy of the butchers after these murders.

Then as night wore on, the tide steadily rose. The butchers had gone home. The cheering was over. The open land at the end of the promontory was under water. The sand that had at first held pools of blood was quickly cleansed. Lonely silence everywhere. Everything was forgotten by the butchers and the eyewitnesses to those cruel murders.

But that ever hotter and ever more ferocious October nevertheless had no gentle way of introducing death to Siti. The butchers— who from the whispers in the next kampong had been possessed by the souls of the generals murdered in a distant city—looked all day and all night for anyone thought to be devil worshippers, meaning the devils who were always flying the hammer and sickle flag and who danced and sang as they beat the generals and their steadfast adherents.

Siti's father Azwar, merely because he never wanted to join the soldiers and the people who claimed to the purest of the pure, inevitably now became the most hated of hunted creatures.

Dozens of people from the next kampong—of course with the soldiers and the raging men in their spotless white robes—attacked the kampong at the tip of the promontory after a very calm evening prayer. They honed their wrath as they stuck out their tongues, waved their swords, and shouted the greatness of Allah over and over, so that everything they did would be cleansed of sin.

To slaughter Azwar, you know, it should have been enough for one soldier to thrust a bayonet into his belly. But delegating this to a weak and timid soldier was not possible. The kampong dwellers out at the land's end greatly loved Azwar. To murder such a favorite, the guiding light of the kampong in everything they did, would drive them wild.

So, in order to mute the rage of Azwar's devotees, there was no other way except for dozens of killers to be alerted.

"Kill Azwar! Save the kampong people from this damned devil!"

"Kill this defender of those who hate Allah!

"Kill him!"

Siti was just then reciting his prayers and discussing with Azwar the difference between the herons at the headland and the famous *ababil* birds that thrashed the elephant army of Yemen, when he was startled to hear all those shouts and cries.

"Could herons turn into fire birds?" asked Siti.

"Anything can happen if Allah permits it," said Azwar. Siti peered through the window and caught sight of dozens of men waving cleavers and bayonets. He also saw dozens of villagers using sampan paddles trying to drive off the killers.

Then cries and shouts were answered by cries and shouts. The waving of cleavers and thrusting of bayonets answered the brandishing of paddles. Blood would soon flow if no one tried to avoid this night battle, lit only by the half-moon.

In all of this, to Siti's surprise, Azwar opened the door and, walking ever so calmly, parted the mob. The kampong people tried to block his way, but Azwar kept trying to keep the mob separated and then hastened to face the wildly shouting killers.

"Go ahead and kill me if you think by doing so you will live free from the most accursed devil!" shouted Azwar in a voice that split the night.

No reply. A cleaver swung into Azwar's back.

"Kill me if you think that by killing me you will become the purest of the pure!"

No reply. A bayonet was thrust into Azwar's belly.

Of course the people of the kampong at that headland could not let Azwar be slaughtered before their very eyes. So, before Azwar's neck was severed, before Azwar's body was dragged away and tossed into the sea, they fought back.

Then the cleavers and bayonets clashed with the paddles. Several people were cut down by the cleavers, several were impaled by bayonets, and others were clubbed by the sampan paddles.

Where was Siti? Siti didn't see this horrible sight. At that very moment, the herons of the mangrove forest around the kampong all flew up at once and surrounded the people locked in combat. There wasn't the slightest crack or gap that allowed Siti to see the blood gushing from bellies or the hacked and stabbed backs. The herons would not allow children as innocent as Siti get a whiff of the cruelty and violence.

But that ever hotter and ever more ferocious October did not have any gentle way of introducing Siti to death. The yelling and shouting of the butchers grew louder. The screams of those being butchered were no less loud. Blood gushed. The sandy soil of the headland reddened right up to its end, right into the innermost recesses of the shells of the snails and gloomy crustaceans.

There was no other way of stopping that useless battle except for the herons of that point of land on the sea to repeat the event of many years before that had been performed by their ancestors. With Allah's permission, the clamoring herons, harshly croaking and rasping a kind of chant, weaved and turned into the direction of the butchers, and, with every weave and turn, scattered flames. The herons, like the mythical *ababil* birds, dropped the *sigil*, bricks of baked clay from hell, on the bodies of the killers. These flaming stones rubbed the air and pierced the bodies of the killers who ran madly here and there—*and praise be to Allah, He permitted and did not crave their killing*—from the distance, looked like arrows of fire that sped through the darkness of night.

At that very moment, Siti saw all those frightful events. Seeing the enflamed bodies of the butchers, Siti asked, "Why have the herons all become so fierce?"

No reply. Siti only saw Azwar staggering—wounded in his belly, back, and neck and endlessly gushing blood—making his way to the mosque and the last of the fiery flashes of the herons, which kept up their croaking and rasping like a chant of praise to Allah that scored the skies in that painful October. Siti only knew that the kampong finally became silent again, as if the incalculable and magnificent cruelties had never happened.

Siti only...

A Pair of Death Sniffers

Moments before the bullet pierced his gut, before the killers
put a wire noose around his neck and dragged his corpse
to the holy tomb, Ahmad had whitewashed the entire
outer wall of the mosque with the color of a burial shroud.
Completely white. Spotless.

He also signed the words and digits *Mecca, 570+1+life+9-6+4x15:9* under the calligraphy *Allah*. "It's completed, Lord, and tomorrow we will perform the Eid prayers here," whispered the caretaker of the mosque as he gazed at the heron flying low and disappearing into a stand of mangrove trees.

Because he'd made the world younger and fresher, Ahmad felt he had the time to reminisce about the first time he came to the dirty kampong almost empty of inhabitants. At the time, he only saw six stilt houses with posts thrust into the earth, around which were pools of sea water, and the mosque, whose foundation was buried in mud, with little snakes, crabs, leeches, and rotting flying fish scattered around the *mihrab*, the Mecca-facing niche.

It had been a long time since anyone had prayed in that mosque. Rather than going through the trouble of scraping out the mud and feeling the cling of leeches, people preferred to pray at home. So the mosque had remained unfinished. Herons were allowed to stalk in, flapping their wings right up to the *mihrab*, and on the walls a light green mildew grew freely. At that time, the atmosphere inside the mosque was like an imperfectly created world: filthy, stinking, full of the carcasses of herons and creeping animals. "Only devils would want to live in this place," thought Ahmad. "But I will be safe here."

Then there was only one thing to do. Ahmad scraped out the mud from the mosque every day, every week. Alone. He couldn't very well ask for help from the fishermen who figured they could pray onboard their boats. He couldn't possibly ask for help from people who found it hard to pray in congregation because they were more often at sea than on land.

In the end, he managed to get rid of the mud. But he couldn't drive away the flood tide. So water just continued to form pools in the mosque. So that the five daily prayers could be performed, he built a kind of stage at the *mihrab* when the floor for the prostrations was usurped by the insatiable seawater. Maybe the way that Ahmad did his prayers was like the Prophet Noah's when the deluge hit. In Ahmad's mind, Prophet Noah—when the seawater leaked into his boat—perched like that, too.

"I will never leave this mosque, ever…"

So from that time on, the folk living on the headland thought a crazy man had slipped into the kampong. Even so, they often sent food across the water to the mosque so that Ahmad didn't starve to death. Sometimes the children—who never considered anyone crazy—gave their share of grilled fish so that Ahmad, who had sworn to eat only food that Allah sent him drifting into the mosque, never greedily devoured anything that wandered around outside there.

But towards dawn, Ahmad seemed to see a pair of angels descend from heaven with blazing eyes and swords ready to be thrust into bellies. He was exceedingly frightened to be in their presence. He felt that in a little while they would turn into great serpents that would coil around his neck and crush the life out of him. "Allah! Allah! Will you be bringing my life to an end when it drizzles just before dawn?"

Just then, a few months before 1983, a year filled with carcasses after the death of 532 men and women considered gone bad, Munawar whispered to Ahmad, "I know it won't be long before you die!"

Munawar was no all-knowing angel, but in front of Ahmad, he always acted like someone who could sniff out death. He even bragged he could sniff the smell of death by breathing in the sweat stains on the shirt that someone had worn. "I've seen a pair of angels shadowing you. Yesterday, when you were at the well performing your prayer ablutions, they were ready to stick you in the belly with the swords of heaven. And your neck, too, was going to be caught in a noose of wire, and you would not have been able to resist His will."

Ahmad, alarmed and annoyed, listened to the whispering of his childhood playmate. But even though he thought Munawar was teasing him, he trembled with fear. Looking long into Munawar's eyes, he seemed to see a bullet pierce the belly of a man who looked every bit like himself. He also saw a soldier strangle him with a wire and drag him to the holy gravesite.

"I'm not going to die just because you want me to…"

"I don't want you to die. I am telling you, one soggy dawn you are going to die."

Ahmad wasn't the slightest bit angry at hearing his friend's prophesy, which sounded more like something serious disguised in a joke. In fact, he embraced Munawar, saying, "I will reject my death. I will kill anyone who wants to kill me…"

Even though he wasn't greatly frightened by Munawar's teasing, every time he saw the police or soldiers moving along the muddy roads that surrounded the kampong, Ahmad felt a certain anxiety. And this feeling was greatly multiplied every time he caught sight of three to four people in the murky distance breaking into his home.

We don't need to see Ahmad as a coward. At the time, even the most powerful underworld lowlife types were scared of the shadowy killers who slipped into the kampongs. And Ahmad was only a small-time thief, just an insignificant bandit who tried to look tough in front of Munawar. So, when he saw more and more tattooed corpses of both men and women sprawled along the roads and in the ditches, their necks garroted by wire, he decided to fight back.

"Before I get killed, I'm going to kill them!"

But killing shadows—someday you'd call them "mysterious shooters"—was no easy thing. It was impossible for Ahmad to grab just anyone passing in front of the house as a rotten thug whose head deserved to be hacked off with a machete. So he was forced to rely on Munawar. He was forced to ask his buddy who was going to die and who could escape the throes of death.

"Today there will be a pickpocket who'll die and a policeman will get his right hand cut off," said Munawar.

And it was true. Badrun and Soleh—petty thieves in the kampong—were stretched out in the graveyard just before dawn.

And totally unexpectedly, that same dawn Ahmad chopped off the right hand of a man who had sneaked into his house. The mutilated hand was still holding a pistol. The hand was still ready to pull the trigger, still ready to kill Ahmad.

The next day, he met Munawar again, "Why didn't you say that I would cut off the hand of that stinking killer?"

"Because actually it wasn't you who was to cut off his hand. Because, in fact, it was your gut that was going to feel his bullet going through you."

Right then, Ahmad wanted more than anything to slap Munawar's face. He felt he was being played with.

"Be grateful that you've still managed to avoid their surveillance. But, believe me, one dawn when it starts to drizzle, they are going to kill you. At that moment you won't be able to avoid death's frenzy. Only then you'll believe that I can smell your death."

Ahmad said nothing. Face to face with Munawar, he felt he was dealing with a lost angel.

"There are still a lot more very bad lowlifes who're going be killed. There are still lots of hands holding pistols that you'll cut off. And I still see a pair of the angels of death tailing you."

Ahmad froze. He imagined dozens of mutilated right hands holding pistols, all ready and eager to pull the triggers. Eager to kill him.

"You needn't be afraid now. You won't die here."

Ahmad shivered. More and more he saw Munawar as an angel who was going to rob him of his life.

"I've got to go into hiding right away," said Ahmad to himself. "And I've got to get away from this damned death-sniffer."

Munawar was no life-snatcher. Munawar never wanted to kill his pal. In 1983, there were no angels that wanted to kill Ahmad, in hiding on a promontory of land in a quiet mosque. So for the time being, Ahmad didn't worry about death. And because he didn't feel as if he was being stalked by death, Ahmad spent all his hours intimate only with laudations to Allah and prayers in honor of the Prophet. Intimate with the little snakes, crabs, leeches, and rotting flying fish scattered around the *mihrab* in the mosque.

Every once in a while, he would listen to the chattering of children about the holy tomb and the mystic powers of Sheikh Muso. Occasionally he would also listen to the story of Azwar, always considered the defender of those who worshipped the hammer and sickle by the soldiers in the town, who once a month would invade his quiet headland. He would also often hear the children talking about Siti, Azwar's son who was now reciting the Quran and pursuing religious studies in Rembang, the city of the revered Kiyai Bisri. But because indeed he did not want to have anything to do with anyone, Ahmad spent his time just getting rid of the mud that had buried the floor, scraping off the moss from the walls, and chasing out the little snakes from the *mihrab*, until he found it in himself to mumble, "Even angels would stop by here. Even angels would prostrate themselves in thanks to Allah in this mosque."

But at dawn everything was different. He felt he was going to meet Munawar. Only, this time he didn't need to ask when he would die. Because all day long he knew only chanting and praying, he could now sniff out when the angels came and when the angels went. He also understood that in a few moments more, Munawar would come with the killers and say, "Now you can't escape death, friend. The drizzle has almost arrived and the killers will drag you to the grave."

Ahmad smiled. He hoped he could right then and there embrace Munawar and whisper, "Yes, the dawn drizzle has indeed come."

Ahmad knew that Munawar had been forced to reveal his hiding place out on the headland by those stinking killers from the town. But Ahmad didn't know that, after they were finished with him, the killers would also beat Munawar to death, so that no one would be left a witness to his murder. Ahmad did not know how such cruelty beyond limit could grow on this earth and could slaughter so indiscriminately.

Then the drizzle fell and cared not about a pair of fellows who perished in that dawn, their stomachs riddled with bullets, their necks garroted with wire, and their bodies dragged to the burial ground without a sound.

Without a sound...

Three Painful Stories of Elisabet Rukmini

The Labyrinth of Cruelty

I know when that moment arrives you will look for me. Like the great explorers, you will comment on every footprint that I have left behind. It won't be easy, because for years I have been close-mouthed, for years I kept my story in the calmness of the mountainside, in the stillness at the end of the promontory over the sea. Perhaps you aren't going to find me. Perhaps you will only discover my faint and unreadable footprints.

In an October without typhus or dysentery, they knocked on the door of every house in Alas, and highhandedly seized and arrested people thought to have plotted to murder the generals during the Dance of the Fragrant Flowers at the Crocodile Hole. Secret soldiers who were never listed in that unit came like the plague. That night and in cold blood, they shot anyone who ran into the forest. With that same coldness, their bayonets skewered the bellies of the wretched people who, when they were interrogated, replied in too round about a way to all manner of questions that shook them to their core.

If you have no desire to taste cruelty beyond compare, hope that you never meet them. Fine, then; if you don't believe me, I'll tell you about what happened to Magdalena Markini. Simply because she wouldn't reveal my hiding place, Magda, my older sister, was burned alive, in our front yard.

It's the truth: I witnessed it from the top of the *rambutan* tree. Before she was set on fire, I saw a soldier bash Magda's head with his rifle butt. And not just that. The moment she fell, another soldier stamped on Magda's fragile head with his boot, so that where her nose and mouth had been was now a big dent.

"Where are you hiding that murdering dancer Elisabet Rukmini?" Magda didn't answer. She made the sign of the cross by touching her fingertip to her forehead, chest and shoulders as she mumbled something.

"Don't trick us with your fake praying!" a soldier said, ramming his boot into Magda's chest. "Didn't you kill God a long time ago already? Why're you now pretending to worship Him?"

Magda gave no reply but once again broke out muttering and mumbling. Perhaps she hoped Christ would come to save her when no one dared resist those pitiless soldiers. And, of course, Christ had been killed and so there was no way he could descend to the earth just to save Magda.

So there was no miracle when a soldier suddenly squatted and jabbed a lighted cigarette into Magda's eye. Magda shrieked, but not a single villager heard her voice. Maybe they had been burned too. Maybe they had gone before the murderous soldiers arrived.

"Again… where are you hiding Elisabet Rukmini? You know what your kid sister did on September 30th?"

Magda, tortured for simply being the older sister of someone suspected to be one of the generals' murderers, shook her head.

"You know the punishment for concealing traitors?"

Magda kept shaking her head.

"All right then. In a minute you're going to know the what the right punishment for you is…"

Then, a soldier splashed kerosene all over Magda. They torched the beautiful body of my older sister, who had always lived in accord with Christ but who never received any help from that Son of Nazareth.

Truly, when I saw Magda running back and forth all ablaze, I wanted to cry out. I wanted to at least divert the soldiers' attention so they would stop torturing her. But I reined in that urge. I had to live. Some day I would have to report the cruelty of those vicious soldiers. I'd never be able to tell anything at all if they killed me then.

So what else could I do but to witness the body of Magda slowly turn into ashes and dust? I could do nothing except wait for the soldiers to go away. As I waited, I didn't pray for my safety. Magda's body slowly melting, her eye unable to shriek when jabbed with a cigarette, or her lips locked shut when bayoneted in her belly—all this made it clear enough which side Christ was on.

The moon wasn't shining at the edge of the forest when I left the burned down kampong. So after climbing down from the *rambutan* tree, I crossed the dark road in the opposite direction the soldiers had gone. Even so, I knew I had to get to safety quickly, and I knew where I had to go.

It wasn't easy in the dense darkness, but I found a place to hide. Because to reach the safest hiding place, that is, a church across from the village, I had to cross through dozens of rose beds full of thorns, ford the river's swift current, and slip into the cave filled with bats.

My sufferings felt worse than the agonies of Christ. To reach the cross, God's staff of salvation for his most beautiful son, Christ of course had to wear a crown of thorns. But what about me? To reach the river, my entire body was stuck with thousands of thorns.

For quite some time, I was trapped in the beauty of those painful rose beds. And for quite some time, having made it through one rose bed, I had to cross yet another.

All this time, my thoughts flew to the church. I meet Romo Sindhu and immediately tell him everything that had happened to Magda. I tell the kindly priest how Christ had not flinched the slightest bit in the face of the soldiers, so cruel and invulnerable.

But, the fact was, my body was still caught in the garden of thorny roses. If in just a few more minutes I could get free of this trap of pain and beauty, I would also have to swim the fiercely flowing cold river. Even if I could best the river, I wasn't at all certain of being able to slip into the cave without a torch.

So of course I felt I'd never be able to report on the barbarity of the soldiers. Because if I managed to leave this trap of a cave, there was no way that the secret soldiers from other units would let me just stroll along to Romo Sindhu's church.

Even so, I was sure Romo Sindhu awaited me patiently. And patiently Romo Sindhu would listen to a wounded woman reporting the distressing news about a kampong that had been incinerated and dozens of its residents brutalized by soldiers in the dark.

I plunged into the river just as dozens of snakes emerged from their hiding holes. They wanted to migrate to other holes. I didn't ask the snakes why they had to move back and forth. And not wanting to come in contact with these disgusting serpents carried along by the current on the surface of the water, I decided to dive down and come up for air from time to time.

The snakes didn't seem possessed by demons or Lucifer; they showed no desire to tempt a descendant of Eve. Since they had other things on their minds just then, they didn't have the slightest interest in nipping or wrapping themselves around a human with wounds. So, bearing the pain, I just let myself be carried along until I reached the headland, until I reached the lip of the cave.

As you know, at the lip of that cave, the water no longer flowed with any force. Nor was the underground river fierce. This helped me get through the final trap fairly smoothly. Still, I couldn't dawdle

there. I had heard from explorers about a whirlpool in the middle
of the cave where that underground river flowed, that could suck
you down as deep as twenty meters. If I were unlucky, I might easily
get pulled under and end up stuck in one of the tunnel passages.

Only, as you also know, a cave will not hurt anyone who explores
the cavities of its body if they obey the rules that were carved, as it
seemed, into their walls.

First of all, never shout out silly words when in the zone of
eternal darkness, that is, precisely the center of the cave. The
echoing and re-echoing of those words would only confuse you
and turn into a humming sound that would hurt your ears. And if
your ears hurt, you will get confused and try to avoid the pain by
slipping into the depths of the underground river. At that moment,
you wouldn't know that the whirlpool will suck you down and sink
you for good.

Second, never kill any animals that live in the cave. They are
very sensitive and know who treats them and their kin badly. If you
kill a snake, that snake will keep your image in its eyes. Its serpent
kin can see your face in the murdered creature so that in a trice
they'll be hunting you. You may go to the ends of the earth, but
those snakes will stay on your trail.

Third, don't ever take or leave anything in the cave. And don't
even think about breaking off a stalactite or stalagmite, for the
moment you do those pointed stones will want to stab you in your
belly.

So, with feelings of respect to all that lived in the cave, I swam
in the underground river. I knew the twists and turns of the cave by
heart, because ever since I was a little girl, I had passed through this
natural beauty about 350 meters long together with my playmates
to get to Romo Sindhu's church.

When we were young, we felt we had discovered heaven when
we emerged at the other end of that cave. And always after that,

Romo Sindhu would tell us, "Yes, you all have discovered heaven!" so that we would often race to the church when Sunday came.

Would I reach the end of the cave? I didn't know. I only felt that Romo Sindhu would greet my arrival with a radiant expression on his face.

Long ago, when I was about twelve years old, after I had succeeded in emerging from the cave's underground river, Romo Sindhu had asked me, "What did you see in the cave, Elisabet Rukmini?"

"I didn't see anything, Romo, except bats and darkness."

"You didn't see a carving of the body of the crucified Christ?"

"I didn't see the body of Christ, Romo."

"You didn't see the body of the grown-up Magda burned by the soldiers?"

"I didn't see the body of Magda, Romo."

"You didn't see your own adult body hunted by the soldiers?"

"I didn't see my body, Romo."

"You didn't see everything that would happen carved into the wall of the cave?"

"I didn't see all that would happen carved into the wall of the cave, Romo."

"Truly?"

"Truly, Romo."

Romo Sindhu was not angry upon hearing my answers. He stroked my hair and softly said, "Some day, when the time has come, you will see all that has been carved into the wall of the cave."

So, what really did I see in the cave in that painful October of 1965? Perhaps because I was hallucinating, I seemed to see my body crucified by those beastly soldiers. Throngs of them thrust bayonets into my stomach, until my body sagged, until I could do nothing at all.

I paid no attention to the strange carvings. I just wanted to see Romo Sindhu right away, a priest who always appeared strong in mind and body. I only wanted to drop down in the church yard and hope that he would take me up in his arms as Holy Mother Mary did with the limp and spent body of Christ.

But, clearly, I still had to get past the vortex in the zone of eternal darkness. The sucking waters were unavoidable, so there was no use in remembering anything at all that deserved to be called life. At such critical moments, I could only trust in what my mother would say, *ngelia ning aja keli*, meaning, *go with the current, but don't let it carry you away.*

So I didn't fight the whirlpool. I let my body be sucked down. I let my body be tossed up to the surface. I let the peaceful current carry me to the lip of the cave, the lip that brought me close to Romo Sindhu's church.

I crawled up to the church door and knocked loudly so that Romo Sindhu would hurry out and carry my feeble body in his arms. But there seemed to be no sign of life inside the church. As if no one heard my knocking on that flimsy door.

"Romo, open the door! Help me!"

But there was no response from within.

*

Where was that most beautiful of priests now? Why did he of all people abandon me at my moment of need? Just as Christ abandoned Magda, why had Romo Sindhu also abandoned me when I so wanted to ask for his help?

The answer was something I never expected. The moment I managed to open the door that in fact had not been locked, I saw Romo Sindhu terribly battered and covered with blood. His eyes that stared in my direction seemed to be holding back his pain.

I could see that Romo Sindhu had been beaten most savagely by several people. Blood also flowed from his stomach. That meant that someone had thrust a kind of spear or bayonet into the priest's tender belly. His chest was also broken and crushed. Someone— perhaps more than one person—must have stamped hard on Romo Sindhu's slender body with his boots. The most frightening thing was that Romo's penis had been obliterated. As if it had been shot at from up close, so that it was now just a mess.

From the many flies swarming over the priest's body, it seemed that these barbarities had occurred quite some time before. I mourned the loss of Romo Sindhu's smile. His mouth had been staved in. His teeth had been knocked out.

In fact, Romo Sindhu's corpse had not yet begun to decompose, but anyone who saw it could not have escaped a stomach-churning nausea. The corpse was that horrifying. Maybe Christ himself could not have prevented that tragic death. The murderers had finished off Romo Sindhu as if they had been slaughtering a goat.

You might think that devils conspired to attack the village in order to kill Romo Sindhu. I don't believe that. I think it was something else. Perhaps, just as Magda didn't want to reveal my hiding place, Romo also did not want to reveal the whereabouts of the parish members suspected of involvement in the murder of the generals. And because he stayed tight-lipped, the soldiers murdered him. Yes, as simple as that.

Perhaps my guess is wrong. But seeing the wounds all over Romo Sindhu's body, wounds very similar to Magda's, I'm sure that the killers all came from the same training camp. That means if Magda's killers were soldiers, then Romo's killers, too, were not far from a military institution.

Of course, don't ask what their unit was. Their plague-like presence would not have been recorded in any document. War crimes tribunals would not be able to sentence senior military officers since naturally there were no records that could implicate them as the brains behind the most vicious murders in this country.

So who murdered Romo Sindhu? No one came forward to answer this question. And no one who knew the answer would ever report such a killing. Knowing about a murder, you understand, will only turn and turn inside one's heart and be entombed like a mummy.

So what could I do at that moment? Nothing. It has never been the gift of frail females to work wonders. Victory and superiority are in the hands of those with the rifles and the boots, and my only capital was the desire to report the brutality of the soldiers to people who don't want to hear about it. Can't change the world with that.

So it was better to do nothing at all. I would play dead, so that when the soldiers came, they wouldn't have to tire themselves out killing me. Oh yes, this was the smart choice. Like a stupid tiger who didn't scent its helpless prey, the soldiers would never touch me. I knew they would be ferocious if they came face to face with a prey that was also ferocious.

But to play dead was no easy thing. I had to regulate my breathing so as not to raise a roar. I had to regulate my heartbeats so no one would hear their thunder.

But damn it all! The longer I played dead the less I could keep from farting. Whether it was the sound of these farts or because the soldiers were naturally keeping a close watch on me for any movement, they suddenly appeared from where they were hiding and jostled each other in their haste to surround me.

"No need to keep hiding! You can't get away again!"

Run? Where would I run to? Maybe my thoughts could run, but I could never have gotten my body to move, even to crawl. So I decided to just remain still. I was sure that once I froze in place like a statue, the soldiers wouldn't make a move. They wouldn't stick their bayonets into me. They wouldn't stub their cigarettes into my eyes. They wouldn't stomp on me with their boots and my mouth wouldn't be staved in and my teeth wouldn't be knocked out.

"Is your name Elisabet Rukmini?"

I said nothing.

"Your name is Elisabet Rukmini? Don't make us kill the wrong person!"

I still said nothing.

"Once again, is your name Elisabet Rukmini? You don't want us to kill you, do you? Come on now, talk!"

There was no need to answer. I knew that perhaps they hadn't actually been ordered to kill me, so I didn't have to obey those damned empty threats.

In such moments I actually have strength. Strength to stifle my anger. Strength to not resist cruelty.

Is it wrong not to resist cruelty?

I didn't need to answer that question. Whether I answered it or not, a soldier still slammed his rifle stock against the back of my neck until I fainted, so I didn't know where they were dragging my body to.

Brutality has incarnated as irresistible strength, so that it would be useless for anyone to try strangle its supernatural powers. So, after coming to again, I no longer cared what had happened. I wasn't afraid anymore of threatening guns or boots. I was no longer afraid of bayonets in my belly. I was no longer afraid whether in one minute or five minutes from then I would be still be breathing or dreaming of freedom.

Really, at that moment I truly, truly was no longer afraid of hearing the stamping of boots and the cocking of rifles. I wasn't afraid of fear.

MIRROR OF FIRE

Have you ever been imprisoned and crucified on a bed of fire? Not only in one cell, but in four prisons and one lunatic asylum during that period between 1965 and 1971? If you have, you surely wouldn't be willing to tell me even the slightest things you experienced bitterly and likely under force. So really, I don't want to tell you my absurd story. Anyone would think I was telling a nonsense tale. I also believe that they, and maybe you too, would think that anything I said was the delirious babbling of an insane person.

But, precisely because I'm not crazy, I've got to tell you how crazy the soldiers and nurses and doctors were who wouldn't believe in my sanity. How not to lose my mind when they were always demanding that I be someone else? How not to go insane when I'm forced to become a murderer in an act I never did?

"We won't execute you today if you'll admit your part in murdering the generals and immediately ask for forgiveness," said the pretty interrogator with the delicate mustache who for some reason was named Karna and not Karina.

"I never killed anyone. I only danced and was a little drunk. After I finished dancing, I was confused and didn't know what had happened."

"Oh, you mean you were unaware you murdered the generals, is that it?"

Even when I answered truthfully, whatever I said was considered wrong, so I preferred just to jabber on with whatever came into my head. Karna looked startled when I said, "I murdered the generals the same way I'd kill rats. Have you ever killed the man you loved most of all?"

Karna shook her head. That gesture had many meanings. Of course, maybe she had never murdered anyone. Maybe she had no man who was the love of her life.

"And also never strangled a cat?"

Karna shook her head again.

"Never stuck a knife into a dog's back?"

Karna smiled. That smile meant that not only had she never stabbed anything, but perhaps she had bashed in the head of that disgusting animal with a crowbar. But the smile that was at first so sincere, quickly turned into a cynical laugh. And just as quickly, she tried to get the better of me by throwing out a question that took me by surprise.

"Before you killed the generals, did you all invite them to have sex first?"

I couldn't manage a quick response to that one.

"Were you able to enjoy it at the time?" asked Karna again, coldly. "Did the generals who were bound hand and foot also get aroused when you fondled them?"

Crazy! What the interrogator with the pointy chest asked was really crazy. Apparently Karna imagined the Dance of the Fragrant Flowers as a horrifying sex orgy. She really thought that, at the time, I was naked and greedily looked on the generals as food to be devoured, with nothing, not even bones, left behind.

"Yeah, I enjoyed it..." I said. "You want to know how I enjoyed that lovemaking?"

Karna nodded. Yes. Her breathing quickened. An arousal that was seething, though restrained. Because I could guess Karna's desires, I took off my red and black T-shirt, my bra, my long black trousers, and my purple panties. Pretending to be deranged, I danced the Fragrant Flowers with my eyes shut.

"Stay seated. Imagine you are a general who wishes to enjoy the wildness of erotic love. I will show you how I and the chosen women fondled and caressed the generals," I hissed.

The stocky woman didn't move. She was so astonished to see me dance. No. No. She was not only astonished at the beauty of my body and the quivers that flowed in each of my dances. As a woman who understood every explosion of lust, I knew then that Karna wanted to be touched by someone who would treat her like a queen. Yes, the touch of someone, woman or man, it didn't matter—with the looks of an accursed animal or an angel imbued with grace, it didn't matter.

Because I felt like toying with that woman, I embraced her from behind. I planted a kiss on the nape of her neck and whispered dirty words. I said to her, that was the way the chosen women and I licked the ears of the generals who were going into their death throes.

"I then stripped off their clothes," I said as I took off all of Karna's clothes. "You'd like to know how those generals felt my kisses?"

The woman resisted not at all. Perhaps Karna thought that to get the most accurate information possible, an extraordinary sacrifice was called for, including letting her body be treated like a general humiliated before the murderers at Crocodile Hole.

However, it just might have been—as the circulating rumors had it—she was indeed a woman who always craved to have sex with women, from any background, who were under interrogation. And because I did want to play games with this foolish woman who really knew nothing at all about Gerwani, I misled Karna with false information and with caresses that were also false.

But it would be a mistake to think of Karna as a stupid woman. She knew that when I kissed and bit her plump lips, it wasn't for real. She knew I was really fantasizing making love with someone else. She knew I saw her as someone who forced me to make love in the park beneath a half-moon surrounded by the grunts and snorting of other couples who had made love oblivious to anyone else. She knew at that moment it was actually I who craved to squeal as I savored the unbearable explosions of lust.

Indeed, I was dripping with the sweat pouring out of me, while she very calmly put back on the clothes I had forced off her. And to my surprise, she called several prison guards over and had them to take me to the cell.

"Transfer her to another prison. This woman is starting to lose her mind," said Karna, who, in everything she did, reminded me of the brutal soldiers who seized me.

The guards handcuffed me. I struggled to break free. They spread-eagled me, then bound my hands and feet. Of course, I kept struggling. I didn't want the guards treating me like the Romans crucifying Jesus on the cross.

I didn't want to be tortured any more, and I screamed out dirty words at them.

"Stop that racket! If you keep it up, I'll burn your bed!'

My bed had not yet been burned. But they moved me to another prison. Being moved to another prison was clearly a blessing. First of all, I could get away from Karna, who had no regard for time—neither nighttime, nor morning, nor afternoon—interrogating me with stupid questions and hefty chest-crushing embraces every time I answered nonsensically about my involvement in the murder of the generals. Second, I could get away from the stomach-churning and heart-racing threat of execution. Third, I'd have the possibility to report the despotism of the soldiers to someone, anyone.

Furthermore, it wasn't only I who was transferred from prison to prison. Later on, when I was with other women held in the camp, I found out there was a doctor who had to be moved from detention in Sukabumi to Bandung, Kebayoran Baru, Pesing, Gunung Sehari, Lapangan Banteng Selatan, and Bukit Duri. Also, the wife of a painter, who after being brought by army truck to Sleman, was also transferred to Benteng Vredeburg, Wirogunan Prison, and finally to Bulu Prison in Semarang.

Compared to them, I was clearly lucky. I had been transferred to three prisons, but all these were in Alas. At first they moved me to a place where I could hear cows lowing in pain.

"Hell," said the guard, coldly.

"Hell"?

"Yeah, there's a slaughterhouse here. Not too different from the Crocodile Hole, eh? No need for you to shrink back like that. After all, you're used to blood. You're used cries of pain, right?"

"But, sir, why do you say this place is like hell?"

"Because this place is going be burned down in a little while and all of you will be turned into ashes along with it," said the guard, again coldly.

Hmm. I knew this was the method used by Soeharto's secret soldiers to make us feel low. And they were experts at creating panic. They looked less like military people than like doctors at a lunatic asylum, who understand all the hidden recesses of our souls.

"Why does it have to be burned down?" I asked, keeping the panic out of my voice so as not to reveal how bad I felt.

"Because you're all dangerous and won't admit to killing the generals," replied the guard casually.

I stopped asking questions. I knew all their questions by heart. They would be answered mechanically and always ended with their wanting us to admit to killing the generals by various razor incisions, by various fatal blows to their heads.

From that time on, I preferred to keep my mouth shut. And from that time, too, I heard them talking about me being moved to another prison.

"There's no use in our keeping this woman locked up here. She's gone nuts. She'd rather talk to herself than to us. We could go nuts ourselves just being around her."

I didn't wait long to be transferred. This time they took me to an old house near the Dutch military cemetery. The air was thick with bats, in the sitting room, the toilet, and even the bedrooms. Who knows how long the bats, which frequently went crashing into the walls, had lived in that all-white house. Who knows how long it had been uninhabited: there was no smell of sweat or anything at all that always stuck to human beings.

At first, of course, I wasn't used to being shut up in a room, with nothing to do but look at the gravestones of Dutch soldiers through the barred window. At first I felt fear when I saw a full moon appear to fall on the graveyard. At first I was bored with listening only to the flapping of batwings and all sorts of strange sounds through the long and stifling night. But as time passed, I ignored the petty torments of these moronic soldiers.

"You still won't admit you took part in murdering the generals? Come on, now, just tell us your version," said an interrogator who looked disgusted when he visited my room.

I kept quiet. There was no point in answering these same old questions.

"I'll release you from here provided you admit to all the things that I will then report to the Commandant," said the interrogator impatiently.

I still kept quiet. I thought it would be better that I spent my days in this place rather than admitting to things I didn't do, just to end up shot by soldiers somewhere else.

Perhaps out of despair, the soldier, who actually smiled at me a lot, called the two guards who had been watching me all along.

"This woman is getting crazier by the day. Shouldn't we transfer her to a special prison for nutcase women?"

The two guards nodded yes.

"Has she been talking to herself in the room a lot?"

The two guards again nodded yes.

"Does she yell and shout wildly?

"Yes, all the time," said one of the two.

"In that case, let's move her tomorrow."

Another transfer? This was clearly a threat. My closeness to the bats made me feel at home in this prison. So the moment the two guards moved to arrest me, wanted to bind me up like a pig to the slaughter, I revolted. This time my resistance seemed dangerously risky. A guard hit me on the back of the neck with something wooden.

Very far off I heard the interrogator's voice giving orders to the guards.

"If that damned woman gives you trouble, just burn her."

Hmm, once again the threat of incineration…

Don't they have anything else to threaten me with?

When I opened my eyes, I was in a room of mirrors set up in such a way that they reflected many bodies. I saw fifteen of me in them. At first I thought that a hole had opened up in my head and my eyesight was getting so fuzzy that I couldn't tell which was the real me. When I spread my arms apart, all the images in the mirrors looked like the people crucified on the hill of Golgotha. When I imitated Jesus praying in the Garden of Gethsemane, the mirrors displayed a figure bowed down in resignation and crying bitterly. And because I loved to dance, I burst out in a kind of dance of very rapid movements copying the comical gestures of Anoman, until I felt I surrounded by ten pretty monkeys leaping and jumping about idiotically.

What was their intention in punishing me with those mirrors with the crazy-house reflections? Were they trying to drive me mad? Did they want to terrorize me with what seemed like so many people following me everywhere? Or maybe they were deliberately frightening me with dozens of ghosts from behind the mirrors, so that I would immediately admit to being involved in murders that I never had committed. Who knows? In any case, at first I let them tease with me with those very irritating mirrors. But when I started to panic, I wanted to smash them. I threw all kinds of things at the glass, but their reflections made my head spin. The mirrors didn't suffer the least scratch, and what was infuriating was that all those things—chairs, ashtrays, plates, spoons, forks and glasses—seemed to bury me. Too bad there was no hammer in the room. If there were, the mirrors would be broken and that would have been the end of my fifteen disturbing images.

At the height of my panic, a woman dressed all in white came in with two guards in crewcuts. Maybe because they were used to the mirrors with the bewildering reflections, they weren't in the least bothered by the other images in the mirrors.

"Do you want to drive me crazy?" I protested right off.

"You're already crazy, why should we have to drive you crazy?" laughed the woman.

"I'm not crazy. I'm only confused," I argued.

"If you're only confused, you wouldn't be treated this way." The woman signaled to the guards to tie me up.

I fought back, of course. I struggled to kick them. But because without realizing it, I saw so many images reflected in the mirrors that an extreme dizziness overcame me. Nauseated me. I felt I had been ganged up on by dozens of people.

As my body grew weaker, I felt the prick of a hypodermic needle into my arm. That made my eyesight go all the more dim. Gradually, a great drowsiness overcame me. Then I heard them whispering what sounded like nonsense, though I could still catch a bit of what they meant.

"She doesn't realize that she is dangerous..." said the woman.

"If she's dangerous, why not just kill her?" said a guard.

"This woman has many secrets that have to be dug out of her before she's eliminated. It's not our job to dig out those secrets. We just have to take her to the lunatic asylum so she'll recover and quickly reveal the secrets of the murder of the generals."

Hmm, secrets? What secrets? That damned woman, as if she knows anything…

But who cares about them? I am just so drowsy. I've got to sleep. I've just got to forget whatever's confusing me…

I was asleep for maybe one or two hours, but it felt like months and months. The moment I awoke, I saw my hands and feet tied to the bed. To the right and left of me there were also beds and other bodies. It looked as if I were locked up in a ward.

Now what game was this? What prison was this now?

No one answered my questions. Hoping for a response from the guards or the doctor, what I actually heard were strange sounds from the other beds. Snoring. Muttering and babbling. Loud shouting. Lewd songs. Lions roaring. Dogs barking. Ducks quacking and pigs squealing.

Surely I was dreaming. Was I in a zoo? They sent me here because to them I was an animal that deserved to slaughtered or tormented? Furious, I tried to free the bonds as I screamed in protest at the despotism of Soeharto's soldiers. Naturally, my wild shouting caused an uproar. People who had been sleeping were awoken. They swarmed around me. They—for some reason they were all dressed the same—were very noisy and threatened me.

"This woman who always claims she has wings has finally woken up…"

"Wings? An angel, you mean? Don't talk like a lunatic. She just belonged to Gerwani…"

Madness! Who were these people? Why were they shut in here with me? Had they also danced with me at Crocodile Hole? No one answered my questions. Of course maybe they hadn't heard them. Maybe they were ignoring them.

Because I kept on shouting and screaming, a smartly dressed man dispersed all the people hemming me in. Then this good-looking fellow whispered softly into my ear, "I'm the doctor who'll be treating you. Whatever you do, don't run off from this lunatic asylum…"

"And if I run off?" I said, baiting the handsome doctor.

"You'll be tied up right away and crucified on this bed."

"No one will free me?" I baited him some more.

"If there's a God, it'll be He who'll free you." Now it was the doctor who doing the teasing.

"According to you, God exists?"

The doctor didn't answer. "Go back to sleep. Obey all the rules. Take your medicine. You have to get better."

"Get better? Get better from what? I'm not sick!"

The doctor laughed. "If you weren't sick, you wouldn't have been brought here."

Now it was my turn to laugh, "Don't joke. I'm only feeling lightheaded and want to sleep…"

"So go to sleep..." whispered the doctor, very softly.

I indeed fell asleep. I didn't know when I would wake up again. I only felt the dangers of being crucified and my body burned were inescapable. Of course, I didn't care. All I wanted to do then was sleep. *Sleep. Sleep. Sleep… and never wake up…*

The God-killers Conspiracy

Every day the doctor and the nurses had to look like they were making a major effort to cure everyone in the drab ward-like room. They never let anyone sleep or laze about in bed. Some of them nimbly attached infusion tubes to bodies that were getting thinner and thinner. Some were doing the same with cables, as if to electrocute animals.

As they went through all the motions they called curative therapy, the doctors and nurses would get very noisy. There were some who always appeared to be monitoring and they walked back and forth from bed to bed. They whispered or yelled at the bodies crucified on the beds, and not infrequently snapped at the ward inmates, who couldn't care less and didn't want to be regulated.

"Don't make so much noise!" I protested the moment I realized that I was now in a lunatic asylum. "Get me out of here! I'm not crazy!"

"If you don't want us to think you're crazy, don't act like them!" a doctor whispered to me.

To get more sympathy from the doctor, I didn't resist. I decided to stay on my back in bed and stare at the other women, who grumbled, muttered, and shouted nonsense.

"Be a nice girl," said the doctor. "If you rebel and shout like them, I'll give you a shot of tranquilizer."

"Tranquilizer? What for?"

"To help you dance. You like to dance, right?" he said impudently.

"I said I'm not crazy. Don't talk nonsense, Doctor. To speed up my death?"

"So you can fly straight up to heaven…" he laughed.

I just let the doctor answer my questions in any silly way. I knew that he didn't see me in the slightest as a sane woman.

"I'm amazed," he said, beginning to ramble on again, "that a woman as crazy as you…. How could the soldiers think you were one of those dangerous Gerwani women? What was the danger?"

"You are right, Doctor, sir. Of course I'm not dangerous. They're mistaken. I'm nobody. I'm only a dancer who likes to sing..."

"If that's the case, go ahead, dance and sing…"

I didn't refuse the doctor, who always spoke gently, as if he could feel empathy with my sufferings. So then I danced. So then I sang. At first I moved sluggishly and sang in a low voice. Dancing and singing with one's heart of course has to be like that. Physical energy, the senses, and rhythm must be controlled so as not to explode self-indulgently. But most people—that doctor included—never waited patiently for me to rotate my belly, shake my hips, swell my chest. Nor did they patiently listen to me murmuring the words of the songs bursting with lust. Whenever I dance and sing, following the words of my heart, they always shout, "Let's see you sway! Let's hear the refrain!"

If I get shouted at like that, naturally I do what they say. My swaying and rocking get really crazy and I puff and pant like a woman being caressed by ten monkeys. And because I can never be stopped, the nurses and doctor would have a reason to inject me with tranquilizers. After that, I would always fall asleep. After that, I would always wake up late at night, when the other women were lying on their backs, like they were crucified to their beds.

What month was it, what year was it in that asylum, when I woke suddenly in the middle of the night, extremely confused and frightened? I felt the faces of the mad women in the ward had changed into the faces of disgusting, slobbering animals. Dog faces. Wild pig faces. Cat faces, but with long protruding necks licking the faces of the other strange creatures. I couldn't live with them. I couldn't live with drooling animals. I had to get away from there. There was no other way; I had to pull out the wires and needles from my body. I had to rip off the infusion tubes.

None of the nurses knew what I was doing. Of course they were supposed to be guarding us, but they were all sound asleep. This made it easier for me to tiptoe out of the ward.

At first I thought it would be easy to get past the mad women. Even though I stepped very slowly, they must have heard the scraping of my feet along the floor, soft as it was. It would wake them up and make my escape difficult.

"Sssst… go back to your place. Wait till they're fast sleep…" I heard a voice I knew very well, Sonya's voice, resounding in my ear.

I intended to immediately escape, but these whispers from beside my bed made me put my plans on hold.

"But they never really sleep deeply," I hissed.

"Wait until two o'clock."

As I waited from midnight to 2AM, I chatted softly with Sonya.

"I used to want to get away, too," Sonya whispered, "but I always failed. They guard us so closely."

"Do you still want to escape now?"

"Of course. I can't live in a place like this. I am not crazy. How can someone who joined Gerwani and who always wanted to fight the devil be considered crazy?"

"Fight the devil?"

"Yes…. Right now God is in very great danger. I've seen a legion of devils led by Lucifer reappear out of the world of darkness. At first they defeat the best people, holy people, angels, and in the end they will kill God."

"Kill God?"

"Yes. Right now for some reason God is very feeble. I heard His voice. He chose me to save Him…"

"To save Him? Don't think you're as strong as all that! How could you save God if you can't even stand up to the doctor in this lunatic asylum?"

"Who says I can't? I'm waiting for the right time. I've heard Him whispering, 'You've got to wait for the very best time to save Me, My child!'"

"Do you mean that at some point you will be freed from this asylum and then you will free God and the blessed angels?"

"I believe just as I believe I've heard God's whisperings. There's only one key. To be free, we have to wait for the proper time. So that's why I can't be in too much of a rush to escape now. But I know that you, too, have the right moment to break free."

Hmm. Although I didn't believe in legions of devils out to kill God or tales of Allah's whisperings to Sonya, what this crazed woman was saying about "the right time to be free" rang true. And so I let her ramble on about the tasks of saving the world that she had taken upon herself now and for the times to come.

"Join me in saving God," Sonya coaxed me. "Join me in resisting the enemies of God. You know who the enemies of God are?"

I shook my head.

"Of course the devils have always been the eternal enemies of God. Only, you must realize, those devils have now become the soldiers who seized us and threw us into this madhouse!"

"But isn't it the soldiers who see us as devils that deserve to be strangled or killed in whatever way they like?"

"Because they've never heard the voice of God, they don't know I am a holy woman sent to change the members of Gerwani into the servants of Allah who will save the world. Have you ever heard the voice of God?"

Again, I shook my head.

"The voice of God, as you know, will guide you in your search for eternal freedom. Only, God isn't saying much these days. He is so busy warring against the legions of Lucifer, it seems he's deserted us." Sonya babbled on. "So help me defend Him. Help me get rid of those devils. Not now. We've got to wait for just the right time."

I giggled. Don't think I believed everything that Sonya said. I don't believe that mankind can save God. I don't believe devils have taken the form of soldiers. I only believed that there'd be a time when I'd be free. Maybe at two o'clock in the morning. Maybe at the moment everyone was fast asleep and no one cared about anyone else.

"Go to sleep now. I'll wake you up in a little while." Sonya stroked my hair. "I promise I'll take you away from here."

Actually, I wanted to refuse her. But perhaps because of the effects of the tranquilizer or because I couldn't pull out the infusion tubes and the wires and needles in my body, my heartbeats weakened, my stomach seemed to churn, and my head felt like it was splitting apart.

"Put the wires and needles back into your body. Reconnect those infusion tubes. You mustn't die. You still have to be with me later on to save God…"

Again I wanted to refuse what she said. But my body was too weak. I was shaky and bewildered.

I only heard the voices of people coming towards me.

"Crazy! Crazy! That nutcase tried to kill herself. She doesn't know she doesn't have to do that. The soldiers are going to kill her whenever they want to execute…" the annoyed voice of a nurse buzzed in my ears.

"Just give her another injection!" said another nurse.

"It'll be an overdose…"

"How about shooting her the juice?"

I didn't know if it was a tranquilizer or an electric shock they ended up giving me. I was too weak and blurry-eyed to tell what was going on just then. I didn't know if when I got the jolt I went into convulsions, foamed at the mouth, and lost all my recollection of things. Also, I didn't know whether, if I got a tranquilizer shot, I smiled sweetly or grimaced in pain. I only knew that when I awoke—perhaps on a new day or perhaps time hadn't moved at all—there were infusion tubes, needles and all different wires stuck into me all over my body.

"Don't be afraid. God has whispered to me: the devils aren't going to kill you yet. They're still going to interrogate you." Sonya stoked my hair.

I don't know why I was so afraid of opening my eyes just then. I was afraid of the nurses poisoning my food. I was afraid that the doctors, bored with treating me, might stick me with an overdose of tranquilizer or juice me with over 131 volts for more than four-tenths of a second.

"You've been chosen to accompany me. So have faith, you won't die today." Sonya planted a little kiss on my brow. "It'll be the soldiers who'll die first. The troops still loyal to Sukarno will revolt. Soeharto will be overthrown…"

I smiled at hearing that Soeharto would be given the boot.

"But of course it won't be easy to overthrow Soeharto. The devils that surround him have to be defeated first. For that, you have to know who are the devils and who are the angels, who's good and who's wicked."

"I suppose it wouldn't be too hard to tell devils from angels."

"As though *you'd* know. Some devils standing right in front of you look like angels. So you have to learn from me how to recognize the face of a devil."

"Recognize the face of a devil?"

"Yes, and you can quickly recognize an angel's face, too. When you've gotten good at it, you can also talk with them. Would you like me to teach you to recognize and converse with devils and angels?"

I nodded. Yes.

"But not now. It's not time yet."

Of course it wasn't time yet. If Sonya had wanted to teach me right at that moment, I definitely would not have been able to take in all that she taught me. Once again, you know, I didn't want to open my eyes. I wanted to be in eternal darkness. I wanted to be freed from light. I wanted…

*

But Sonya wasn't going to let anyone stay in eternal darkness. Sonya deeply hated the darkness. Even when she slept she wanted to be under a bright light. And that day, when each person was given the opportunity to stroll about the garden, she pulled me to the middle of the field.

"I'm going to teach you how to recognize devils and angels." Sonya told me to imitate everything she did.

I did as she ordered. Because she stared at the sun without blinking, I did that same stupid thing and hurt my eyes while I was at it.

"Keep looking until your eyesight becomes special. Until you can see something that other humans can't!" She kept her eyes lifted skyward.

Once again, I did what Sonya told me to do. But because I wasn't used to staring directly at the sun, I kept shutting my eyes. At first there were no changes at all. That meant that when I looked into the starry skies, I wouldn't discover an ocean filled with whales. Or when I looked at a mountain, I wouldn't find coral reefs filled with fish. But gradually, a startling change occurred. Looking at the sun over time, I actually felt I had lost it. Looking at the sun over time, I saw instead a hundred wild pigs all crammed together in a mass grave. I saw the pregnant bellies of these pigs stuck by spears so that the gushing blood welled up in the grave. Oh no! Oh no! That sight could change quickly. These pigs turned into a group of women digging their grave before their heads were bashed with rifle butts, before their pregnant bellies were bayoneted by crazed soldiers.

"Now look at me!" Sonya ordered. "What do you see?"

"I see a face that is so pretty and that you have a pair of beautiful wings." I replied with the first thing that came to mind.

"Don't lie to me! Of course I have beautiful wings, but I don't have a face. Every time you look at me you will forget pain." Sonya tried to set me straight on this.

I didn't challenge her words, although I knew that she, like other human beings, did have a face. What really happened was that Sonya's face often changed according to her whim. So frequently did her beautiful face change—especially to look like Holy Mother Mary—that no one would ever be able to gaze at Sonya's real face.

"Now look at those doctors!"

I scrutinized them.

"What do you see?"

I didn't answer her.

"Now see those soldiers that have been infiltrated into this madhouse? You see them looking like devils, don't you?

Again I didn't answer her.

"There's only one principle: you only need to concentrate and be convinced that whatever you see is real. Look at everything with your soul. Not with your eyes. Tonight I will teach you to talk with angels, devils, and people who've died."

Then we laughed together like a couple of little kids who had found a lost toy. Of course no one would have thought we were doing anything out of the ordinary. At the asylum, we could do whatever we wanted to. Just so long as we didn't kill our fellow patients, we would be seen as still normal and in character.

Then, all that day I did try to learn to see things that other people could never witness themselves. At that time, I found out that there was a pair of spirits in the toilet who always asked whoever was in there to whistle their hearts out when passing water. I saw three pairs of snakes that came from years gone by, hiding in the roots of the rambutan tree. I saw, just as twilight approached, legions of devils racing about in the fields, and they appeared to be trying to catch Sonya and me.

"Now listen very carefully to any sounds which you've never heard before. I'm positive that you've always had a talent for hearing supernatural voices!" Sonya closed her eyes. "You are hearing whatever the patients want to say and do, right?"

I imitated Sonya. At first I only heard the sounds of the snoring patients. But gradually I could hear various kinds of voices gently filling my heart. I listened and found out that someone was going to commit suicide at 11:14 PM. I listened and found out that someone going to strangle a nurse at 9:46 AM. I listened and found out that someone was going to rape a woman at 11:17 in the toilet.

"Now listen to what the Soeharto soldiers are going to do to us," ordered Sonya.

I couldn't hear a thing. Not a signal of anything.

"Don't panic. Sometimes we really cannot penetrate their hearts. And of course there is a supernatural power that makes the soldiers unreadable by us. But keep on studying and watching and listening with your heart. Someday, at the right moment you'll be able to see the face of God and can converse with Him…"

"Converse with God?"

"Yes, why not?"

I couldn't keep from laughing. I was sure at that moment Sonya was joking with me. It didn't take her long to sense my uneasiness. Without my asking, she told me what could be done if a soul has been entrusted to save God from fragility.

"Even seeing God battle the devils every day is not difficult… to say nothing of just seeing and hearing Him asking your help!"

I just kept nodding yes as I took in Sonya's sermon, which was indeed very convincing.

"On the other hand, what's most difficult is hearing the voice of your own heart…. You've got to study hard how to listen to the true voice of your heart…"

I smiled. I didn't want to listen to the voice of my heart. That night I only wanted to hear the voice of Magdalena Markini, my big sister, who was burned alive in the yard of her home by soldiers, simply because she didn't want to say where her kid sister, a mere puppet accused of murdering the generals, was hiding. I could hear the voice of the fire that burned her body up. I could hear the sounds of Magda's bones crumbling and being devoured by the fire. I…

"Don't drift off. You can stop anything you don't want to hear and see!" Sonya gave the salvation command.

I was shocked. I got gooseflesh. I trembled.

For days, for months, oh no! no! maybe for months or years during that wasted period from 1965 to 1971, I was always trembling, always covered with goose bumps, always shocked by all the different things I saw and heard. Unlike Sonya, I never got good at controlling whatever slipped ever so quickly into my heart. Soeharto was by no means overthrown. Sukarno became increasingly frail. Slaughter occurred everywhere, and I and Sonya could still do nothing at all.

"God is becoming more and more of a shell," Sonya said to me sadly, "and we can do less and less to help Him…"

I kept quiet. I could never imagine the Almighty being unable to confront Lucifer and the furious legions of devils that never stopped trying to bring the Kingdom of Heaven crashing down.

"There's only one way to bring all this to an end," Sonya whispered into my ear. "The rebellion must be quickened. We've got to kill the devils in this lunatic asylum!"

I stayed silent. Sonya's task was such a weighty one. Actually, more and more I was hearing and seeing the legions of devils, the would-be God-killers, conspiring and visiting us nightly. Again and again, they injected me with tranquilizers. Again and again they ran electrical currents through Sonya, who grimaced in pain.

That was when I often shrieked out, just before the doctor came, just before the nurses bound and crucified me on the bed.

"Are You still willing to help me, God?"

The Wolf in Almira's Class

Yes, of course they will throw you into the madhouse.
No need to be afraid. All you have to say to whomever
examines you is that anything considered beyond the limit
and nonsense is also the truth. You've got to be brave and
speak up. Don't just be mute...

There were no snakes, but since morning there was something that kept hissing when you asked them to tell about the astonishing things that they dreamed of last night. Nor were there goats, but there was something that suddenly crept up on its hands and knees, right up to you, bleating loudly. Of course there were no wolves, but in Grade IV of the Merah Putih Elementary School, all in uproar just then, something was howling and howling, as if calling for the souls of the ancestors.

"Teach me to keep patient and not see them as animals, oh God," you whispered softly, as you listened to the chatter of the students that was hard to follow, but which they had no trouble understanding.

Of course, it's not only now that you seemed to be in the zoo or the wild forest. A week ago, you had to play the role of Eve, who was forced to understand Edo's snake language when he so painfully read *This is a chicken* on his writing slate. Edo always just hissed and said, "This is a snake."

"Chicken, Edo, chicken."

"Snake!"

"Chicken, dear!"

"Snake, *hsssssss*, snake!" shouted Edo.

"All right, snake, *hssssss*, snake," you said gently.

When you entered the crannies and crevices of Edo's language and world, that most introverted of students was no longer crawling on the floor. He'd sit prettily in a chair and then draw anything at all that had to do with snakes. At first he drew a pretty girl with hair of snakes who was being led by the hand by a prince with snakes for hands, and finally he'd draw the sun as a circle throwing off rays of snakes.

"What do those snakes eat, Edo?" you said softly as you pointed to the picture of the hens with the brown wings on the writing slate.

"Chickens, Missus Prita, chickens."

"So what is this, Edo?" you said, pointing to the writing: *This is a chicken.*

You smiled at hearing Edo's reply, but just at that moment, you wondered why he always wanted to imitate everything a snake would do. Did he perhaps live at home with a mother who worked as a snake dancer? Or maybe after school, Edo only played with the snakes that were raised by the family in the garden behind the house?

You couldn't answer that question yet. You then promised to go and visit Edo's family and as quickly as possible to find the nicest way to free this snake child from the coils of influence of those crawling creatures.

You hadn't finished with Edo when, three days later, you had to creep along on all fours like a goat following Ongky's movements. Ongky didn't want to sing before he asked you to play butting heads. You also had to bleat loudly so that Ongky would then quickly get up and want to sing in front of the class that each day was filled in its turn with the different behavior of your eight special students.

"Teach me to keep a sincere heart in all my lessons with these beautiful little angels of yours, oh God. I truly look at them as I would look at Your calm face," you try to whisper in prayer.

God, like other gods of long ago, wanted you to look at more than just His face only. Thus, He sent you Almira. That morning, before Almira started howling, she kept bashing her head against the classroom wall, painted reddish maroon. And not only that, she clambered up on the bench and then, jumping to the teacher's desk, snatched your glasses from your face and threw them down on the floor.

"What do you want to tell us about, Almira? What did you dream about last night?" You still tried to stay patient.

Almira only howled. She hadn't been willing to speak with anyone for several days.

"You met a wolf?"

Almira grimaced. She drooled. Her eyes burned savagely.

"Tell us all about everything that happened in your dream, dear." You tried to draw near to her.

Still no answer. The class that earlier had been in uproar was now hushed and still. Edo didn't hiss. Ongky didn't bleat. Selma didn't cry. Safa didn't slam her hand down on the table. Sirna just sat dazed. Kafka and Juve gaped and gawked. They thought they'd become victims of Almira's teeth.

"Come here to Teacher, dear…" You tried to cool Almira's rage.

Too late! Almira had already whetted her fangs and now a pair of wild eyes stabbed into those of Selma. Almira looked like she wanted to rip and tear Selma's neck apart.

Feeling mortally threatened, Selma shrieked. The shriek resonated so quickly that it made the whole class cry out. Totally confused, you witnessed Almira's ferocity and Selma's terror. You couldn't kill one student to save another. You thought hard so that you and the students wouldn't be staring at Almira's pointed fangs ripping apart Selma's delicate neck. Nor did you want Almira to go on howling, calling other wolves to attack the school with its flimsy fence. Nor did you want Almira's loud howls to make Gesti, the owner and principal of the school—and in your mind a cruel dictator—scrutinize everything you did with your students. You didn't want Gesti forbidding you to teach with methods not found in the teaching manual.

But what succeeded in overcoming the problem of Edo, who only hissed, and Ongky, who only bleated, couldn't be used for Almira's problem. Almira not only looked like some rare vertebrate that perhaps lived all its life in the same cage as wolves. Almira in fact behaved like a wild creature from heaven that would bite anything that appeared to be a sweet devil. Just then, maybe Selma looked like a sweet little lamb for the slaughter.

You could have simply throttled Almira and threatened the wolf child against ever doing anything that endangered anyone again. But you didn't want to be like Gesti, who once tied Almira to the flagpole just because she bit that tyrannical school leader on the hand.

You also didn't want to roast Almira under the fierce rays of the sun, as you muttered, "Die, you worshipper of wolves. Die, you child who cannot be a dear child of Allah…"

As a guardian of the class of little angels that might be considered demons with special needs, you actually did protest Gesti's actions. Paying no heed to your whispered concerns, the irascible woman just said casually, "Only the Sun God can change a wolf into a human. Let those wretched devils leave her."

You didn't see devils in Almira. Rather, you witnessed delicate wings sprouting out of the wolf child's shoulders. Wings that would let Almira fly away from school, away from the torments of the school principal.

Even so, she wouldn't flap her wings, and you couldn't help that little girl who really was very sweet. Apart from the strap that entwined her body so tightly, you couldn't oppose the principal who paid you all of Rp750,000 for everything you did in class, because you were still counted as a novice teacher. You exploded in anger only when Gesti dunked Almira's head into the school's water basin. "Have pity," you whispered, "have pity on the little angel whose wings have now folded back up."

Because you found it ever more difficult to witness that very painful scene, you found the courage to keep Gesti from doing something even more reckless. You snatched Almira from Gesti's hands and immediately embraced the wolf child, who was still skewering Gesti with her devil eyes.

"Teach her properly," said Gesti. "If you can't, then get out of here and never teach in this school again!"

You didn't want to argue, and so you obeyed. You led the wolf child, now soaking wet, to the classroom, even though you were afraid to meet Almira's eyes. Yes, you were afraid half to death, but you began to understand that to teach Almira, you had to enter the hidden places of her world. From that time on, wherever Almira invited you, you were ready and willing to go into a world that sometimes went beyond the limits, beyond the rational, and that shook your consciousness.

So, when now Almira behaved like a wolf again and tried to attack Selma, there was no other way: you had to play the part of a mother wolf that forbade her darling daughter from tearing to shreds the neck of another creature. Because you understood that the wolf child had to be fed milk, you even tried unbuttoning your blouse to make Almira quickly come to you.

You failed. Almira didn't pay any attention. She still wanted to kill Selma.

Just then you remembered how hungry wolves would immediately devour meat thrown in front of them. But in class there was no meat or fresh, dripping blood. So, you whispered, "I have to sacrifice myself. This may be the last way to save Selma."

Then, to the astonishment of the pupils, you gave out a loud howl, and suddenly furiously bit into the back of your own arm, filling your mouth with your own flesh and smearing it with your own fresh blood.

Almira was shocked. She turned toward you. She crawled slowly. Slowly she approached you. Slowly she tried to gorge herself on the meat from your mouth.

Disgusting? No. No one would think of you and Almira as wild animals. Instead, they would think they were witnessing a pair of human beings showing the world the beauty of their love and affection.

But at that very moment, Gesti and some attendants from the lunatic asylum were spying on what you were doing with your little angel. Having thought you mad for sometime now, they burst in and immediately tied you up.

Then all was quiet when from the distance—just when they were dragging you out of the classroom—you heard Almira calling and calling out to you. "Mother! Mother! Why are you leaving me?"

You didn't want to answer that question. You only wanted to glare fiercely at Gesti and howl.

"*Aoooooooooooooo!*"

Glossary of Foreign Terms, Place Names, and Personages (both real and mythical)

ababil

A flock of heavenly birds said to have saved the city of Mecca in 571 CE from an invading Yemeni army by striking the enemy's elephants with *sigil*, bricks of baked clay.

abaya

The long cloak-like outer garment worn by women for everyday wear, particularly outside the home, in many Muslim countries and societies.

Abilawa

In the Javanese *wayang kulit* versions of the Indian epic *Mahabharata*, Abilawa (aka Jagalabilawa, "Abilawa the Butcher") was the name taken in disguise by the "giant" Wrekodara (aka Bima), one of the five Pandawa brothers.

ajma

Believed to be the most nutritious of the dozens of varieties of dates, and planted by the Prophet himself to be eaten when breaking the fast.

Al-Baqi (Cemetery)

In Medina, Kingdom of Saudi Arabia, the burial place of many important family members and companions of the Prophet Muhammad (c. 570-632 CE). The tomb of the Prophet himself is in the nearby Nabawi Mosque.

Ali Sadikin

(1927–2008) Indonesian general and progressive governor of Jakarta for the period 1966–1977, marginalized by the Soeharto government for his criticisms of it.

Anoman

Also "Hanuman". "The White Monkey", leader of the army of fellow warrior monkeys in the *Ramayana*.

Arjuna

In the *Mahabharata* epic, among the Pandawa (the "good" side) are the refined archer main hero, Arjuna, and his mighty brother, Bima (seen above as Abilawa the Butcher). Karna, raised among and loyal to the "evil" Kurawa, is a sympathetic and tragic figure. Except for the Brahmin Durna, these figures all belong to the *ksatria*, or warrior, caste, and are bound by its norms and laws. Here, in Mas Triyanto's reworking of one of the themes of the *Bhagavad Gita* section of the *Mahabharata*, Arjuna expresses to Kresna his reluctance to kill his relatives, the Kurawa.

Bilal	A former slave of part-Abyssinian stock (580–640 CE) and one of the earliest converts to Islam, chosen by the Prophet Muhammad himself to be the first muezzin.
Bisma	In the *Mahabharata,* grand uncle and would-be reconciler of both the Pandawa and Kurawa clans. Mortally wounded by Srikandi on the Kuruksetra battlefield (qv).
Crocodile Hole	Indonesian: Lubang Buaya. See Gestapu.
De Fakkel	(The Torch) was the magazine of the Independent Socialist Party (SDAP, in Dutch) which was founded in 1932 and whose radical editorial tone was the cause of a break between moderates and the leftists of this party.
Destarastra	Eldest brother of Pandu in the *Mahabharata* and the father of the Kurawa clan, rival of the Pandawa, the scions of King Pandu.
Diponegoro	Pangeran (Prince) Diponegoro (1785–1855), the eldest son of the Sultan Hamengku Buana III of Yogyakarta waged a holy war to overthrow Dutch rule and to regulate the Islamic religion in Java. Diponegoro was exiled by the Dutch to Makassar, Sulawesi, where he died in 1855.
Drupadi	The wife of Yudistira, the eldest of the five Pandawa brothers, in the *Mahabharata.*
dukun	In the Malay and Indonesian world, a traditional healer, expert on local *adat* (customary law), spirit medium, and, in some instances, practitioner of black magic.
Durna	In the *Mahabharata*, the sage and teacher of the scions of both the Pandawa and Kurawa families. (Also Drona and Dorna.)
Eid	*Eid al-Fitr*, the Islamic holiday at the end of the fasting month.
Garuda	A Sanskrit-derived term for a mythical bird related to Jatayu in the *Ramayana*. The garuda is a symbol of the Republic of Indonesia and is in the national emblem as well as being the name of the national airline.
General Su-	Likely a reference to General Sudirman (1916–1950) with his emblematic head cloth. He was the revered top commander of the Indonesian republican military forces in the war of independence against the Dutch (1945–49).
Gerwani	Indonesian acronym for "Gerakan Wanita Indonesia", The Indonesian Women's Movement. See Gestapu.

Gestapu	Indonesian acronym for "Gerakan September Tigapuluh", the September 30 Movement. On the night of September 30, 1965, a putsch of mysterious origins and motivations (for which the Indonesian Communist Party and its local sympathizers were scapegoated) struck down the top command of the Indonesian army. Three generals were killed outright and three others (together with an aide de camp) were taken to a place on the outskirts of Jakarta called Lubang Buaya ("Crocodile Hole"). There they were allegedly tortured, sexually humiliated and then sadistically murdered by leftist military and paramilitary personnel, most prominently by drugged-up members of Gerwani, who were said to have taunted them with a nude dance called Tarian Bunga Harum ("Dance of the Fragrant Flowers"). This lurid account has long been the object of scholarly skepticism.
habbah	A kind of un-hulled grain. Pilgrims visiting the Al-Baqi' (see "Al-Baqi") cemetery are recommended to feed the hundreds of pigeons that always flock to this graveyard complex.
Hamzah	Full name: Hamzah ibn 'Abd al-Muttalib, the paternal uncle and early companion of the Prophet Muhammad. (Also see "Hindun".)
Hariman Siregar	Indonesian political activist and human rights advocate (1950–).
Hindun	Hindun was the daughter of 'Utba ibn Rabi'ah, one of the top leaders of the Quraysh, the dominant tribe in Mecca, at the time when the Prophet Muhammad was just beginning his mission. 'Utba, violently opposed to Islam, fought the Muslims, but was killed in the Battle of Badr (624 CE) by the paternal uncle and early companion of the Prophet, Hamzah ibn 'Abd al-Muttalib. The enraged Hindun vowed revenge, and according to tradition, she incited the young Abyssinian slave, Wahsyi ibn Harb, to kill Hamzah, which he did in the Battle of Jabal ["Mount"] Uhud (625 CE). After this defeat of the Muslims, Hindun is said to have triumphantly cut out and eaten the liver of Hamzah. In later years, both Hindun and Wahsyi converted to Islam.
Imogiri	"Cloud Mountain", the sanctified hilltop burial ground in South Central Java of the kings of Mataram beginning with founder Sultan Agung (d. 1646) and including most of his successors, the rulers of the rival kingdoms of Yogyakarta and Surakarta (Solo), together with prominent members of their families.
Jabal Uhud	Site of a battlefield defeat (625 CE) of Muslim forces in the early days of Islam. (see "Hindun".)

Jaka Tarub	The hero of a story by the same name wherein this crafty young man tricks a heavenly nymph, Nawang Wulan, into marrying him by stealing her dress while she and her six companions are bathing in a pond.
Jatayu	A character in the *Ramayana*; the birdlike demigod that tries to rescue Sita from Rahwana and is a symbol in this epic of undying loyalty.
Java War	The Java War (1825–1830), waged by Diponegoro against the Dutch. This conflict nearly bankrupted the Netherlands East Indies government, but in the end Diponegoro was treacherously arrested during a goodwill visit to the Dutch officials during Lebaran, the Javanese-Islamic holiday of Eid al-Fitr upon the completion of the fasting month.
joget	A variety of popular street dancing forms in Java.
Ken Dedes	A legendary Helen of Troy-like kidnapped beauty and queen consort of Ken Arok, the first ruler of the kingdom of Singhasari, East Java (1222-1292 CE).
Khun Sa	Khun Sa (1934–2007), of Chinese and Shan (one of the minority peoples of Myanmar, Laos and southern China) parentage, was famous as the dominant opium drug lord of the Golden Triangle and, after 1985, as commander of the so-called Mong Tai Army which championed the independence of Myanmar's Shan, while staying heavily involved in the international drug trade. Khun Sa died of health complications while living as a free man in Yangon, Myanmar.
Ki, kiyai	Javanese male honorific *ki* (abbreviated from *kiyai*) signifies a figure revered for his profound knowledge of spiritual and mystical matters. Because of their erudite knowledge, puppeteers (*dalang*), are commonly referred to and addressed as "*ki dalang*". Though the term predates the conversion of Java to Islam, it is now widely used for religious scholars and the rectors of Islamic boarding schools as well.
Kliwon Friday	Traditionally in Java, the days of the week are indicated as a combination of the seven-day week and the five-day market week.
Kresna	The Javanese name for Krishna, a character in the *Mahabharata*, especially in the *Bhagavad Gita* section; Arjuna's divine charioteer and spiritual guide.
ksatria	A member of the warrior caste in Hindu India and societies influenced by Indian culture, notably Java and Bali.

Kunjarakarna	The protagonist in a verse story of salvation through the Buddhist Dharma dating back to the pre-Islamic period of Java and subsequently incorporated into the *wayang kulit* repertoire.
Kurawa	See the entries for *Mahabharata,* Destarastra and Arjuna.
Kuruksetra	Site of the final battle in the *Mahabharata.*
Kuta streets	A reference to the terrorist suicide bombing in Kuta, south Bali on October 12, 2002, that killed 202 people and wounded 240. A near-simultaneous bombing occurred again in Kuta and the nearby Jimbaran Beach Resort in 2005 on its third anniversary, this time claiming some 20 dead and about 125 wounded.
Lebaran	Indonesian term for *Eid al-Fitr*, the Islamic holiday at the end of Ramadhan, the fasting month.
Mahabharata	Counted as India's greatest epic, the *Mahabharata* relates the fatal rivalry of two branches of one family, the Pandawa, fathered by Pandu, and the Kurawa, fathered by his eldest brother Destarastra, and has long been a major cultural and philosophical wellspring and source of role models for the Javanese.
masnawi	Or *masnavi*: refers to the Arabic poetic form of rhyming couplets as well as to the crowning literary achievement, composed in thousands of these couplets, of the Persian (or Tajik) Sufi mystic and poet, Jamaluddin Rumi (1207–1273).
Merah Putih	Literally, "Red and White", the Indonesian national flag.
Merapi, Mount	Literally "Mountain of Fire", Indonesia's second most active volcano which, together with its nearby twin Mt Merbabu, towers over the Central Java plain, itself made fertile by frequent eruptions and containing the palace cities of Yogyakarta and Surakarta (Solo). Mt Merapi is also a very important focal point in the spiritual landscape of many Javanese in their traditional pre-Islamic beliefs of great mountains being the home of gods and powerful spirits.
mihrab	The niche in the mosque wall that faces in the direction of Mecca toward which the congregation prays.

Ned Kelly	Ned Kelly (1854–1880), the celebrated Australian iron armor-wearing "bushranger" and gang leader of Irish convict lineage, arrested in the town of Glenrown, Victoria State and hanged in Melbourne. Australia's "iron outlaw" was the subject of a celebrated series of 27 pictures by Australian artist, Sir Sydney Nolan (1917-1992), as well as several movies.
Pasopati	Arjuna's magic arrow.
Petruk	In Javanese mythology, Petruk is the middle child of the comic and awesome Semar, also traditionally believed to be Ismaya, the guardian spirit of Java. Collectively, these four lively grotesques are known as *punakawan*, the retainers and sometime advisors of the gods as well as mouthpieces for *ki dalang's* own social and political commentary throughout a *wayang kulit* performance.
Quraysh	The dominant tribe in Mecca, at the time when the Prophet Muhammad was just beginning his mission.
Raden	A Javanese male title of an intermediate level of nobility.
Raden Patah	A historical figure (d.1518) said to be related to the ruling family of the Hindu-Javanese Majapahit empire (c.1293–1500), and founder of the trading city of Demak, on the north coast of Java, near Semarang.
Raden Saleh	Javanese painter (1811–1880) of Yemeni-Javanese extraction whose exotic Delacroix-like paintings were well regarded in Europe. His most famous painting is the 1857 poignant *Capture of Prince Diponegoro.*
Rahwana	Demon antagonist in the *Ramayana* (see "Sita").
Raja Pemangku Bumi III	A fictitious ruler, named in the style of the sultans of Yogyakarta.
Rama	A leading character in the *Ramayana* and the husband of Sita.
raudah	Literally "heavenly garden", the area of between the niche of the Masjid al-Nabawi (The Prophet's Mosque) that faces Mecca and the tomb of Prophet himself within the mosque.
Rendra	Internationally recognized *avant garde* playwright, poet, and political activist (1935–2009).
romo	"High" or "polite" Javanese for "father, elder brother", or other revered senior male figure, and also the standard term of reference and address for a Roman Catholic priest in Javanese-speaking areas of Indonesia.

Second Dutch Military Aggression	Operation Kraai ("Operation Crow"), launched by the Dutch on December 1, 1948, aimed at crushing the Indonesian revolution in one lightning blow by seizing the republican capital of Yogyakarta. President Sukarno and Vice-President Hatta surrendered, but General Sudirman's forces remained resistant and elusive in the countryside. With US opinion turning strongly against a colonial war in effect funded by Marshall Plan aid, the Dutch declared a unilateral ceasefire, and the Rum-Royen Round Table agreement was signed on May 7, 1949, leading to Indonesia's formal independence from the Netherlands.
September 30, 1965	See Gestapu
serimpi	A female dancer of the royal Javanese dance form of the same name.
Sita	A main character in the *Ramayana*, Sita is the wife of Rama who is abducted by the demon Rahwana. Sita is held by Rahwana in his palace while Rama besieges it with the aid of an army of warrior monkeys, led by the White Monkey Anoman. Rahwana is killed, Sita is rescued and, in one tradition, must undergo Rama's trial of her by fire, to prove her fidelity and purity.
Sultan Ngamid	Or "Sultan Ngabdulkamid", a title adopted by Diponegoro during the Java War (1825-1830). At that time he bestowed the name "Diponegoro" upon his eldest son.
sharia	Canon law governing all aspects of Islamic life and applicable only to Muslims, Syariah is based on the teachings of the Prophet in the Quran and the oral traditions of his sayings and exemplary life, subsequently collected into what is known as the *Hadis* and *Sunnah*, respectively.
Sydney Nolan	Australian artist (1917–1992) who painted a celebrated series of 27 symbolic pictures of the life of Ned Kelly (see above).
Takroni	African immigrants in the Kingdom of Saudi Arabia who can no longer return to their native lands but for whom citizenship in the kingdom is impossible.
Tibum	An Indonesian acronym for *ketertiban umun* ("public order"), and a popular way of referring to the officials enforcing public order regulations.

tuan

An honorific used by many Malay- and Indonesian-speaking people when speaking of or addressing an adult Western male.

Tuntang

A forest located about 40 kilometers south of the coastal city of Semarang, the provincial capital of Central Java.

Wahsyi ibn Harb

The Abyssinian slave who killed Hamzah in the Battle of Jabal Sur but later converted to Islam. (Also see "Hindun".)

wali

In Islamic law, a person who exercises guardianship or has authority over someone else. It can also refer to someone who speaks with religious authority. In Indonesia, and especially in Java, the legendary Nine Wali (*Wali Songo*) are celebrated as having introduced Islam to the archipelago sometime in the fifteenth century, and are revered as saints in the Javanese Sufistic tradition.

wayang kulit

Literally "shadows of leather", the shadow theater of Java and other areas of Indonesia.

zamzam

The well of water located inside the Sacred Mosque at Mecca.

Publication History

English Title of Story	Original Indonesian Title	Source
Night Train Sorcery	Sihir Kereta Malam	*Pelita*, September 15, 1991
Children Sharpening Knives	Anak-Anak Mengasah Pisau	*Media Indonesia*, 1996
Enter My Ear, Daddy	Masuklah ke Telingaku, Ayah	*Republika*, February 28, 1999
The Silent Eyes of the Takroni Woman	Mata Sunyi Perempuan Takroni	*Kompas*, April 7, 2002
Like Drizzle, Pointed Red	Seperti Gerimis yang Meruncing Merah	*Kompas*, November 23, 2003
Sand Mirror	Cermin Pasir	*Kompas*, September 8, 2002
Womb of Fire	Rahim Api	Majalah *Pantau*, February 2004
The Resistance of Sita	PerlawananSita	*Cempaka*, November 12, 2005
Sultan Ngamid's Wings of Mist	Sayap Kabut Sultan Ngamid	*Kompas*, April 12, 2009
The Ghost in Arthur Rimbaud's Head	Hantu di Kepala Arthur Rimbaud	*Koran Tempo*, November 19, 2006
Handcuffs of Snow	Belenggu Salju	*Kompas*, July 22, 2007
Mother's Quiet Light	Cahaya Sunyi Ibu	*Jawa Pos*, October 21, 2007
The Devil of Paris	Iblis Paris	*Kompas*, February 3, 2008
Prophet Bowl Delirium	Delirium Mangkuk Nabi	*Koran Tempo*, March 8, 2009
Natasha Korolenko's Fiery Circus	Sirkus Api Natasja Korolenko	*Jawa Pos*, May 3, 2009
Everlasting is Arjuna's Sorrow	Sepanjang Masa Kesedihan Arjuna	Majalah Sastra *Pusat*, 2010
Kufah's Flying Fish	Ikan Terbang Kufah	*Kompas*, November 7, 2010
The Eleventh Wali	Wali Kesebelas	*Koran Tempo*, January 15, 2012

English Title of Story	Original Indonesian Title	Source
Siti's Fire Birds	Burung Api Siti	*Kompas*, October 30, 2011
A Pair of Death Sniffers	Sepasang Pengendus Kematian	*Koran Tempo*, January 6, 2013
Elisabet Rukmini's Three Painful Stories	Tiga Kisah Perih Elisabet Rukmini	*Koran Tempo*, June 10, 2012
The Wolf in Almira's Class	Serigala di Kelas Almira	*Kompas*, July 7, 2013

Biographical Information

TRIYANTO TRIWIKROMO was the winner of the 2009 Language Center Literary Award for the short story collection, *Ular di Mangkuk Nabi* (The Snake in the Prophet's Bowl). Ten of his short stories in the *Kompas* Short Story Choice from 2003-2012 were published in book form as *Celeng Satu Celeng Semua* (One Wild Pig All Wild Pigs, Gramedia Pustaka Utama, 2013). His short story "Cahaya Sunyi Ibu" (Mother's Quiet Light) was carried in the 2008 Golden Pen Literary Award for 20 Best Indonesian Short Stories. His most recent book is *Surga Sungsang* (Wrong Side Up Heaven), a novel published by Gramedia Pustaka Utama in 2014.

From 2012 to 2013, Triyanto was involved in implementing the *citybooks* program that was produced by deBuren, a renowned Belgian cultural organization. This program facilitated the translation of ten long poems of his about Semarang, the provincial capital of Central Java, into Dutch, English and French. His short stories have been also translated into Swedish and English.

Triyanto Triwikromo was born in Salatiga, Central Java, on September 15, 1964 and graduated from Diponegoro University in Semarang with a master's degree in literature. He worked as a lecturer in Creative Writing at his alma mater and as managing editor at the daily newspaper *Suara Merdeka*. In addition to composing poetry (which, among others, was published in the bilingual edition *Mud Purgatory* in 2008), he has written collections of short stories, *Rezim Seks* (Regime of Sex), *Ragaula* (Aini, 2002), *Sayap Anjing* (Dog Wings, *Kompas* Book Publishers, 2003), *Anak-Anak Mengasah Pisau* (Children Sharpening the Knives, Masscom

Media, 2003), and *Malam Sepasang Lampion* (The Night of a Pair of Paper Lanterns, *Kompas* Book Publishers, 2004).

He participated in the Utan Kayu International Literary Biennale in East Jakarta in 2005 and 2007. After that, he was a participant of Wordstorm, the Northern Territory Writers Festival in Darwin, Australia, and in January–February of 2008, in the Gang Festival as well as being a writer in residence in Sydney, Australia. That same year, he was also a speaker at the Ubud Writers and Readers Festival in Ubud, Bali. Together with Budi Darma, Eka Kurniawan, Nugroho Suksmanto, and Chavchay Saifullah, he wrote *LA Underlover* (Katakita, 2008), a collection of short stories about the interaction of Indonesians with Los Angeles people. In 2010, a collection of his poetry *Pertempuran Rahasia* (Secret Combat) was published by Gramedia Pustaka Utama. Triyanto's most recent work, published in 2015 by Gramedia Pustaka Utama, is a collection of his poetry, *Kematian Kecil Kartosoewirjo* (The Little Death of Kartosoewirjo).

GEORGE A FOWLER lived and traveled widely in the Asia Pacific region for over thirty years, first as a Marine, then as a student of Chinese and Malay, and finally for twenty-three years as a commercial banker. He co-authored *Pertamina: Indonesian National Oil* and *Java, A Garden Continuum* while living in Indonesia in the early 1970s. George received a BA from St Michael's College, the University of Toronto, in 1975, and a Master of Arts in International Studies (China Studies) from the Jackson School of International Studies at the University of Washington in 2002.

He has translated Marah Rusli's classic Indonesian Malay novel *Sitti Nurbaya: A Love Unrealized* (Lontar, 2011), *Old Town* by Chinese writer Lin Zhe (Amazon Crossing, 2011), *The Golden Road* and *Life Under Mao Zedong's Rule* by Hong Kong writer Zhang

Da-Peng (CreateSpace, 2012 and 2013, respectively), *The Rose of Cikembang*, a popular novel of the late 1920s Netherlands East Indies by the Indonesian writer Kwee Tek Hoay (Lontar, 2013) and *Ceremony* by famed Dayak poet and novelist Korrie Layun Rampan (Lontar, 2014).

George and his wife, Scholastica Auyong, currently live near Seattle, where he is a full-time freelance translator of Chinese, Indonesian, Malay, and Tagalog, and is finally learning Vietnamese.

Translator's Acknowledgments

This translation would have not been possible for me without the assistance of the author, who never failed to generously provide me with clarifications of certain obscure Javanisms and poetic turns of phrases in his writing. It has been an honor to have been given the opportunity to bring these entrancing, powerful, and sometimes disturbing stories to a wider global readership. For that I have to thank John McGlynn of the Lontar Foundation. Thanks too, once again, to Wikan Satriati of Lontar for her timely expert liaison and linguistic assistance. More generally, any success I may have had over the years in my Indonesian and Malay translation endeavors, whether literary or commercial in nature, is to a great degree thanks to the feedback I have unstintingly received from the various members of the international translation listservs Bahtera and Teraju in those languages, respectively. My discussions with Graham Fuller, linguist extraordinaire and widely recognized writer on modern Islam, continue to be a valuable source of ideas on translation.

And, once again I have been fortunate indeed to have had as my copy editor Diana Darling, resident of Ubud, Bali and author of the wondrous and wise novel of that island, *The Painted Alphabet*. Let no translator fail to pay homage to a good editor.

Finally, as always, I express my deepest gratitude to Scholastica Auyong, my wife, best friend, and road manager of my journey through life.

CPSIA information can be obtained
at www.ICGtesting.com
Printed in the USA
FSOW01n2052250116
16042FS